## ALL AND ALWAYS

"It is only that you have been so distant lately." They were both in front of his desk. Lavinia saw that he was watching her with equal intensity.

"We have spent no time together except at meals when everyone is present." She let her eyes fall to her hands. "I thought that you had lost interest once I said yes, Captain."

He lifted her chin so that she had to look at him. There was nothing distant about him now. The touch of his finger on her face was like a crumb of bread for someone starving.

Hunger made her raise her mouth to his and the spiral of arousal made the kiss a feast. She put her lips on his and the feel of him, the taste of him, was so satisfying that she gave him all of herself, full and unguarded . . .

# BOOK YOUR PLACE ON OUR WEBSITE AND MAKE THE READING CONNECTION!

We've created a customized website just for our very special readers, where you can get the inside scoop on everything that's going on with Zebra, Pinnacle and Kensington books.

When you come online, you'll have the exciting opportunity to:

- View covers of upcoming books
- Read sample chapters
- Learn about our future publishing schedule (listed by publication month *and author*)
- Find out when your favorite authors will be visiting a city near you
- Search for and order backlist books from our online catalog
- Check out author bios and background information
- Send e-mail to your favorite authors
- Meet the Kensington staff online
- Join us in weekly chats with authors, readers and other guests
- Get writing guidelines
- AND MUCH MORE!

**Visit our website at
http://www.kensingtonbooks.com**

# The Captain's Mermaid

## Mary Blayney

**ZEBRA BOOKS**
Kensington Publishing Corp.
http://www.kensingtonbooks.com

ZEBRA BOOKS are published by

Kensington Publishing Corp.
850 Third Avenue
New York, NY 10022

All Kensington titles, imprints and distributed lines are available at special quantity discounts for bulk purchases for sales
promotion, premiums, fund-raising, educational or institu-
tional use.

Special book excerpts or customized printings can also be created to fit specific needs. For details, write or phone the office
of the Kensington Special Sales Manager: Kensington Publishing Corp., 850 Third Avenue, New York, NY 10022. Attn.
Special Sales Department. Phone: 1-800-221-2647.

First Printing: September 2004
10 9 8 7 6 5 4 3 2 1

Printed in the United States of America

*For Meg Grasselli*

*With thanks for sharing
her love of art,
the Regency,
and at least a hundred lunch hours*

# Chapter 1

## The Mermaid

*Talford Vale, Sussex*
*August, 1811*

Her feet were bare. And she did not care who knew it. Lavinia Stewart tried to take some little pleasure in the cool, velvet feel of the close-cropped grass. But she would forever miss the warm grit of Jamaica's white sand beaches.

As she hurried toward the lake, she glanced up through the trees, watching the sun struggle to break through the clouds. Even on a day that her brother declared "damned hot," the Sussex sun managed only a poor imitation of the great gold heat that had warmed her days for her first twenty-two years. Until fifteen months ago.

Her uncle's death had changed everything. England was different from her home in Jamaica in a hundred ways. Ladies never showed their feet or any more of their limbs. Going barefoot was a truly pathetic gesture of defiance on her part, but it was all she dared venture.

She'd reached the shelter of the trees when she heard the carriage move down the drive and out the gate. Her brother was gone. Off to Scotland in his endless pursuit of pleasure.

It was a relief, she insisted. A relief that he spent so little time here at Talford Vale. He might be her only brother, but their last confrontation had left her shaking with rage—so angry that she had no desire to see him ever again.

She would have no Season. Despite the fact her mourning was well over, Desmond had told her that there was no trip to London in the offing.

How had he phrased it? "It's not as though you're a beauty." He ticked off her failings as though she had no feelings at all. "At your age you are beyond the first blush, nigh on the shelf, and you know there's no money to speak of."

No money for her, he meant. And that meant no chance of vouchers for Almack's. He said that even if she were in London—"all decked out"—it was unlikely she would receive invitations to any but the most inconsequential gatherings.

He'd laughed when he said it, promising that there were plenty of unattached men at his house parties. But his friends, both the men and the women, were of loose morals with little interest in family.

He'd patted her on the shoulder, told her that she would always have a home with him, and that she could show her appreciation by continuing to care for his children.

She sat down, pressed her back against the tree trunk closest to the water, raising her knees and resting her head on them. She loved Harry and Sara, but she had hoped for more in life than caring for someone else's children.

Memories of Jamaica were dimming, like a dream that fades quickly. All those plans she and her uncle had made for a trip to London. All those dinners he had hosted for the visiting naval officers and midshipmen. Only practice, Uncle insisted. She was bound for London, for a Season or two among the *ton*.

The officers seemed to enjoy those evenings as much as she did. They were all charm as though their world was little more than cruising from one port to the next in search of beauty.

All but the lieutenant she had come upon one evening, standing on the veranda. His hands were clasped behind his back and he watched the night-dark sea as if it were alive with action.

It was as though he was standing on the deck of his ship, completely alone. Did he wish he was? She'd almost asked him, but had decided to leave without interrupting, convinced that flirtation was not what he wanted.

How could a man be so alone when living closely with so many others, she'd asked, and the younger men, the midshipmen, had laughed. "Impossible to be alone," they insisted, unless you were the captain. Then you did live in a world all your own.

She understood more now about the difference between being alone and being lonely. Her life was the perfect example. And destined never to change. The townsfolk were nothing more than civil, her brother's debts and reputation having preceded her. In no more than five years he had managed to reduce the name of Stewart to one of no consequence and of less value.

Without invitations to even the local assemblies, how would she meet anyone eligible?

She had heard that a wealthy naval officer owned Talford Rise. But naval officers were constantly at sea. They left their wives to fend for themselves, often for years at a time. What kind of family was that?

Indeed she had never seen the naval officer who was her nearest neighbor. Never even heard that he was in residence. Which only proved her right.

She raised her head. So was this her future? She looked around as though she could find the answer in the warm breeze or in the blades of grass at her feet.

She wiggled her bare toes. Oh, how she longed for some

freedom. Any little bit of freedom to call her own. Lavinia regarded the lake and wondered how cold the water would feel.

She stood up and walked closer, then sat on the wall that was an artificial bank and dangled her feet over the edge. Oh! Not as cold as she thought. The upper natural lake would be colder, with its chalky depths and the river water coursing through it to the waterfall, but the water of this artificial lake was quite lovely. Not the liquid heaven of the Caribbean, but not so very cold at all. She held herself motionless. In a moment she felt some small fish nudge up against her toes, tickling her, their curiosity making her smile.

She considered joining them, swimming and splashing in the water the way she had as a child. Her dress was old, her hair pinned up, and she could tell anyone who cared—not that anyone would—that she had fallen in.

On impulse, Lavinia slid into the clear, quiet water and began to swim. Alone, but not lonely. She floated for a while, letting the water cool her back as the summer air warmed her face. The water was a caress, welcoming her, enveloping her, embracing her. She flipped over, startling two fish into a jump, then swam slowly, her head only a little above the water, her limbs moving gently, barely unsettling the surface.

By the time she climbed out, she was thoroughly chilled, but her temper had eased and any thought of tears long gone.

She had found her freedom. Not the incredible independence of the naval officers. She squelched the thought. It was part of her past life. She would build a new life, making what family she could with Harry and Sara, just as she and her uncle had made a family. She would find pleasure in that, in swimming, and in the little freedoms she could find.

Lavinia hurried toward the house, her teeth chattering. Next time she would come better prepared. She shivered even as the sun burned through the last of the mist.

# Chapter 2

## The Captain

*Aboard HMS Confidence, Bay of Biscay*
*August, 1811*

The sun burned through the last of the mist. The two ships had played cat and mouse in and out of the fog for two days, but with the haze gone, further evasion was impossible.

Captain William Chartwell had not wasted those two days. He had the measure of his counterpart and knew how to best him. This would be his victory, the *Dorsay* his prize.

The distance between his *Confidence* and the French ship disappeared with all the speed he wished. His decision to set a head-on course had been unconventional, if not downright reckless. The ships would meet on opposite tacks. At last the ship, bearing the emperor's flag, was committed to the game.

The *Dorsay* was a ship of the line. It carried a good twenty guns more than Chartwell's *Confidence,* which made her more powerful than the English frigate, but far less agile. And that was the key.

Watching through his glass, Chartwell could see confusion aboard the French ship and he could judge the moment when the captain's indecision showed itself and when he decided to hold course to see on which side the *Confidence* intended to pass.

Perfect. On his own deck both larboard and starboard crews manned the guns. The French captain's glass would give him no clue of Chartwell's intent.

He could feel the anticipation of his crew simmering in the air, their tension from eagerness held in check.

"Ease the helm," Chartwell called to the helmsman. "Steer for a close aboard starboard-to-starboard passage."

"Ease the helm, aye, Captain."

It took a long moment for the Frenchmen to discern the imperceptible change in course. Through his glass, Chartwell could see that his choice of a downwind approach further confused the enemy. Indeed, it was part of his plan to even the odds between the two ships.

Some of the *Dorsay* watched their captain, waiting for his command; others eyed the Frenchmen and the scramble of action that meant the *Confidence* had the advantage.

When the *Confidence's* mainmast drew abeam of the *Dorsay's* bow, the French ship's size swung from her single biggest advantage to a deterrent. The English ship's starboard crew came alive as Chartwell nodded slowly and yelled, "Let fly!"

There was a deafening thunder as the forward-angled guns raked the hull and deck of the *Dorsay.* Chartwell breathed in the burnt powder smell. It sharpened his senses the way a woman's scent seduced him. His heart beat double-time as he focused on the battle.

The smoke of the guns curtained the action, but he had been part of such battles a hundred times. He did not need to see to know what was happening. With the *Confidence* lower in the water than the larger *Dorsay,* the force of his guns would do serious damage to the *Dorsay's* hull and guns.

The returning French fusillade whistled through the *Confidence's* sails, riddling them with holes. One lucky shot cracked the foremast at the crosstrees, but it fell into the water on the larboard side, clear of the action.

A second roll of thunder began. The Connies' expertise was a testament to weeks of exercising the guns on quiet nights with no enemy in sight.

As the gap of water between the two ships disappeared and the relentless roll of the guns continued, Chartwell considered his next move. "Bring her hard over."

"Hard over. Aye, sir."

The ships were less than five feet apart.

"Prepare to board," Chartwell bellowed through the trumpet, and before the words had reached the foremast, he could see his first lieutenant responding.

Carroll MacDonald leapt to the rail and raised a boarding axe, followed by men who were not at the guns.

The two ships collided with a grinding crunch, as thorough a call to arms as his shouted command, "Boarders away."

The words were a mere formality. The yards and sails entangled with brutal cracks and a screech, the fouled yards committing his frigate as surely as his command. The Connies fought as one, the heart of their captain as firm a part of the crew as their combined strength was a part of him.

Chartwell drew his sword and raised his pistol, taking charge of the hands aft. He and MacDonald landed on the opposite ends of the *Dorsay's* main deck at almost the same moment.

Hand-to-hand lasted less than five minutes. The *Dorsay's* captain had been hit and killed in the first round; the crew disheartened by the continued raking from the guns. The ship herself was holed and, indeed, by the time the French struck their colors and the second-in-command offered his sword in surrender, the ship sat noticeably lower in the water.

Chartwell looked about for MacDonald, annoyed at his absence. Climbing from the *Dorsay* back aboard the *Confidence,* he called to his boatswain, "Dolley, find Lieutenant Mac-Donald."

With five concise commands he set about untangling the tops, separating the ships, moving the wounded, and saving his latest prize. He stood with his arms across his chest, a slight smile the only sign of his pleasure at the ease of the action.

He named his second midshipman head of the prize crew with orders to rendezvous in Portsmouth.

In only slightly more time than it took to overwhelm the *Dorsay,* the ships were apart. Chartwell saw his boatswain come up from below just as it occurred to him that he had not yet seen his first lieutenant. "Where the hell is MacDonald?"

When Dolley shook his head with a solemn face, his captain sobered, every bit of elation at the victory draining from him. He stared at the man, willing a different message, but Dolley was as honest as he was ugly. "He's below with Mr. Pettison. A gut wound, Captain. The surgeon says that there is naught he can do but make him comfortable."

Once again the crew drew its mood from their captain and as he hurried past on his way below, their laughter trailed off into anxious silence.

The surgery was as much a study in chaos as the ship was a study in battle. The surgeon's work went on long after the enemies struck their colors. Blood and gore spattered the deck and bulkhead. Smells of every imaginable offense assailed the senses, overridden by the metallic smell of blood.

MacDonald lay on a chest in a far corner. His ten-year-old son stood next to him. Angus MacDonald clutched his father's hand, his eyes wide in shock.

*I know exactly how you feel, boy*, Chartwell thought. *This cannot be happening.*

"Always thought I was born to be hanged," MacDonald spoke steadily, but he could not raise his voice above a whisper.

"You die like this and I will hang you." It was a weak joke, but grief had such a hold on him he could hardly think.

The man smiled.

*God give me half his valor.*

"Be honest, Captain. Be honest with me and yourself."

"You came through fire at Trafalgar and a dozen other grand meetings. To buy it in nothing more than a skirmish is a damned insult." The anger was misplaced, Chartwell knew it was, but if Carroll wanted honesty he would have it.

"All in the King's service, William."

It had been years since they were lieutenants together, when they had used each other's given names. It brought back a raft of memories, of good times and trials.

"I'll be meeting Jeannie, William. She'll be at the pearly gates waitin'."

"I've no doubt your wife will be there, arms wide to greet you." They both smiled at the thought. Jeannie MacDonald was one of the few women William had ever known well enough to respect.

Carroll MacDonald turned to his son and his eyes filled. "Angus."

The boy stepped closer. William moved to the other side of the chest, nearer Angus. The child leaned into him but he did not let go of his father's hand.

"Boy, your mother and I will be waiting for you. In a different place, but we will see you again. Never forget your mother's laughter or mine. Remember it is our love run over."

Angus MacDonald gave a nod and pressed his lips together, but the tears ran down his cheeks.

"He's your boy, William. We spoke of this before. Get him out of the navy—it's no place for him."

The boy buried his head in Chartwell's smoke-tinged coat and began to sob.

"If that is what you want, Carroll."

"It's what Jeannie wanted. He has her heart. As intrepid as any man's, but too curious, too independent to accept the discipline of the navy even though he came aboard young."

*The same age I was*, William thought. "I will take him to Talford Rise. I promise I can make a home for him there."

Carroll smiled. "And maybe one for yourself as well."

The captain shook his head and would have argued, would have told him the navy was all the home and family he needed. But with this last most important business done, MacDonald closed his eyes, though he was still smiling even as his breathing grew more labored.

William knew death came in battle, knew that as surely as he knew that God was on their side. But this insignificant triumph came at too dear a price. He wanted to move the clock back, rethink the pursuit.

*Spare this friend.* It sounded like a command. *Please*, he added, as if a miracle depended on the niceties. He tried again. *Dear God, please spare this friend. I have so few.*

As MacDonald's breathing faltered—MacDonald who was his brother in all ways but blood—William felt rage pour through him. He wanted to slash the heart out of a dozen Frenchmen.

Instead he let his own eyes water and sat heavily on the crate that the loblolly boy pushed under him. He settled Angus MacDonald on his lap and let the boy hold onto his father's hand until it grew cold.

# Chapter 3

## The Children

*Near Talford Rise, between Portsmouth and London*
*August, 1812*

Angus MacDonald lay flat on the branch, close to the trunk of the tree. It felt much the same as stretching out on the yard of the *Confidence*, but without the rhythmic rise and fall. And only twenty feet separated him from the ground, not a hundred with the world visible to the edge. Leaves gave shade, and while he could feel the warmth of the August day, he could see no more than the boy and girl below. Since spying on them was his current goal in life, he considered that he was exactly where he most wanted to be.

"*Animal disputans*." The boy spoke the Latin phrase, then pulled some stones from his pocket and began to skip them on the lake not five steps away.

"Some kind of fighting animal?" The girl gave her translation as though the very thought disgusted her.

*No, you stupid girl*, thought Angus. Animal *is man and* disputans *means fighting. It means a man who likes to fight.*

"It means argumentative man."

The girl stuck her tongue out at her brother. "Men might be animals, but women are not."

"Sara, you are so stupid."

"I am not."

*You are too.* It was all Angus could do not to yell his agreement with the boy who he knew was Harry.

"I'm two years older than you are." She spoke with as much frustration as anger.

"And you are hopeless at Latin."

"Because you are the one teaching me. If Papa would let me have Latin lessons, I bet I would be speaking it in whole sentences and not just stupid phrases like you do."

"*A minori ad majus.*"

"I am not lesser and you are not greater," she all but shrieked.

Angus snickered at the insult and did his best to hold still lest the quivering branches betray him.

"You might try arguing in French, Sara."

The two spun around at the sound of another voice. The woman, their Aunt Lavinia, stood before them, smiling.

"You would be on equal footing. For you do share French lessons, *n'est ce pas?*"

"He is such a stupid boy, Aunt Lavinia."

"No, he is not, Sara. He is actually a very bright boy, but perhaps not quite ready to be a teacher."

Angus loved the woman's voice. It was always so calm and soft. He was sure his mother must have sounded like this.

Harry had not spoken since his aunt had arrived but came closer to her. She stretched out a hand to him and he took it, grabbed her other one, and proceeded to swing on them, pivoting on his feet, his head thrown back to the sky.

"Oh let me," exclaimed Sara. Harry actually let go and gave her a chance. Before long the three of them were laughing.

"I know for certain . . ." Aunt Lavinia said breathlessly.

"*Certum scio . . .*" Angus mentally translated with some pride.

"Mrs. Wilcox has made some lemon tarts and they are just from the oven. If you go up to the kitchen and knock on the door and are very, very polite, I suspect that she might have a couple to spare."

Harry took off as if in a race. Sara followed and she too began to run when Harry called out, "If we hurry, Sara, they will be warm. And after, we can go to the swing."

The aunt did not go with them. Using his favorite from an amazing collection of rude words, Angus swore as he realized that he was trapped in the tree until she went back to the house. And she showed no sign of leaving.

Indeed, she walked back over to the very tree he called his own and sat down, her back against the rough bark. She pulled her knees up and he noticed that she was barefoot. How odd. He had never seen a woman's bare feet—not even his own mother's. He stared at them intently and decided they looked exactly like his, except cleaner. The thought that he had anything in common with a girl made him feel sick.

Before he could decide if a tattoo on his ankle would adequately distinguish his foot from hers, she moved a little. She did not stand up, but settled more comfortably and put her head on her knees.

Even from high above her he could see the curve of her neck, where some strands had escaped the knot of hair on her head, and a patch at the shoulder of the old gown she was wearing. She seemed tired, like the prisoners who were taken aboard the *Confidence* after a battle.

She sat motionless for so long that Angus began to wonder if she had fallen asleep. Could he climb down without being caught? Just as he reached out his own bare foot for the trunk of the tree, she raised her head.

He froze, his heart thudding so loudly he felt sure she could hear him.

She did not look up, but stood and walked closer to the water. She stepped down from the cement ledge of the artificial wall and raised her skirt so that it would not get wet.

Reaching down, she grabbed the hem of the dress and drew it over her head. Angus blushed at the sight of the woman in only her small clothes. And when she turned and tossed the dress onto the grass, the rise of her barely covered breasts was the last straw. He was so shocked that he yelled as he lost his balance, and only kept from falling and from certain injury by a desperate grab at the branch. He dangled there like the monkeys he had seen in Africa, with no hope of remaining undiscovered.

"Who are you and what are you doing in that tree?"

Aunt Lavinia's voice was neither calm nor soft. When she came into view the aunt had her dress back on and stood directly below him, her hands on her hips, her eyes blazing.

"Let go of the branch," she commanded.

He shook his head.

"Let go. Stretched like that it is only a few feet."

He tried to judge the truth of it.

"Of course if you break your leg, it will be only what you deserve."

Angus let loose his hold, but only because he felt as though his arms were coming out of their sockets and he could not hold on a moment longer. Maybe he could land on his feet, not break a leg, and run faster than she could.

She stopped his fall with her arms, eliminating the possibility of escape. As soon as his feet were on the ground, she grabbed his ear and pulled him fully upright.

His eyes teared at the painful twist but he did not cry out.

"You are from the Rise, are you not?"

"Yes, ma'am." Clearly caught, there was no point in a lie.

"Let us see what your mother has to say about this."

"My mother's dead."

That gave her pause, but she would not allow herself sympathy.

"We will talk to your tutor then."

He mumbled something but she did not hear.

She let go of his ear, grabbed his arm and pulled him along, up and around the lake that the two properties shared. It was less than a quarter mile to Talford Rise and she marched him along, muttering all manner of threats under her breath, as though he were a prisoner of war and she was a sadistic jailer.

He would not end up in prison, but would get the switch for sure.

They had reached the grass verge that edged the circular drive when she spoke aloud. "What is your name?"

"Angus MacDonald."


*This is beyond anything*, Lavinia Stewart thought. What kind of child hides in a tree to watch her swim? What kind of parent allows such behavior? At the least an uncaring one. Or worse, one depraved and debauched. She thought of that after she knocked on the door, too late to reconsider confrontation.

What did she know of this household? Very little. The villagers were polite, but not inclined to include her in their gossip. She was not sure if that was because of Desmond's reputation or the family's place in society.

The owner of Talford Rise was in the Navy, but was he at home or at sea? Most likely he was at sea with a thousand men at his command. Did he even think of the child he had left behind? Anger overtook any anxiety. No wonder the boy sought out mischief.

The man who opened the door could hardly be a butler. No porter either, not that a house this size would need one. Dressed in rough cotton pants and a shirt with no cravat, the man had a red scarf around his neck and a queue down his back. And an empty sleeve where his left arm should be.

"I want to speak to this boy's tutor," she spoke, with all the authority she could command, gratified when the man reacted with surprise.

"He has no real tutor." There was a long pause before he thought to add, "ma'am."

"Then I will speak to his father."

"His father is dead."

Her heart softened but she steeled herself against sentiment. "Surely he does not live here without an adult in charge."

"That would be the captain, ma'am."

"The captain is here?" She made to look behind him as though she could see him there. "He is not at sea?"

"No, ma'am. He's here."

"All right. Tell the captain that I will speak with him."

The man agreed with an uncertain nod and left them standing on the front steps with the door open.

They stood in silence, Lavinia doing her best to retain her sense of authority, but as she waited she grew increasingly aware of her appearance. Her hair. She raised her free hand and felt it halfway down her back. She had on a dress that belonged in the rag bag. And bare feet! He would think her indecent, no better than her intemperate brother.

The man who came to the door was not at all like the naval officers of her Jamaica days. She remembered carefree smiles; he was not smiling. She recalled the enthusiasm of youth; he had left youth behind long ago. And he was bigger than any midshipman she had known. Not the kind of big that meant fat, but rather the kind of size that came from a great height and Saxon blood.

He wore no queue. His hair was cut short, the blond as bleached by the sun as his skin was browned by it. A fine web of wrinkles at the corner of his eyes attested to years aboard ship in all climates. There was a v-shaped scar on the edge of his cheek and another that went through his eyebrow. Neither mark was disfiguring, but they gave a hard edge to an appearance that was already less than friendly.

He was dressed in buckskins and a shirt that was rolled up at the arms. Had he just come from the stables? He wore a cravat that he had loosened and she could see the hollow of his throat and yet another scar that ran from the edge of his collarbone under the linen of his shirt. His undress, so close to matching hers, should have made her feel better. Instead it made her feel unprotected.

He glanced at Angus and slowly gave her his attention, his gray eyes cool and impersonal. "Yes?"

To keep her standing there and to speak curtly was so rude that her anger rekindled. He might be an officer, but you could not call him a gentleman. He had not even introduced himself.

His butler was hovering in the background, clearly intent on reporting every word belowstairs. It only increased her discomfiture and further fueled her anger.

"This boy, Angus, has been trespassing on our property at Talford Vale."

He eyed Angus and the boy straightened and spoke as if the captain had asked a question. "I guess I was, sir."

The man waited, his silence as good as a demand for an explanation.

"It's the best of the climbing trees for miles, Captain."

Lavinia looked around at the innumerable towering trees that surrounded the property and back at the boy. "There are a hundred trees between here and the lake and you think the best one happens to be at the lake where I swim?"

"Swim?" The captain's ennui disappeared. "You were going to swim?" Even the butler was surprised.

"Yes." She had no need to explain. To tell them that she had grown up swimming. That it was one of the most treasured of her childhood memories.

"That would tempt any boy." He smiled a little. "And most men."

She blushed, feeling the color rise from her throat and redden her cheeks. "Who do you think I am? Some dairymaid eager for attention?" She included the butler and the boy in her question, but there was only one person whose answer she cared about.

He raised his eyebrows, inviting some other explanation.

"This is Aunt Lavinia, Captain."

That a further clarification should come from the child surprised them both.

"You see, sir, she is Harry and Sara's aunt and cares for them when their father is away."

"And Harry and Sara are?"

"Mr. Stewart's children. Mr. Stewart who owns Talford Vale."

"So this lady is Miss Lavinia Stewart?"

The captain's icy gray eyes held hers and she nodded.

"Miss Lavinia barefoot Stewart."

Lavinia blushed again as both the boy and the butler looked at her feet. Deeply embarrassed, she curled her toes in an effort to hide them. She had been going barefoot in the warm weather for a year. It seemed as natural as the summer to her. His comment made her aware of how unseemly it would appear to most everyone else.

"Forgive my confusion, Miss Stewart."

It was a command, not a request. The autocratic tone annoyed her. Again she nodded, gritting her teeth with the effort to at least appear polite. Blast her temper. It was quite her fault that she had come looking so far less than her best.

"My name is Chartwell, Captain Chartwell, currently on leave from His Majesty's navy."

She gave a slow nod to his perfunctory bow, but could not bring herself to be any more gracious.

"You must also forgive me for not inviting you inside. Mine is an all-male establishment. We do not receive calls from unaccompanied ladies."

An all-male household? What could that mean but that it was as depraved a place as she suspected? The boy, the poor boy. What was his life like? No wonder he ran away.

"Exactly how many days have you spent up in that tree, Angus?" the captain asked.

"Not that many." He stared at the ground and Lavinia knew it for a lie.

"Often enough to know more of the family than is polite."

He shrugged and muttered, "*Errare humanum est.*"

"To err is indeed human, and since you were caught, you pay the price."

Angus shifted with some discomfort and Lavinia almost asked what the price would be.

"And have you observed swimming before?"

"Oh no, sir. I swear, sir. Never before, sir, and I would have left if I could have gotten away without being seen."

The captain appeared to accept the truth of that. To her he said, "I will see that it never happens again." He gave his attention to the boy. "You know what this means, do you not?"

"The lash, sir." He spoke with confidence, a step beyond certainty.

"The lash," Captain Chartwell agreed.

Lavinia could not control her gasp. "Surely you are not going to whip him?" Despite her protest, the captain nodded, as did his butler.

"Surely I am. He knows the penalty for such a breach of manners."

"Three lashes," the boy answered glumly.

Even the butler did not object, as if his agreement would make her see it as reasonable.

"But that's a horrible punishment for one so young! Would not bed without dinner be adequate?"

The captain laughed, actually laughed, and she thought he was a devil—his greatest pleasure her discomfiture. "If you could know the number of times we have seen bed without dinner and counted it good fortune, you would hardly call it a punishment."

The boy was smiling too. He pulled his hand from hers and stepped to the captain's side. The man rested his hand on the head of the boy he was about to beat and the child leaned into the embrace. The tableau lasted only for a moment, until the man removed his hand, crossed his arms, and shook his head, as though affection was a trap he would not fall victim to.

"Off with you. The switch is in the library. Wait for me there. You go with him, Dolley." He spoke the last without turning around, obviously certain his order would be obeyed.

"Aye, sir," Dolley and Angus chorused. The boy was not smiling now and Lavinia bit her lip.

She knew she should say goodbye. Turn and leave. "Captain, I'm afraid your experience at sea has hardened you."

"Yes, I'm sure it has." He waited, all patience, for her to continue.

"How can you have convinced that child that he deserves such punishment?"

"Because he knows that he is wrong." He moved from the doorway, closer to her. "And Miss Stewart, this is, quite simply, none of your business. I suggest that you go home." He moved even closer so that she had to look up. His nearness took her breath, the male power of him enveloping her. He smiled, but it was more suggestive than friendly. "Of course, you are more than welcome to come inside."

She waited, afraid of his meaning.

"If your concern for Angus is merely a pretense," he chose his words carefully, "shall we say, a front for a personal interest, then there is no need to be so circumspect."

# Chapter 4

It took her a moment to unwind his meaning. When she did, the blush returned, along with shock at his suggestion. "I assure you, sir, my only interest here is that poor boy."

"Then good day to you, Miss Stewart."

A dozen rude thoughts crowded her mind. Instead of speaking, she stormed down the steps and onto the grass verge. She could feel his cold gray eyes follow her even as distance broke the power of his masculine aura.

His manners hardly improved after Angus told him who she was, but it was clear that he was used to treating people as beings who existed only to serve his needs—whether they be men or women.

*Of course you are welcome to come inside if your interest is more personal?* She stopped short, wondering if that insult meant that he had been as physically aware of her as she was of him. When he had stepped toward her it was as though some unseen force urged her closer. She had resisted, but she could still feel the wanting. She shuddered, appalled. The idea of sharing tea with him was intolerable, much less anything more intimate. Shying away from a specific definition of "more intimate," she banished the memory of his mouth and the firm set of his lips.

The boy. This was all about the boy. Mr. Chartwell was a captain in the Royal Navy, used to command, and here he had no one to order about but one small boy.

She wanted to reach out and rescue Angus MacDonald—to take him back to Talford Vale, add him to her version of family, and keep him safe. Though there were times when the place she lived was no more a haven than Talford Rise appeared to be.

Earlier today the gardener had threatened her with a pitchfork when she had gone out to pick some flowers. At this very moment the housekeeper was confined to bed with a sick headache, and she had seen the butler pinching one of the maids as she carried water up the stairs. No, the only advantage Talford Vale had was her presence, and there were times when it seemed like a weak bulwark indeed.

She'd needed that respite by the lake, that hour of solitude to restore her equanimity, to ease the fatigue that came from doing the work of the incompetent and unmotivated, and to rebuild the defense that kept the children secure.

She walked through the woods and out of the captain's sight, disgusted with herself, embarrassed that her misplaced anger had brought such nasty consequences for the child.

Surely the responsibility to protect extended beyond one's family even to an ill-mannered scapegrace who climbed trees. He lived in an all-male household. He had no mother. Or any family, female or otherwise, in his life.

There must be some way she could draw him from the awful influence of that man. She shuddered at the thought that he was the kind of person who drew pleasure from floggings, from killing people, from battle.

The grass tickled her feet as the air cooled her cheeks, but her heart was not soothed. She reached her favored swimming spot and stopped. It was too late to swim. She had promised the cook that she would go to the village and speak to the butcher.

How many ladies of the ton cringed at the thought of talking to the butcher? They both knew there would be no chance of payment until Desmond returned and wanted some true service. Until that unknown date, no one would starve, and the household would have to make do with second-rate cuts of meat made edible only by the genius of Mrs. Wilcox.

She considered the "best climbing tree for miles" and wondered how much time the boy had spent up there. If he knew the Latin phrases that Harry was so fond of tossing about, he must have been at it for a while. Could he be that hungry for knowledge?

The idea came to her as she walked back to the house.

Chartwell watched the woman, Lavinia Stewart, as she made her way along the grass to the woods that separated the two estates. More plain than pretty, the dark brown hair cascading down her back was her one true claim to beauty. And her eyes. Though he expected that when they were not flashing with anger, they would be self-satisfied and placid—like her life, like her expectations, like her world.

He had insulted her. Quite deliberately. Offending women came naturally to him, he decided. Look how he had upset Mariel Whitlow just two months ago. Left her sobbing on her brother's arm, surrounded by a house full of curious guests.

True, she was part of a family he detested for reasons both numerous and ancient. A family he would never see or deal with again, but Lavinia Stewart was different. She was a neighbor. He winced. He should not have been so crude. It had been a graceless way to eliminate unwanted attention.

Dolley came up behind him. "Sussex is full of women like that, Captain."

"And is it your experience as my majordomo or as my boatswain that informs you?"

"Women take to meddling as easy as boys do to climbing trees."

"Oh, yes, meddling women." He smiled, his back to Dolley. For a moment, only a moment, he thought Dolley meant that the neighborhood was full of women who were totally unaware of the appeal of long brown hair, full breasts, and bare feet.

"You know, Dolley, despite her meddling, you have to admire her willingness to defend the child who had insulted her."

"Sounds more like she could na' make up her mind."

"Oh, she has made up her mind, I have no doubt of that. It will be interesting to see what her plan of attack will be."

"She'll be back?" Dolley spoke in such horrified accents that this time the captain laughed aloud.

"Indeed she will. I've spent a lifetime studying my adversaries. And I can guarantee that at our next meeting she will be fully armed. No more bare feet, but shoes, pelisse, hat, and gloves, and at least two servants for support." As she disappeared into the woods, his attention was drawn to motion on the drive. He continued speaking in the same tone. "Do you see that rider turning in at the gate? Rides like a sailor, does he not?"

Once he had the man in sight, Dolley had to agree. "Aye, sir. Like a horse is a torture tool and not made for our convenience." He shook his head in sympathy. "Do you think he's from the admiralty, sir?"

"We'll know soon enough."


She had waited more than a day—close to two days— Lavinia reminded herself as Mr. Arbuscam raised the knocker at the front door of Talford Rise. The tutor was entirely too tentative. The sound barely echoed. The complete lack of response frayed the already strained nerves of the three standing at the door.

Lavinia would not countenance being ignored. She had waited all those hours so that her decision would not be based on temper. But even after a period of calm reflection, she was as certain that what she was doing was right and best for the boy.

Mrs. Wilcox was not as confident. She was wringing the front of her cloak as though it was her usual apron. "He will know me for the cook at first glance. No gentleman would believe me a maid, Miss Lavinia. Never."

"Yes, he will. You look the part completely." Except, perhaps, for her sturdy round build. But where was it written that all lady's maids must be slim and thin-faced?

Mr. Arbuscam would never admit to nerves, but his timid effort with the knocker betrayed him.

The tutor raised the knocker again. This time it was much too loud, so loud that Mrs. Wilcox jumped at the sound.

The door was opened almost immediately. The butler did not recognize her even when she stepped to the front of her small group.

"We would like to see Captain Chartwell."

"He's busy."

She allowed herself into the front hall by the simple expedient of walking so close to the man that he had to back up. She had seen it done, though never actually tried it before.

It seemed the province of irascible old ladies. She was not old, but it could be she was becoming irascible. No matter, it worked and she was in the entry hall of Talford Rise in an instant. The butler had not let go of the door as she announced, "We will wait."

He mumbled something like, "Taken without a shot fired."

"I beg your pardon?"

He shook his head and she decided it was some sort of navy welcome.

He would have closed the door on Mrs. Wilcox and Mr. Arbuscam, but the two came to their senses and herded through before he could leave them stranded on the steps.

"Wait here." He thought for a moment and bowed. "If you please, miss."

Before he had gone more than two steps, Mrs. Wilcox whispered to Mr. Arbuscam.

"Why this house *is* exactly the same as Talford Vale."

Indeed, the wide square entrance hall was identical, with the staircase rising along three walls. The doors opening from the hall were familiarly placed. As Lavinia counted them, one opened and the boy, Angus, came into the hall.

He at least recognized her immediately and mumbled a greeting. It was rather like a strangled "ma'am," but Lavinia took that for welcome and answered with a smile and a nod.

"Good morning, Angus. It's a lovely day, is it not?"

He nodded vigorously, but clearly a further discussion of the weather was beyond him. He hurried to the front door, pulled it open, and shut it tightly behind him.

Lavinia stared at the empty door as if it would give her some clue as to the wisdom of her mission. None was forthcoming, and she gave her attention to the house.

There were some differences. The Rise was significantly cleaner than the Vale and in far better repair. No stains where water had leaked through the plaster. No worn places on the elegant staircase. But even given those differences, one could see that it was the exact same design.

"You have never been here before?" The butler had not left to announce them, clearly more intent on their comments than making their presence known to the captain.

Both servants shook their heads.

"The two really are the same," Mrs. Wilcox volunteered. "My father and grandfather worked on this building. After it was done, they stayed on at the Vale. They always said that the two houses were the same down to the last nail."

The one-armed man's keen interest drew the other two servants closer, leaving Lavinia within earshot, but not part of the group.

"Me dad told me that the two brothers were close and very tight-fisted."

"If money mattered so much, why would they not live together?" the butler asked.

"One brother was married and his wife did not want the other brother in the same house," Mrs. Wilcox confided, clearly pleased to be privy to a bit of gossip. "So the married Talford built the Rise and the other Talford used the same design for the Vale. They even agreed to share the lake and water supply."

"It is an odd arrangement to be sure," Lavinia spoke in a tone she hoped would put an end to the discussion. She stared at the butler whose only interest appeared to be Mrs. Wilcox.

If the butler was immune to her hint, Mrs. Wilcox was not. Recalling her role as a lady's maid, she stepped back to take a place next to her employer. "Sir, would you please tell the captain that Miss Stewart is waiting?"

Lavinia had to bite her lip to keep from smiling. While not precisely coy, there was a wheedling tone to Mrs. Wilcox's words that was very close to flirtation.

The butler bowed to Mrs. Wilcox as though she were the honored guest.

"The name's Dolley, ma'am, Arthur Dolley." With something very like a blush burning beneath his bronze skin, Dolley walked across the hall to the door that led to the library.

Lavinia took the opportunity to consider her surroundings. The hall was empty of statuary or paintings as though the owner had not had the time or the inclination to leave his mark on the place. So unlike Talford Vale, which was littered with disagreeable statues and second-rate art.

There was, however, a pile of items by the front door: a trunk and sword case and a box no bigger than a hat box, though this one was square rather than round and made of some beautiful dark wood.

Mrs. Wilcox spoke again. "Do you suppose they are going away?"

Lavinia only nodded, her attention now drawn to the butler who had knocked at the door she knew led to the library. When there was no call to enter, he eased the door open and stopped with it only slightly ajar. No servant of any standing would have behaved so.

He was no more a butler than Mrs. Wilcox was a lady's maid.

Two voices drifted out from the library. Two men. One of them had his voice raised in anger.

"I have no time for this discussion," Captain Chartwell spoke in accents even more frigid than the ones he had used with her. He really was a most disagreeable gentleman. "The Admiralty sent a message calling me to London yesterday and I am due there within two days of receiving it."

That explained the trunk and other items by the door.

The other voice, also male, was more quiet. "If you had answered the letter, there would be no need to waste your time. You have only to tell me if the boy is your legitimate child. You may not wish to acknowledge your connection to the Marquis Straemore, but it exists nonetheless. And if the boy is your son, then he is part of the family as you are." Despite the captain's brusqueness, the stranger was all affability. A man, a true gentleman, who relied more on charm than authority.

"How do you even know of Angus?" The captain's voice rose again.

The stranger laughed, though the question was far from friendly. "Mariel's fiancé, Edward Hadley, was present at that card marathon. A game they say you would have won if the boy had not come to call you away." He paused. "Is that confusing enough for you?"

"Angus is my ward."

"Not your son?"

"He is my son in all ways *but* blood."

There was a long silence and Lavinia could imagine the intensity of Chartwell's eyes and wondered if the other man was squirming yet.

"One more thing."

The stranger was either confident or insensitive to insult. Chartwell remained silent.

"Come to Braemoor, Chartwell. Come speak with James. He would like to meet you."

"He does not exist for me. None of you do."

"The marquis is not well. When he is gone—"

"Never," the captain cut him off.

"By all the gods of stubbornness, you are so like James that I can almost see him in your place."

Ah, now the visitor's exasperation was showing.

"Goodbye" was Chartwell's single-word command.

There was another long beat of silence before the stranger spoke. "For the moment."

Dolley pushed the door more fully open just as the man left the room and came into the hall. In the moment before he looked up, Lavinia recognized more frustration than anger. It disappeared the minute he noticed their small group. He greeted them with a smile that was all flirtation.

"Madam"—he bowed to her—"I am sorry my business kept you waiting."

"We have only this moment arrived." She gave him a small curtsy.

"I am Lord Morgan Braedon." With a mischievous smile he continued, "Come on a matter of family business." He bowed a little again. "And sorry to have left him in such bad humor, but you know how difficult relatives can be."

"Get out, Braedon. And stop spreading gossip."

The captain was in the hall and his temper was showing.

Lord Morgan Braedon appeared unmoved by the anger in the captain's voice. "Travel safely, William, and we will meet again." With a polite nod to her, the man was out the door Dolley had moved across the floor to open.

*William. His given name is William.* It was one small bit of information that Lavinia held on to amidst all her questions. How were the two related? Why was the captain so rude to Lord Morgan? If Captain Chartwell was a scion of a marquis' family, why had he gone to sea? Was he a legitimate brother or base born?

"Miss Stewart." He spoke her name as though the two words were a true test of his patience.

Captain Chartwell pushed open the door of the room he had so recently left and gestured with an open hand. "Come in."

*Please,* she added for him. He was the rudest man, but if he was willing to see her, she would hardly make that complaint aloud.

She stopped at the threshold. "I am sorry to take your time when you are clearly preparing for a trip."

He did not speak but his look implied, *Then why are you here?*

She answered as if he had asked. "The very fact that you are called away makes my errand even more important."

It took all her effort not to wring her hands. Oh, this was a mistake. The timing was all wrong. He was in a foul humor—of course that seemed the norm—but she was slowing his departure to his senior officers, to the Admiralty.

"Come in," he ordered again, "and stop wasting my time."


Angus watched the man come down the front steps. He was dressed like a lord and talked like one, but Angus would not let that intimidate him. Dolley had told Chasen that the man had been determined to talk to the captain about "the boy." Angus needed to be sure that he would not be made to leave the Rise. He stepped out from behind the bushes and called to the stranger.

"I beg your pardon, sir."

The man's surprise dissolved into a smile that was all the reassurance the boy needed.

"Sir, are you from my grandparents' place in Scotland?"

"No. My name is Morgan Braedon and I live near Bath."

Angus wondered why some stranger from Bath would care

about him anyway. "My name is Angus MacDonald, truly it is. The captain and my father were best friends. My father died and I am to live with the captain," he said with emphasis. "I am to live here at Talford Rise with him." He thought a moment. "Until I am twenty-five." That last was a made-up bit, but he thought it sounded convincing.

"I see. He is like a father to you."

"Yes, sir."

"But there is no blood between you?"

"No, sir."

The man came closer. "I can see that you care about him. Well, my boy, the truth is that I do, too. If you ever think he needs help, will you write to me?"

Was this some kind of trap? Angus wondered.

"You do know how to write, do you not?"

"Of course I do. I can even speak Latin." Honesty compelled him to add, "Some Latin. I cannot actually talk in it. Not yet."

*"Et nunc et semper.* I want you to think of me if he is ever in need."

Angus understood that. "Now and always."

"Good."

Angus had not meant to agree to write, only to show that he knew the words, but the man's delight at his agreement made it impossible for him to clarify.

"The captain is very like someone close to me. And neither of them will ever admit that they need help."

Angus could not actually imagine the captain ever needing this man's help, but nodded anyway. "Yes, sir."

"Remember my name. Morgan Braedon. If you direct the letter to Braemoor, Sussex, it will find me."

# Chapter 5

"Let me be sure that I understand you, Miss Stewart. You are demanding—virtually ordering—me to send Angus to be tutored at Talford Vale along with your nephew?"

Facing the man again, hearing the animosity in his voice, Lavinia wondered how she had ever thought this would be easy. An aggressive address had seemed like such a good idea until three minutes ago. Should she have considered a more conciliatory tone? A catch-more-bees-with-honey-than-vinegar approach? It had not worked for his previous visitor. Nevertheless, she tried to relax a bit. "I would say that I am proposing it, Captain Chartwell, certainly not commanding."

"Oh, you are commanding, Miss Stewart. There is no mistaking that tone of voice."

"If my tone is demanding, it is because yours is insulting."

He gave a slight nod as if applauding her grasp of his intent. So much for conciliation.

"You do not think I can make suitable arrangements for Angus myself?" he asked.

She tried to control the laugh that came from nerves as much as from skepticism, but it came out worse, more like a snicker.

His eyes lost any inclination to question and hardened at the sound.

"Not to put too fine a point on it, but, no, I do not think that you can have made adequate arrangements. You have been in residence these last six months and Angus must climb trees in order to learn Latin."

"And you are prepared to assume the responsibility? How presumptuous of you."

She did indeed wish that Lord Morgan Braedon had left him in a sunnier mood. The two of them sounded like Sara and Harry on a bad day. She reminded herself that the captain was about to leave and Angus's well-being was more important than winning a war of words.

"My right, sir, is that of a concerned adult."

The captain looked down at his arms folded across his chest. "Not the inclination of a meddlesome, bored spinster with nothing better to do than interfere in my life?"

"Bored and meddlesome?" She was speechless. "Nothing better to do?" If he only knew of the chores waiting for her. "Believe me, Captain, interfering in your life is as distasteful to me as that hideous picture on the wall."

He glanced at the painting as though he had never noticed it before, a brace of dead birds with leaves for background. He probably thought it was artful, when ugly was too kind a description.

"Does your interference stem from some misguided notion that our two properties continue to be linked by something other than the lake?" He pointed to the atrocity on the wall. "Does Talford Vale have the same painting on its library wall?"

"No. The two houses might be identical in architecture, but the Talford brothers have been dead for fifty years. The library at the Vale is furnished in quite a different style and it has nothing like that painting." It had, instead, pictures that would embarrass any well-bred woman. Paintings she kept covered when her brother was away from home.

She searched the room for Mr. Arbuscam and found him in a corner where he was doing his best to imitate a statue. "I will not be distracted, Captain. Harry's tutor agrees that it would be beneficial for both children, do you not, Mr. Arbuscam?"

The man cleared his throat and Lavinia pretended it was the hearty gesture of support she had hoped for.

She faced the captain. "I insist."

"Oh, you do, do you?" Captain Chartwell placed his hands on his desk and leaned across it. "Miss Stewart, were a man in my command to be as obstinate and insulting as you are, I would have him at the gratings and hold the whip myself."

She stared at him. His eyes, angry and imperious, held hers as surely as his hands could. She did not know what else she could say to convince him, but threat or not, his intimidation served only to increase her determination.

The relentless gaze pulled the truth from her. "I want to keep him safe."

"Safe?"

"Because he is a child, a boy who needs a mother."

His whole disposition changed. For the shortest of moments it was as though he was the one who felt the whip.

There was a knock at the door and the one-armed man leaned in. "Er, Captain, sir?"

With a jerk, Captain Chartwell turned to the door.

"It's gettin' on, sir."

Without waiting for an answer, the butler closed the door as though the four words were a world of explanation.

Turning to the window behind the desk, the captain stared out, his back to his guests. When he faced her again, his countenance was an impenetrable mask.

"One thing I have learned in this life is not to question providence even when it wears an interfering face."

Lavinia bit her lip to keep from insulting him in return.

"Angus can join in the lessons, but only if you will take him into your household while I am away."

His sudden capitulation left her speechless, a gasp of surprise as close as she could come to answering. He ignored her shock.

"And I want Dolley, the man who just left, to go along."

"All right." If he thought that his qualifications would make her rethink her plan, he was wrong. She was already mentally moving furniture and wondering how Harry would feel about sharing his room. Where would she put the servant?

"I have business at the Admiralty. I was going to leave Angus here with Dolley, but had some doubts as to who would supervise the supervisor. Dolley is a good worker, but untrained."

That was no surprise to her. Did he think Talford Vale was a place to learn the business of butler? She held her tongue. "How long will you be away?"

He considered the answer for such a long time that Lavinia snapped at him. "A week? A month? A year?"

He nodded, thinking. "Miss Stewart, the letter the Admiralty sent has already been destroyed. Any information I give you is not for village ears. Angus knows this, as does Dolley."

"Of course, though it's hardly likely that Napoleon has spies in our village."

He did no more than raise his eyebrows at her, but she felt suddenly naive.

"Three weeks."

All that caveat for two words? "Thank you." He was not the only person who could speak in short sentences.

"When I return, I will have Angus home and then decide if the lessons will continue."

Lavinia inclined her head. "I never thought I would have any reason to ask God to bless the lord of the admiralty, but he has enabled me to have my dearest wish."

"I will pass your words onto Viscount Melville."

She ignored the sarcasm. She had what she wanted and could at least try to be gracious.

He directed her to a seat across the room where Mr. Arbuscam and Miss Wilcox were settled and sent for Angus.

It was not an easy interview. At first, the boy refused to even consider the move. "I want to go with you. You always need powder monkeys, or I can help the surgeon."

The captain was not behind his desk, but seated on a window seat that made him only a few inches taller than the child.

"Not this time." There was no command in his voice. "I'm to have a brig, not much bigger than a sloop, and only the smallest crew."

"But that's an insult, Captain. You should have a triple decker or a frigate like the *Confidence*."

"No insult, Angus. This is a quick in-and-out action, no more than three weeks, but they need someone who speaks French."

"*Je parle français.*"

Lavinia tried to repress a smile. Angus spoke well enough, but with the worst imaginable accent. She devoutly hoped that the captain was not the one who had taught him.

"The Admiralty wants someone who speaks French like a native, Angus. We really must do something about that accent."

He did not address her, but Lavinia made a mental note to include Angus in the French lessons she gave Harry and Sara.

"You know this is what your father wanted. And you know just as well that you would rather learn Latin here than put up with a bunch of rowdy midshipmen."

"I'll hate Latin if you are not here." The boy's back was to her, but Lavinia could see his fists bunched at his sides and hear the tears beneath the anger.

The captain put his hand on the boy's head and with a mournful sigh Angus gave in and moved to sit beside him on the window seat.

"You will obey Miss Stewart and Mr. Arbuscam."

Angus flicked a glance at Lavinia. "Yes, sir."

"You will not teach Harry or Sara one bad word."

Angus avoided her eye. "Yes, sir."

"You will keep a journal so you will remember every detail of your adventure."

"More like I'm going to jail," he muttered.

"I was thinking it would be like the letters a midshipman must write."

Lavinia relaxed a bit. For the first time it felt like they were working together for the child's welfare.

"Prison or adventure, Angus. It is your choice."

"Yes, sir." The boy was silent a moment and then asked, "Can I sketch as you do? Instead of writing?"

"That is up to Mr. Arbuscam."

"Yes, sir."

As Lavinia watched the exchange, the truth of the situation struck her.

There was real affection here.

And it was mutually shared.

Despite the beating and the neglect, the captain seemed to regret the parting as much as his ward.

"I never lived with a woman before, sir."

The captain would not look at her and tried to contain his smile. She pretended that she was not listening.

"You remember your mother."

"Not really."

Even the captain had no answer for that.

"Miss Stewart will not be your mother, but she will be a suitable female influence."

Angus wrinkled his nose.

"I tell you, Angus, it's the girl, Sara, who will be the true bane of your existence." And this time the captain did look at her.

"A girl, sir?" He said the words as though they were the worst punishment imaginable.

"Your mother was once a girl. Mrs. Tuttle was once a girl."

"The gunner's wife?" he asked as though it were impossible.

"Indeed. But I was never a girl and you never will be either even if you breathe the same air for ten years."

Angus considered the truth of that before he answered. "If she hits me, what should I do?"

"Treat her like a lady, Angus. For she will be one someday. Best start practicing before you learn bad habits. Hold your tongue and never raise your hand to her."

"Yes, sir." The big sigh that came with the two words made it clear that this was the biggest challenge of all.

The captain smiled a little. "Should she annoy you beyond bearing, I am sure her brother will devise any number of suitable retaliations. As a matter of fact—"

At that, Lavinia stood up and spoke before the captain could share any more of his wisdom. "I do believe that we should be going."

The captain rose and the boy did too. "Go and collect whatever you think is necessary."

It was Lavinia's turn to protest. "You are going to let him pack for himself?"

"Hmm. I'll have Dolley help him." Before they left the room the captain spoke again. "Mr. Arbuscam, go with them. You can decide what books might be useful. And Mrs. Wilcox, you go too and advise Dolley on what clothes Angus will need."

There was a flair of panic in Mrs. Wilcox's eyes.

"Thank you, Mrs. Wilcox," Lavinia added with pointed emphasis. "Anything we forget, we can send someone to collect."

Mrs. Wilcox gave a small curtsy and crossed the room as quickly as her large size would allow.

"One more thing, Angus. I am sending Dolley with you to the Vale."

"You are?" For the first time a hint of excitement replaced the dejection.

"But of course. I would not want you to forget me."

Any sentiment Lavinia might have felt at the admission

was cut off by his parting comment. "Miss Stewart, wait here. I have something else to discuss with you."

"Have you never heard of the word *please*?"

The door closed behind him and Lavinia was almost positive he had not heard her question. How long had it been since he had felt the need to be polite to anyone? What kind of example was that for the boy? And exactly how many bad words would Angus pass on to Harry?

She walked over to the shelves and scanned the titles, wondering if the books had come with the house and if they were as awful as the painting.

They seemed conventional enough and she was about to pull out Sir Joseph Banks's work on his travels with Cook when Captain Chartwell came back into the room.

Lavinia pushed the book back onto the shelf and waited for him to speak. Before he could, Mrs. Wilcox burst into the room.

The woman hurried over to her, wringing her hands. Lavinia faced her so that her back was to the captain. "He has a hammock, miss. He says he has to have a hammock. He says he cannot sleep in a proper bed."

Lavinia rolled her eyes. They had yet to leave the house and already the boy was trying to best her. "Of course let him bring the hammock." She would let him win the small battles and hold herself ready for the big ones. Besides, she had no doubt that within the week he would be sleeping in a bed.

Mrs. Wilcox bobbed a curtsy to the captain and hurried out of the room.

The captain's gaze traveled very slowly from the closed door to where she stood. "She looks more like a cook than a lady's maid." He moved across the room as he spoke.

Lavinia followed him. "Mrs. Wilcox is a loyal, trustworthy servant."

"Sit down."

*Please,* she added mentally.

As he spoke he sat, not waiting to see if she would obey.

"If I do not come back, I have instructed Dolley to take Angus to his mother's family."

He began writing, but when she did not answer "yes, sir" he stopped and looked up.

"If you do not come back?" She repeated his words with some disbelief. "What do you mean if you do not come back?" Before he could explain, she understood. "You mean if you die?" She could not help the incredulous edge and hoped he would not think it hysteria.

"Or am captured and held for exchange."

All her outrage evaporated as she understood what his assignment meant. She tried to match his sangfroid. For her it was a facade. In him it appeared bone deep.

"Why is he not with his mother's family now?"

"They live in Scotland, Miss Stewart, and they are too old to care for a child his age and temperament." He wrote a few words and continued. "And his father entrusted him to my care." His eyes were intense and direct. "On his deathbed." He emphasized the pronoun. He did not return to his writing but waited for her reply.

"I know that death in war time is real, Captain. It is only that you speak of it so matter-of-factly."

"It has been a part of my life since I was the boy's age."

She nodded, understanding a little better. "If something does happen, do you have family that Dolley or I should notify?"

It was a simple question. She wondered why it took him so long to decide and wondered more when his answer was only one word: "No."

"But Lord Morgan Braedon, the gentleman who was leaving as we came in. He said . . . "

There was such hostility radiating from him that she stopped midsentence. "You will listen to this very carefully, Miss Stewart. I will not know or be known by the Braedons. Not ever."

"Yes, sir." It seemed the only possible response to his insistence.

He gave his attention to his letter. It was a personal and painful communication, she could tell that. Ah, she thought, most likely a farewell to someone. At least there was someone somewhere he cared for who cared for him.

Lavinia stood up and walked to the window and let him have some privacy. Was it a mistress or a fiancée? *Goodbye, my darling. Live on but never forget me.*

When she turned around again he was reaching for the sand. He folded the paper and put it inside another piece of parchment on which he scribbled a direction and handed it to her.

She took it and read the words written on it: "Miss Lavinia Stewart." He had addressed the letter to her. *She* was the only person who cared if he died?

"The Admiralty will send word if there are complications. In the meantime, keep the letter somewhere safe and out of Angus's sight." He paused and added, "please."

# Chapter 6

"Was a time when I could have done the sewing for you, miss." Dolley hovered close as though he could give her advice on the best way to mend the tear in Angus's shirt.

"You are a help in so many ways, Dolley. That is the very reason I have time for this."

"Will you come closer, miss?" He gestured to the three children who sat waiting near the papier-mâché model of the Mediterranean Sea and the surrounding countries that the boys had fashioned earlier in the week. "Me and the captain have had some rare adventures."

"No, thank you, your voice carries very nicely. If I stay by the window there will be enough daylight to sew. I can save the candles for when they are truly needed."

He nodded and moved to the center of the room.

Mr. Arbuscam was seated nearby. Even he was interested in a story that Dolley insisted had real historical value.

Lavinia was grateful for anything that would keep the two boys sitting quiet. They stayed up half the night talking and, despite that, morning would find them running wild through the house, only calming when Mr. Arbuscam insisted that they come to the schoolroom for lessons.

Even those sessions seemed to end in turmoil. Once, Angus had tackled Harry with a flying leap and held him down when Harry had teased him about his interest in learning.

Harry swore he would never compare Angus to a girl

again. The two vented all their energy in a scuffle that left Harry with a bruised cheek and Angus a torn shirt, neither one the winner which was, apparently, just the way they wanted it.

The truth was that Angus did have a hunger for knowledge and despite his exuberance she found she could not regret her invitation that he join Harry for lessons.

She set the last stitch in the boy's shirt and put it on the table next to her. She reached into the basket and pulled out one of Sara's Sunday dresses. Sara was growing so fast. Lavinia examined the lace that would lengthen the dress by two inches at the hem. Attaching it required no creativity and was about all she had the energy for.

"Captain Chartwell and I met for the first time when we served on the *Speedy* under Captain Cochrane in 1800." Dolley began his story. "I was rated able seaman and he had just passed for lieutenant."

Lavinia shook her head. She could not imagine Lieutenant Chartwell as autocratic as he was as a post captain. What was it about command that had made him so intractable?

"Captain Cochrane favored him, he did."

What had the famous man seen in the new officer? Was Captain Chartwell as guarded in his younger days? She tried to draw a mental picture of the young Chartwell. Fewer scars. A more ready smile. It was hard to know what he had been like in his younger years without some idea of his family and his life before the navy.

"Captain Chartwell was raised in France, you know."

No, she did not know.

"And he speaks the language as good as any Frog." Dolley spoke with some awe.

Mr. Arbuscam cleared his throat and Dolley glanced at him, puzzled.

Lavinia interpreted. "Mr. Arbuscam prefers the term Frenchmen to Frog, Dolley."

"Oh, aye, miss."

"You were saying that the captain was raised in France?"

"Yes. The captain was living over there until the revolution came on too nasty. But he was English—as English as Lord Nelson."

"Was his father French?" Lavinia asked. And, if he was, how had William Chartwell come to fight for England? It was very odd, for his name was not at all French.

"Could be he was."

"Maybe his mother and father went to the guillotine and the captain was rescued and brought back here?" This was Harry's contribution, but Sara agreed with a solemn nod.

"No way o' knowin', 'cause the captain never talks about it." With that, Dolley put an end to the speculation and left Lavinia wondering if the captain ever spoke more than two-word sentences.

"He went into the navy when he was twelve, maybe younger. He was real quiet at first. Never talked much until he lost his French way of talkin'. That accent used to land him in all kinds of fistfights."

"Oh, how awful," Lavinia said. "A boy away from home and nothing but fights to show for it?" She could see him. Tall for his age, grieving for his lost family. Angry.

"Fightin' is how they find their place, miss."

Ah, thought Lavinia. That would explain the fistfights between her boys, despite the obvious friendship.

"He first went to sea aboard the *Chartwell* under Captain Bessborough."

"Was the ship named for someone in his family?"

This question came from Harry, though Lavinia was curious too.

Dolley shifted on his feet, a little uncomfortable. "No, the captain took the name Chartwell from the ship."

"But why?"

"No one knows. He gave a midshipman a black eye for

calling him by the other name. Captain Chartwell was only a boy when he did it, but he got his first taste of the cat for it. But no one ever called him that other name again."

"Oh, how awful."

" 'Tweren't that bad. He was a big boy, like I said, big as a midshipman from the start. Soft in the middle he was, but that was gone soon enough. He was Chartwell from then on."

"What was the other name?" Harry asked with cautious curiosity.

"Never asked and he never told me, lad. But there always've been stories about that he is connected to one of the great families and that his mama ran away and died in France. That's why he was in an orphanage there."

*Could his name have been Braedon? Or was he not a legitimate Braedon at all? Had his mother given him a French name? Yes, that could be the reason he had changed it to Chartwell. Were there any clues in his note, the one lying restlessly in her glove drawer?* She wanted to read it quite desperately, but would not allow herself to invade his privacy that way. Honor was not the sole province of men.

Sara called out a question that drew Lavinia's attention back to the discussion at hand. "If you first met him in 1800 how do you know all this?" she asked with a natural suspicion grown from dealing with a brother who was always making up stories.

" 'Cause, young miss, a friend of mine was on the *Chartwell* and wound up with us on the *Speedy.* Stories pass that way, even though not many of us can do much more than read a bit of the Bible and write our names."

Dolley glanced at Mr. Arbuscam who smiled. Lavinia wondered if Dolley was one of his students as well. Good. If he was to be the house steward for Talford Rise he would need to have full command of numbers and letters.

"Tell us about the *Speedy*, Dolley, and about Captain Cochrane." It was Angus who spoke, but Lavinia noted that

Harry was the one who had pushed him into speech with a sharp jab to his side.

The *Speedy* was not what Lavinia wanted to hear about, but this lesson was not for her.

"*Speedy* was a brig. A brig is not a big ship. No more than fourteen guns and them miserable little four pounders. Had a crew of about eighty. A small ship for sure, but any sailor knows that the most important weapon on any ship, big or small, is the man who is master and commander. And Cochrane is the best. He weren't much of a teacher, but watchin' how he went about it was all an officer needed to see. Our Captain Chartwell learned it all in that one cruise from May 1800 until July 1801 when the *Speedy* went down off Malaga."

"The *Speedy* sank? With the captain and you aboard?" Lavinia bit her lip to keep from uttering "how awful" for a third time.

"Not the first or the last time it happened to us, miss."

*Did he mean that for consolation?*

"But that's a whole different story."

Lavinia shook her head. "It sounds as though we will have entertainment for days to come."

"Be my pleasure, it would." The idea made Dolley smile. He turned his full attention back to the boys. "*Speedy* wasn't much of a command but Captain Cochrane was so damn—beggin' your pardon, miss—so darn proud of *Speedy* that it was contagious. Not a one of us would have left him for less than a place with Nelson."

He went on telling them of days of patrol marked by the occasional skirmish and finally the great defeat of the Spanish xebec frigate *El Gamo.* "The finest bit of battle between two ships that I ever did see."

"You said *El Gamo* had thirty-two guns and three hundred nineteen men?" Harry asked.

"Exactly," Dolley said.

"And the *Speedy* had only eighty-four officers and men? How could they win against a ship that much bigger than they were?"

"Genius, pure genius, luck, and a clever trick or two. I tell no lie, Master Harry. I would swear to every word on a stack of Bibles." He nodded. "That's why when Captain Chartwell thought to take the *Dorsay*, I knew he could do it." He was about to go on when he realized what else had happened on that voyage and cast a stricken eye at Angus.

"I'm sorry, lad. I should never . . ."

"It's all right, Dolley," Angus explained while looking at Harry but including all of them. "My father died that day. He boarded the *Dorsay* and was shot. But the captain and I sat with him 'til the end. He's with my mother and I have the captain." He looked at Dolley, dry-eyed and relaxed. "The capture of the *Dorsay* is a good story too, Dolley, but finish telling us about the *Speedy*. Tell us what Cochrane did with all those prisoners."

*He's with my mother and I have the captain.* It did not seem like a fair trade to Lavinia. The light was fading fast and she put her needle aside and began to fold the mended clothes.

As Dolley went on about pointing guns down hatchways she let her mind drift. She did not care a bit about prisoners of war or incredible victories. She cared so much more about a boy, motherless, facing life with too little love.

But Angus seemed content. How was it that he had not stayed at sea, building a life like his father's and Captain Chartwell's? Was it because a hero-worshipping boy was a burden aboard a ship? Or could it be because the captain's own experience had been a cautionary tale, one that he did not want Angus to share?

Whatever the reason, Angus and Dolley were here at Talford Vale, and because of it the number who cared about the captain's safe return was growing.

Was this the first time that the captain had ever put to sea and left someone behind, whether boy, man, or woman?

Most likely this was a first. How else to explain the daring that Dolley described? Had a lack of family made Captain Chartwell more willing to take such chances? She trusted it was different with Angus as a part of his life.

The captain could take all the risks he liked. But he had better come back. Lavinia smoothed the shirt that she had crushed into a knot. There were people waiting for him. Not family exactly, but a boy and a man. And now a woman who cared enough to worry while they waited.

The rude and taciturn captain might not be appealing, but he had once been very like Angus, a motherless, love-lost boy. And that image was a sure way to her heart.

The onshore breeze cooled the air, but sweat dripped off William's head. Fever was inevitable; death was not.

Angling his body against the rock, he settled himself into the sand above the tide line. Eventually his crew would find him. His orders covered all manner of contingencies. But it would be hours before they put the boat to shore.

He let himself drift off again, dreaming of her. A barefoot woman with hair down her back. He liked her better that way. Better than when she was dressed to impress him with her wealth and privilege.

Was she as comfortable at a dinner party as she was in the water? If she was a graceful swimmer, did that mean she was light on the dance floor?

Why was she not in London? Had she ever had a Season? Had she been ruined? Was it possible that Harry was her natural son and not her nephew after all?

Surely his fever could be blamed for that flight of fantasy. Despite the loose hair and bare feet she seemed every inch a lady. Not that he had known that many.

Lady or not, imagining her here with him eased the pain that fired from his hand up his arm.

The mission had been a ruse. His only consolation was that even the Lord of the Admiralty had fallen for it. Damn Starret. He was a liar and a traitor. A double agent, bold enough to use the Admiralty to make good his escape to France.

William raised his hand to his head and pulled his cap over the bloody bruise on his forehead. The bullet should have left him for dead and eliminated any evidence of Starret's deception.

But Starret was an actor, not a marksman, the wound no more than a graze that had knocked him unconscious. The slice of the knife through his palm was more cause for concern.

William longed for home, longed to get as far as he could from the duplicity that weighed heavily all around him.

He could not stay at Talford Rise more than a night. He would have to go to London as quickly as possible to make his report. And there was every chance in the world that they would try to blame him for the bad intelligence. There must be a way to phrase his report to salvage his career and not accuse the Admiralty of some failure none of them could name. If not, he would be spending a great deal more time at Talford Rise.

In the quiet moments before sleep he had missed the boy, missed the way his curiosity led to such wild mischief. He was like his father in that. In their early years together Carroll had made the miserable parts of a midshipman's life bearable.

Should he have warned her? No. Lavinia Stewart was so sure that her maternal touch would cure Angus's impropriety. And maybe it would. Maybe what the boy needed was the one thing his all-male world could never give him: a woman's love and caring. He had lived his life without it and until she had said the words, it had not occurred to him that it could be something Angus was missing.

Had she convinced him to abandon his hammock and sleep

in a bed? Had affection been a more effective discipline than a swat with the cane?

The crunch of footsteps on the sand brought him fully awake. He saw no boat drawn to shore and heard the unmistakable sound of an armed soldier, his gun rattling at his side as he moved along the shoreline. Most likely a routine patrol if the man did not have his gun in hand at the ready. He should be able to bluff his way out of this. He reached for the bottle of wine and hoped it was an adequate bribe if one were necessary.

William concentrated on the sound and forgot all about Angus and his newly formed household. At the moment he had more pressing problems than his ward's need for discipline.

# Chapter 7

"You want me to give 'em a thrashing over the berries, miss?" Dolley made it sound as though she had suggested they be cast out forever.

Harry and Angus stood before her, their stained hands and mouths the evidence of their crime. Their eyes were round with shock. Good. It was about time they showed her some respect.

"This is the last straw, Dolley. The endless hours of chaos. We'll be finding goose down for months after that last pillow fight. Sara is afraid to go to bed without pulling the sheets back completely, and a bird remains loose in the house somewhere." She threw up her hands in disgust. "The list is endless and no amount of rebuke has worked.

"And now the berries are gone. The berries that had ripened to perfection. The berries Mrs. Wilcox had planned to use in a syllabub"—she raised a finger for emphasis—"despite repeated warnings that they should be left untouched, unsampled, and not eaten."

They were watching her. All three of them. And in complete silence. Finally, they were paying attention.

"Mrs. Wilcox is the only employee of any value here. And she is talking of leaving." Lavinia knew that she could go on for an hour, but made herself stop.

"She's gonna quit over some berries?" Angus asked, surprise clearly overriding his worry about a beating.

"Some people take their work seriously." She glared at

him, her usual tolerant affection had totally evaporated. "The switch will teach you both some respect."

Dolley cleared his throat. "Miss, I'm sorry to have to be telling you this, but I can't use the cane on 'em."

She whirled around to him. "And exactly what do you mean by that, Dolley? You've spent years in the navy. And your adventures are punctuated regularly with accounts of punishment, yours and everyone else's. Surely you know how."

Dolley shifted from one foot to the next and would not meet her eye. "I'm that sorry, ma'am, but them stories is before I lost my arm." His empty sleeve twitched as he moved the stump that was his right shoulder.

He'd used that trick so often that the gesture no longer unnerved her. He was lying. She knew he was.

"Ma'am, I never learned to use my left hand that way and there's no strength there or true aim."

The boys were not smiling, not yet, though they were looking infinitely relieved.

What she really wanted to do was take a stick to the man who had left the boy without telling her exactly how inventive and rebellious he could be.

Captain William Chartwell was at sea, no doubt beneath blue sky and sunshine with men who raced to obey his every wish, while she was stuck here in a bad dream.

"If you cannot do it, Dolley, I will have to do it myself."

Dolley was as surprised as the boys.

"If I do not discipline them, what will be next?" She pointed at the boys. "You two. Go to the house."

Angus and Harry began to march slowly down the path to the side door.

"Wash your hands and face and come to the library," she called after them.

She sent Dolley for the switch and went into the library. He was back quickly, which was a relief as it did not give her time to rethink her decision. She sent him off with orders to send the boys to her.

The worn piece of hickory felt sinister, the end smoothed from years of use. Her hand shook with dislike, but she stood firm.

Assuming an authoritative stance, she drew a deep breath and practiced by slapping the cane against the upholstered sofa.

The stick made a resonant "thwap" as it hit the padded arm. The sound brought a memory instantly to mind and she threw the stick across the room as if distance would ease her revulsion.

She recalled driving with her governess to one of the sugar plantations. Witnessing, actually seeing, one of the estate slaves being whipped mercilessly, his back bleeding, his screams fading to moans.

Her governess had pulled the shades on the carriage but there was no escape from the ghastly cries. She felt as sick as she had all those years ago and knew she could not whip Harry and Angus no matter how heinous their crime.

How could the captain do it? How could he order men to be lashed? Dolley had described it a dozen times. What was it about men that made them willing to use force to make their point? Could he use the whip on a woman? If he married, would he use it on his wife?

No, for had he not told Angus never to strike a woman, to start practicing so that he could learn how to properly treat a lady? Or had the captain told Angus that because of his own experience? Was the captain too old to learn any other way to exert his influence if someone were to defy his command?

There was a tentative knock on the door.

When she called for them to enter, the two boys stepped into the room, as tentatively as if they feared waking a sleeping baby. Their faces were clean, their hands dripping wet.

"Aunt Lavinia?"

"Yes." She considered her one-word answer and the tone a

good imitation of the captain. Imperious. Yes, that's what it was.

"Aunt Lavinia, we went and apologized to Mrs. Wilcox."

"You did?" She should not let her surprise show, but it was too late for that.

"Yes, miss," said Angus. "She boxed our ears and said that we must help her with kitchen chores for a week."

"She did?" Apparently Mrs. Wilcox had a more maternal sense of discipline than she did.

"Yes, Aunt. She said that if we are going to be such bad boys we needed to do woman's chores to calm us down."

Lavinia was not at all sure that would work, but, since it would free time for her to tackle other chores, it was worth trying.

"Very well." She walked over and picked up the switch. She ran it through her hand once or twice and slapped the sofa as she had a few moments before.

Harry jumped. Angus did not. He was probably used to the sound.

Traitorous tears filled her eyes and she waved a hand at them. "Do not ever make me this angry again. Not ever. Do you hear?"

"Yes, miss," Angus spoke.

Harry nodded, speechless.

She turned away. "Go. Both of you." She could barely speak the words amidst her tears.

They all but tripped over each other as they hurried from the room. As the door closed, she heard Angus ask in his version of a whisper, "We're the ones scrubbing pots. How come *she's* crying?"

The door clicked quietly behind them and Lavinia sank to the couch and sniffed as the tears kept falling. This misery is what came from her arrogance. She had been so certain that having the boy in her care was what was best for him and it may have been. But it had more than doubled her responsibilities.

Dolley had been a great help, but there were simply not enough hours in the day for her to clean what she and the children needed, urge the servants to do the rest of the house, avoid the gardener's demented wrath, convince the village merchants that they would be paid, and, all the while, worry that Desmond would come for a visit with yet another group of his dissolute, self-indulgent friends.

Well, she could be self-indulgent. Tomorrow she would turn a blind eye to the chores and spend some time in Angus's hammock. But it was hardly a permanent solution.

She needed someone, anyone to help her escape from this trap. And marriage was the only way out. He did not have to ride a white horse or look like a god. He had only to be honest and kind and willing to take on Harry and Sara. He had only to use his presence to give her protection.

She used the edge of her gown to wipe away her tears. She might as well ask for the moon.


William came to the edge of the lake that separated Talford Rise from Talford Vale. He stopped, taking a moment to absorb the picture that was as sweet as his dream. The sight made the long trip from France and up from Portsmouth worth the effort.

Lavinia Stewart lay in the hammock, which had found a home on the piazza of the boathouse, built out over the mooring and dock space. The vantage point gave a broad overlook of the lake and caught any breeze rising from the water.

Dolley came up behind him.

"I see Miss Stewart convinced Angus to sleep in a bed." As William spoke, he turned and looked at his butler. Dolley's smile had been a welcome all its own. His old boatswain was full of news, as though the time ashore suited him.

"She has him in a room with Master Harry, Captain, but for his part Angus managed to convince her that the hammock is not entirely worthless."

There was no mistaking what she was watching, if she did indeed have her eyes open. Angus and Harry were rowing vigorously to the far end of the pond, trailing a dozen or so ducks as though they were an enemy convoy and, not coincidentally, moving as far from her supervision as they could.

"She told them not to throw rocks, but they will not give up on the chase."

As they watched, the boys continued after the ducks while the ducks paddled toward the protective reeds with equal determination.

Moving slowly across the grass, his eye on the boys, William headed for the opulent boathouse. He lost sight of them as he stepped into the elegant chamber that led to the portico.

"Tell them not to chase the ducks."

He stopped, startled, until he realized it was Sara's voice carried to him from where she was sitting near her aunt.

"This room is like a giant bullhorn," Dolley spoke quietly.

"Indeed." William raised an eyebrow. "Do Talford Vale and Rise share the same listening holes, Dolley?"

"I would hardly know about that, sir," Dolley answered, trying for indignant.

The girl's voice interrupted William's reply. "It'll serve them right if the ducks attack them, won't it, Aunt Lavinia?"

William could hear the malicious satisfaction in the girl's voice. No doubt Angus had earned every ounce of her longing for revenge.

"Hmmm" was the only comment her aunt made.

"They have to learn everything the hard way," Sara said.

William smiled, sure that the girl was answering for her aunt.

"She did tell 'em to mind the ducks. Told 'em more than once," Dolley said.

"Has it been difficult?"

"Not after she threatened 'em with the hickory."

William felt a twinge of guilt for not warning her.

"That bad they were, sir. But she never had to use it on 'em. She cried and that was the worst torture in the world."

"Indeed." He tried to visualize the stalwart Miss Stewart in tears. The picture did not come easily.

The boys' yelling distracted them. One could almost insult them and call it screaming. William stepped down and moved around to the front corner of the building. He stopped at the low retaining wall in time to see the boys rowing madly away from a duck intent on pecking any exposed part of their bodies.

William's laughter drew their attention. Angus let out a whoop and William raised his unbandaged hand in greeting.

He could see that Angus's yell had brought Lavinia to her feet, but she was looking out at the boys and not back to where he stood. At that moment, Harry stood up in the well of the boat. Angus reached for him and tried to tug him back down, but Harry jerked out of his friend's reach. The boat leaned to the right, and before any of the adults could shout "sit down" both boys were in the water in a windmill of arms and legs.

"Run for a float, Dolley. Have Chasen bring blankets."

Dolley took off. William moved down the bank, in the shadow of the boathouse, but closer to their overturned boat. He could see neither boy and hoped it was only the overturned boat that was blocking his view.

Lavinia raced past him and had quite literally ripped off her dress and one petticoat by the time she reached a point of entry closest to the upturned rowboat.

She did not see him and he doubted it would have stopped her. She was, indeed, as ferocious as a mother duck when it came to protecting her young. Did she know that Angus had never learned to swim?

The boys' heads popped up, thrashing wildly as they struggled to find a handhold on the hull of the flat-bottomed boat.

William considered it a good sign that Harry had enough breath and energy to bellow "Angus can't swim" even as Lavinia made a sleek, shallow dive into the water, her hair streaming behind her, looking every bit like a mermaid playing dress-up in a woman's chemise.

How deep was the clear green water? Over the boys' heads, that was obvious. He moved to the spot where she had waded in, and followed her into the water, boots and all, and never mind the white of his uniform pants. If he could wade out close enough, he could haul up either boy one-handed. He had gone only a few yards when the water deepened suddenly, putting an end to that plan.

It would be a fool's act to follow her farther. He could keep himself alive in the water, but with his wounded hand he would be no help at all.

She knew the water. She could swim. If a man had gone to the rescue he would not feel this frustration, but would let him do the job he had committed to. She reached the boys and he waited to see what she would do.

# Chapter 8

She had no idea what to do once she reached the boys. Try to right the boat? Swim to shore with one and return for the other? They were not so very far from the bank bordering the Talford Rise property. She eyed the shore, mentally measuring the distance, and saw a man wading out toward them.

"Wait, Miss Stewart. Dolley has gone for a float," the man yelled, and with that voice of authority came recognition.

Captain Chartwell was home? Was here? He was watching her?

"Welcome home, sir," Angus called out as if in confirmation.

"Go back, Captain." She flipped to her back for a moment as she answered. "You'll ruin your uniform. I can manage." As though his uniform mattered more than the boys. But the truth was, with him nearby, she could manage. She was not alone and he would never let them come to harm.

She moved slowly in the water, catching her breath, lost more from fear than exertion. There were no more shouted instructions from the shore and Lavinia glanced back again. And laughed.

The captain was standing still as a statue, except this statue, with his arms folded across his chest, was knee-deep in water. The narrowed eyes and set jaw gave him the look of a man judging a contest.

"Do I have to wait for Dolley, Aunt Lavinia? There are fish eating my toes."

Both boys were holding on to the boat and Angus laughed, as though he was not in danger himself. "A shark's what's nibbling your toes, Harry, a great big one and next he'll bite your whole leg off. Dolley's seen it happen."

"But not in a lake in Sussex," Lavinia reminded him. "Stop teasing him, Angus."

"I'm not afraid," Harry insisted. "It's only that I can't see what's down there."

"You have never learned to swim, Angus?" Lavinia asked, recalling Harry's earlier shout.

"No, ma'am."

"Remind me to teach you the next time you come to stay."

"Yes, ma'am, and thank you." He grinned as though this was a great adventure and she knew that, torture though it could be, this boy would always be welcome in her home.

"Harry, do you want to swim with me to the edge where the captain is waiting? It is only a little way before you can stand on your feet and wade out."

"All right," Harry said doubtfully.

"Can you hold on for five minutes more, Angus? Surely Dolley will have help here by then."

"Oh yes, miss. I can hold on and I do know how to float even if this is not salt water."

Lavinia and Harry made their way to the edge of the lake. Harry swam until the captain grabbed his arm and helped him as he stumbled ashore.

Just as Lavinia began to swim back to Angus, Dolley showed up and tossed her a float attached to a rope. She put her arm through it and swam to Angus who grabbed the float with some expertise.

Once there was something he could do, the captain was anything but a statue. He pulled the float and Angus toward shore. Dolley stood behind him and tucked the length of rope under his shoulder stump, drawing the excess from behind the captain as he pulled. There was a third man as well. He was tending to Harry, a pile of blankets dumped on the ground nearby.

As they reached the bank, Lavinia realized that she was less than half-dressed and the water made her clothing transparent.

She moved back into the water and called to the captain, "I'm going for the rowboat."

"Wait," he said over his shoulder. "Dolley, take Harry to his house. Chasen, you take Angus back to Talford Rise. Give me that blanket before you go."

They all scurried to obey and in less than a minute Lavinia and the captain were by themselves.

That did not make it any easier for her to leave the water.

"Where is Sara?" she asked.

"Gone to have Mrs. Wilcox warm some soup for you." He opened the blanket and held it out. "You have to come out sometime. Unless you really are a mermaid come ashore to plague the minds of men."

She plagued him? It sounded like something a London beauty might claim. Or maybe he merely meant that she annoyed him. Who wanted to be "plagued" by anything?

One huge shiver shook her.

"Come out of the water." It was his command voice and with a shuddering breath as much from the cold as the embarrassment, she obeyed.

Water trailed behind her, pulling her waterlogged garments tightly against her, outlining every detail of her body. She knew her nipples were peaked, but only from the cold. She hoped he knew that. For he was not looking away, but right at her.

She stepped into his waiting arms, or rather into the blanket that he held. He wrapped it around her so that the opening was in the back and for one long moment they stood close together. Just to help warm her, just to make her feel safe. She was sure that was all it meant, but he did not let go and she could feel his hands on her almost bare back.

She could have sworn he whispered, "mermaid and mother duck," but if she looked up to question it, their lips would only be inches apart. An embrace was one thing, a kiss entirely another. Did he think her morals as free as her brother's?

She pulled herself from him and turned round to fix it so that the edges of the blanket were at her front where she held them tight around her neck with one hand. She bent down to pick up the clothes she had tossed to the ground.

She straightened and glanced at him but would not meet his eyes. "You were here all along? You saw what happened?"

"Yes."

"And you let me do the rescue? I don't know whether to be flattered or appalled."

"You had it well in hand." He made no further offer of help, turned from her, and started to walk away. Lavinia was annoyed. He was so completely lacking in sensibility.

She loosened the blanket, not quite as chilled. In fact, her temper was warming her nicely. "You looked absurd standing there in water up to your knees."

"Indeed." He glanced at her over his shoulder and then spoke with his back to her. "I have been in water deeper than that and managed to give orders."

Of course he had, she thought. Even near drowning he would probably give commands. "Is that it?" She followed him. "You are so used to being in charge that actually doing the work is beneath you? Surely you were not afraid?"

He faced her again. A muscle ticked in his cheek and Lavinia stopped, but did not apologize.

He stepped toward her even as she moved away. With one hand he took one end of the blanket that had slipped down to reveal her shoulder. Pulling it up, he cinched it tightly under her chin.

"Bare feet is one thing, Miss Stewart. But standing here baiting me when dressed in nothing but a wet chemise and one of my blankets is as foolish as it is . . ." he paused, "as foolish as it is absurd."

He might call her absurd, but neither one of them was laughing. His eyes held hers and they were both steely and expressive. His large hand burned hers where it lay over her smaller ones, both of them holding the blanket tightly around her.

"Is it only me that brings out the shrew in you?"

If she wanted feeling from him, she had it. He seemed genuinely puzzled and frustrated. At least she hoped that was what he was frustrated about. Given their proximity, any other kind of frustration could prove dangerous.

Before she could answer, Sara came running across the lawn and flung her arms around her aunt's waist. "Aunt Lavinia, I am so glad you are safe. I was so afraid you all would drown."

She watched the captain even as she soothed the child. Was this enough answer to his question? It must have been, because the anger he had held in check faded, leaving him looking tired and bruised. Despite her annoyance, she wondered how long it had been since he'd slept.

He moved away, brushing his pants as though the water stains were dust he could easily remove. "Dolley will come tomorrow for Angus's clothes."

She watched his retreating back. Did he not say "thank you" any more often than he said "please"?

"We will expect him for his lesson tomorrow," Lavinia called, loud enough for him to hear even if he were a county away.

Captain Chartwell raised a hand, in acknowledgment she supposed, but did not answer her. Angus had better come, she decided, or she would go and collect him herself.

Sara pulled at her arm. "His hand, Aunt Lavinia. Look."

She noticed the white bandaging for the first time. How

had she not seen that his left hand was covered across his palm and around his thumb?

He had been injured? He had only been gone a few weeks. It was only to be "a simple in-and-out action." Apparently it had not been as simple as he and the Admiralty had hoped. She shivered again, and this time she knew it was not from the cold. While she was dealing with fractious boys and unmanageable servants, he had been facing an enemy intent on injury. And she had implied he was a coward.

She hurried after him, calling to him.

"Yes, Miss Stewart?" The three words hinted at a barely controlled anger and when he turned back to her, her words of sympathy died at the flare of temper in his eyes.

An apology was in order, but she shied even from that. "About the letter you left. The one I was to open if something were to happen."

"Yes."

"You are returned safely. Should I destroy it?"

He started away again before he answered and she stopped following him. "Keep the letter. Keep it for next time."

He hurried back across the grass, and was most of the way to the Rise before anger gave way to embarrassment. She had handled the situation with the boys admirably, as well as any man could have. How was it that he was leaving, having not said thank you, having insulted her?

She was more than a mermaid. She had been Diana the huntress or Poseidon's daughter. He wished he could name some great heroine of the Greeks. She had been all of them as she came from the water with both boys safe.

Just as suddenly the image of triumph had faded, replaced by thoughts far from noble. The way her breasts filled her light corset. The way the wet chemise clung to her legs and thighs, outlining her most feminine parts.

When she had called him a coward all his pleasure ebbed. He had hardly acted the hero, but did she truly think that he would have not helped if she had been in distress?

Angus came barreling out of the house, down the steps, and across the grass. His hair was wet, but he was in dry clothes. Clearly the mishap in the lake barely registered on his scale of "disasters averted."

"Oh, sir! Oh, Captain, you are here. You are back." He came to an abrupt halt, straightened, and with a grin announced: *"Esse homo multarum literarum."*

"Great learning? Is that so? *Exercitatio optimus est magister."*

"Practice is the best teacher—but I practice all the time, sir!"

"Indeed?"

"During lessons, sir, really, though Mr. Arbuscam could make even the Trojan War boring. And sometimes when Harry and I wish to trick Sara, we will plan in Latin."

Angus was all but dancing around him, then suddenly stopped short. "Your hand, sir." He stared at the bandage, shocked out of all proportion to the injury.

"It is nothing. A deep splinter during a small disagreement. It turned putrid." He had decided in the carriage on the way from Portsmouth that a splinter was a far easier explanation than a stab wound.

Angus nodded in understanding, but his high spirits had disappeared. He walked around the captain as if inspecting for any further injuries, and then took his other hand.

They walked in silence, William fully aware that this little injury reminded Angus that his guardian was no less impervious to harm than his father had been.

"Is your uniform ruined?" Angus asked timidly.

William shook his head. "My uniform is soaked worse than this in a rain squall. You know that. I'm so used to wet boots that dry feels odd."

They reached the door and the boy moved to push it open. William brushed his hand across the boy's head and pulled him close for a moment. "*Hoc certum est.*"

"What is certain, sir?"

"I am not the only one who saw battle. Come up while I get out of this uniform and tell me about the duck attack."

William had changed into buckskin breeches and a linen shirt long before Angus finished the telling of his adventures of the last two weeks.

He pulled his favorite coat from the clothes press. As he struggled into it he noticed that the cuff was beginning to fray. He had yet to find another steward half as good as Crask and wondered if he had recovered from the fever that made it necessary to leave him behind in Brazil. A valet must be next on his list of staff if he was to continue ashore.

"I know taking the berries was bad, sir, and believe me, we were punished. Cleaning pots is the worst sort of work and it is endless."

"Well, that is why it is called punishment. Would you have preferred the switch?"

"Well, no, sir," Angus said after actually considering the idea. "But it was like a double punishment. Mrs. Wilcox never stops talking; her insisting that Miss Stewart works too hard and we should help her instead of making her life miserable."

William stopped buttoning his jacket. "She works too hard?" Doing what, he wondered. She was swinging in a hammock when first he saw her.

"She says that Miss Stewart does the work of three housemaids." He ticked the chores on his fingers, for all the world a male pint-sized version of the dreaded cook. "She starts the bedroom fires on the mornings we need it, brings hot water, helps with breakfast, keeps the school room clean, mends our clothes, airs our beds, and helps with the cooking."

"There are servants, aren't there, Angus?" When did the lady of the house call on the neighbors, do fancy needlework, and write letters?

"She says Miss Stewart's brother hires sluts who do nothing when he is away and are only good for one thing when he is at home." He narrowed his eyes and asked, "Would that mean that the maids at the Vale are like the women who spend time aboard when the ship is in port?"

"Probably." And that was an odd makeup for a household with a woman and children.

"That's what I told Harry."

What could he say to that? No doubt young Harry was far more worldly wise than he had been a fortnight ago.

"You are to go to lessons tomorrow."

"But of course, sir! Miss Stewart is expecting me." Angus made it sound as though there was no decision to be made.

"This schooling suits you?"

"Yes, sir. Very much, sir. Harry is the finest. And," he went on with real excitement in his voice, "we are to start on the geography of the Americas."

William spent some more time listening to the boy's description of his studies, which seemed to involve Dolley as much as it did Mr. Arbuscam. Finally, he sent Angus to supper and then to bed. As he left the room, Angus asked one last question, "Do you think Harry will be in trouble for standing up in the boat, sir?"

"Washing more pots?"

"Or forbidden to see me?"

"You will find out tomorrow."

"Yes, sir."

William let him leave on those two sorrow-filled words. He might be dejected, but it would not last long. At least the boy was no longer worried about the possibility of his guardian's death.

# Chapter 9

William made his way down to the library, but was not ten minutes with his sketchpad when there was a tap at the door. At his "enter," Dolley came halfway into the room.

"You have a report as well, Dolley?" William closed the pad and dropped the bit of lead with which he had been sketching.

The man gave his boatswain's sharp nod and came up to the desk. He stood ramrod straight with his hand behind his back. Did he even know he had assumed the old familiar position of report, the one they had shared for years aboard ship?

"Sit down, Dolley." Easier to make that offer than to remind him that times had changed and he was ashore for good.

Dolley said, "Thank you, sir." He relaxed his rigid posture, but remained standing. "I know times is different, sir, but I could never sit. Not in front of you, sir."

William accepted that Dolley knew the right of it better than he did. "How was life at Talford Vale?"

"A woman in command is a whole different world, sir." His butler hesitated. "She means the best, but it's hard to tell her commands from her suggestions. And at Talford Vale there are two women in charge: Miss Stewart and the cook, Mrs. Wilcox."

"I thought Wilcox was her maid." He leaned back in his chair. "Or are there two of that name?"

"She's no maid, beggin' your pardon, sir." Dolley took a step closer. "You had the right of that. Maude Wilcox is the cook. And the only servant in that house worth a measure of grog." Dolley cleared his throat. "And a right nice handful on a summer night."

William sat forward again, clasped his hands in front of him as he considered the last sentence. "Be careful, Dolley. This is no brief port call and she has Mrs. in front of her name."

"Aye, sir, and I asked. She's been a widow these past six years."

William nodded and wondered if it had been a mistake to send his butler to the Vale. It was very possible that Dolley's loyalty would be tested. And this was one servant he did not want to lose.

William folded, unfolded, and clasped his hands as he considered the problem. "You know, don't you, Dolley, that Gibson is determined to go back to sea?"

"Yes, sir." Dolley appeared disappointed at the change of subject. "But it'll be hard to find a spot for a one-eyed gunner."

William leaned back again, his hands folded across his middle, tapping his thumbs. "I could speak for him."

"That will be all it takes, sir. But if he goes, his brother goes with him. And he's the one cooking."

"Oh, yes, I've noticed. And if both Gibsons leave, we'll be needing someone new in the kitchen."

William could tell when a grin split Dolley's face that he had reasoned it out.

"Finding staff is part of your job," William continued, more than satisfied with Dolley's growing excitement. "This time I would like a cook who has perfected something more than spotted dick and peas."

"Do you think she would come, sir? Our kitchen is the same or maybe even a sight better than at the Vale. It might do, Captain. If she'll have me." He jerked his empty sleeve.

William shook his head. "You're as fine a man as any even

with one arm, Dolley." His butler straightened even more, if that was possible.

"I don't know, sir. It might not be that easy. She is Miss Stewart's favorite and she might not take losing Mrs. Wilcox with a smile."

"Then it will be a test of her feelings for you, will it not?"

"Yes, sir," Dolley spoke without conviction, but his indecision did not last long. "Come to that, sir, I was thinking that maybe it be time for you to marry."

"Good God, Dolley." William stopped smiling. Here was proof positive that one mistake—sending Dolley to the Vale—could take on catastrophic dimensions. "Has three weeks in a female household made you a matchmaker?"

Dolley swallowed the insult, shifted from one foot to the other, and plunged on. "I mean Miss Stewart, sir."

"I guessed as much." He let his exasperation show, but Dolley was not deterred.

"You see, Captain, I was thinking that if you married Miss Stewart, Maude might come here with her." He continued, "But you see, if I married Maude, it could be the other way and Miss Stewart would marry you."

William did not smile, forbade himself to smile. He hardly thought Lavinia Stewart would marry him in order to follow her cook, no matter how fine her puddings were.

"Aye, sir, I can see you think that is nonsensical, but I been watchin' her for a while now and I know a sight more about what goes on there. Mrs. Wilcox is as near as Miss Stewart has for a friend, not counting Harry and Sara."

"They are hardly peers, Dolley. And there is a town less than a mile away."

"Her brother owes money to every shop there. The vicar's wife avoids her even on Sunday. And Mrs. Newcomb and her sister are the only ladies who give her the time of day." He spoke as though he were a matchmaker on a mission. "Miss Stewart is good and kind with the children and anyone else who earns her approval. The swimming is not what a lady usually does, but she is right and proper for all that and her bare feet."

If so, why was she unattached, so firmly on the shelf? He'd been wondering that for weeks.

Dolley hurried on, clearly under the mistaken impression that he was making headway. "She does not suffer fools easily, sir. The maids earn an earful and so does the crazy gardener. She's the only one who can force him to give over the vegetables from the kitchen garden. A real blistering she gives 'em."

"Yes, I've had one of those myself. So where does that leave me? With the serving girls and the crazy gardener?"

"Oh no, sir, you are in a class all by yourself."

At the moment he suspected that class was somewhere *below* the ineffectual servants.

"Maude says that Miss Stewart's brother hardly ever remembers her or his children. Only comes to the Vale when he wants to entertain his London friends."

William stood up. This was more than he needed to know, wanted to know. Standing was a sign that the interview was over. Dolley knew it too, but continued anyway. "Of course, you'll be making your own decision on that, sir."

William lowered his head in what might have been a nod and remained silent. Dolley still ignored the tacit order.

"Was hoping you might have a report for me as well, sir."

"A report for you?"

Dolley straightened to attention again and did not look away. "If you please, sir."

"Dolley, just because you are ashore does not mean the chain of command is any different. You report to me, not the other way around."

The old boatswain did not reply immediately and when he spoke, William knew he had been working up his courage.

"Like you said, sir, I'm ashore. I report to you, here as well, but it's different havin' no idea what's happenin' out there."

William would not be swayed by Dolley's mournful eyes. "Under any other circumstances I would tell you. But the report on this mission is meant for the Admiralty's ears only."

"Aye, sir." He spoke slowly, understanding dawning. "It's 'cause you speak French so well, isn't it, sir?"

He ignored the question. "And if these missions continue, that is all you will ever know."

"It'll be enough, sir." He spoke with conviction as though acknowledging an order.

William came around the desk. "It is true that you are ashore and acting as both butler and house steward, but those roles are as important as any aboard ship. And the pay is better."

Dolley nodded, but he did not look convinced.

"And you must admit that the villagers regard your word with as much respect as any seaman."

"That they do, sir." Dolley's stiffness eased as he considered the elements of his new position.

"And a Christmas bonus is more sure than prize money."

"Thank you, sir," he said, nodding and looking considerably happier. "Will you be wanting some supper yourself, sir?"

"In an hour, and bring it in here, Dolley.

"Aye, Captain."

"I go to London first thing tomorrow to make my report to the Admiralty." As he spoke, William went back to his desk, sat down, and pulled the sketchpad closer. "Nothing in writing for this one. I'll return as soon as I can. No more than five days."

"Aye, sir," Dolley said, acting as though he was privy to the secret.

"You and Angus will stay here, but he will continue his studies at Talford Vale."

"Aye, sir." Dolley left the room, mumbling under his breath.

William picked up the lead but did no more than hold it for a moment and wonder about this new lot in life. He had a household to keep happy. Not only Angus, but Dolley as well and possibly even Mrs. Wilcox.

But not Lavinia Stewart. William opened the pad and ripped out the quick drawing of a woman rising from the water and crumpled it into a ball. The last thing his mind or body needed was a reminder of her wet chemise, her lush body.

The Admiralty would value his sketches of Garrett and the lay of the land. He banished the thought of Lavinia Stewart's lips and began to draw the village where he had last seen the double agent.

Dinner was brought promptly and was still hot. That was the best he could say for it. The unimaginative boiled chicken and eternal peas satisfied his hunger and nothing more.

He had fallen asleep over a brandy and a weeks-old newspaper when Dolley found him a few hours later.

"Captain, sir?"

William woke instantly and gave Dolley his full attention.

"Angus has gone missing." Dolley came into the room. "His bed's not been slept in and he's nowhere in the house."

"Surely not run away?"

"Oh no, sir. But I expect he may have gone off to Master Harry."

"Aha. What time is it?"

"Near midnight. If you will, I can run across and see if he is at the Vale."

With a nod from William, Dolley was off and back in fifteen minutes. "Master Harry is gone too. I told Miss Stewart we would find them, but I heard her tell Sara that she was going to dress and go look for them herself."

"Go to bed, Dolley." He tossed back the last of his brandy and rose from the chair.

"They are up to some mischief, sir."

"But only boyish mischief. That I can deal with even with a bandaged hand and it is an easy guess where they are."

Dolley smiled with comprehension. "The hammock at the boathouse."

The full moon made walking easy, layering the pathway with shadows almost as keen as the sun's. He was crossing the grass when he saw Lavinia Stewart approaching from the Vale.

Her steps were slow. Indeed, she even stopped to look at something in the grass. He deliberately snapped a twig so he would not frighten her. When she saw him, she stopped abruptly but, after a moment, raised her hand in recognition if not greeting.

Why did she ever wear her hair up in a tight knot when this long flowing flood of it was so much more appealing? The dark hair was a complete contrast to her loose-fitting white dress. How had he ever thought her plain? She was not elegant, but she was lovely in the way a madonna was or a child of nature. She brought to mind Mélusine the mermaid princess of childhood fairy tales.

He resisted the fairy tale image. He had never believed in them anyway. Lavinia Stewart was more like a siren. She would draw a man so she could flay him with words as surely as a siren lured men to their death.

They came together without speaking and walked as one to the boathouse. He could see the hammock swaying slightly and a small form leaning against the doorframe.

Lavinia stopped their progress just as the boys' conversation drifted back through the mural-walled anteroom.

"Sara said he had his whole hand wrapped in a bandage."

William saw her glance at his hand.

"He said it was a splinter."

"A splinter?" Harry scoffed. "A little splinter would never need a bandage like that," Harry said.

"Not a little splinter. On a ship sometimes they are as big as a man. When a cannonball slams into the ship and breaks it all to pieces. It can kill you easy."

Lavinia looked at him for confirmation. William's only answer was a casual shrug.

"Angus, if it was a splinter that big his whole hand would be gone. He'd probably be dead."

"Yeah, I know." He was silent a minute and William knew he was worrying again. "I expect that it was more the size of a nail like the kind they used when they crucified Jesus Christ."

That silenced Harry completely and William saw that even Lavinia winced at the comparison.

William shook his head. "No need for a town crier with Angus to spread the news."

She reached out as though she would take his wounded hand in hers but thought better of it. "Is it healing as it ought?"

"Yes." He had to force himself not to put his hand behind his back.

The boys must have heard them because by the time they walked through the chamber and onto the cement portico, Angus had flipped from the hammock. Harry straightened next to him.

William gave them the concentrated stare that had cowed men much older.

"You could not wait twelve hours to see each other?" Lavinia spoke very quietly, with a maternal authority that was probably more effective than his glare. "Why must you worry the captain, me, and Dolley, too?"

He thought the shade of disappointment in her voice was masterful.

"We were afraid you would not allow us time to play together," Harry said and Angus agreed.

"The thought never entered our minds until two minutes ago," she said.

The captain added, "What happened today was nothing more than an accident." With a glance at her he went on, "We know that falling out of the boat was not deliberate."

Lavinia finished the thought, "We know that as well as we know that this behavior was meant to deceive us."

"Yes, ma'am," they both mumbled.

"How lucky for Miss Stewart and me that Mrs. Wilcox has endless pots to wash."

"Oh, Aunt Lavinia."

William was the one who had mentioned the pots, but Harry must have thought his aunt was more inclined to forgiveness.

"Harry, that whine only annoys me more."

"There is always the lash," the captain said, even though he realized that time in the kitchen would be more helpful to Miss Stewart. "I brought a new switch home with me."

Harry cringed, but Angus smiled a little.

"But perhaps not, for I know Miss Stewart finds the lash upsetting. We will not give you a choice. You will report to Mrs. Wilcox after your lessons tomorrow."

"I think it exactly the right punishment, Captain."

Angus responded with a firm "yes, sir," and Harry with a resigned "yes, Aunt Lavinia."

"Go to bed." He stepped back so they could move past him, but made no move to leave himself.

"Yes, sir," they chorused.

"In your own homes," Lavinia added.

He could see her considering if she had covered all possible mischief. He called out, "Go directly. No detours."

The two stayed close together until the last possible moment. When they did separate, Angus ran while Harry moved as slowly as was humanly possible.

Lavinia Stewart watched the boys until they were out of sight. William watched her, taking in every detail—from the shining hair to the shabby dress and pale pink slippers, wet from the grass. William wondered what she would say when she realized that it was just the two of them with nothing but the moon for a chaperone.

# Chapter 10

She watched until Harry was out of sight and then focused on him. The light of the moon showed her a little surprised. "We actually agreed on something, Captain."

"Yes, Miss Stewart." He folded his arms across his chest, wondering at the tameness of this opening volley. "But I know from experience that when faced with a greater threat, even enemies can become allies."

"I suppose I deserve that." Clearly stung by the analogy, she turned from him as though seeking comfort in the water or the grass edging the bank. "I must apologize for my behavior today." She spoke stiffly, not looking at him.

By the stars, was she trying to make amends? "And my apologies to you, Miss Stewart."

"Please, Captain," she went on as if she had not heard his apology. "If Angus and Harry are to continue lessons together, I, for one, would like to make an effort to be civil." She raised her chin a little, awaiting his response with more challenge than courtesy.

"Indeed."

"Indeed, sir. Indeed?" She made an inarticulate sound of frustration. "Is that all you can say? What exactly does 'indeed' mean? If that is all I am going to hear when I try for civility, it is not worth the effort."

He almost said "indeed" again; instead he raised a hand to his forehead and knew better than to blame the incipient headache on his after-dinner brandy. "You say you want peace, but I see that you are determined to stop short of surrendering your colors."

"Would you speak in a language I can understand? I was never in the navy."

He could tell by her tone, by the way she stood square in front of him, that he was failing this test.

"You are not entirely convinced that this effort at civility will work, so you offer peace with one hand and with the other you hide a gun behind your back."

She laughed, a short exasperated sound, but not the burst of temper he had expected.

"You doubt my sincerity?" She held out both her hands to him. "You have spent too much time with people who dissemble. I mean exactly what I say. I apologize. I was overwrought with worry for the boys and you were a convenient target."

He could hardly return her honesty when it meant admitting the feel of her in his arms had undone him. He cursed the moon for a fickle chaperone. "I can understand your frustration with them, Miss Stewart. It was the final mischief in what must have been a trying time. I can understand perfectly."

"You can?" He watched as her gaze moved to his hand. "I suppose you can. I see that you have had trouble of your own. Were you able to complete your mission before your ship came under fire?"

Her eyes met his and he found he could not lie to her. She was making the effort. He was the one being difficult.

"All I *can* say is that the mission did not go as any of us expected, but for all I know that may have been part of the plan as well."

"How could they send you on a mission like that?" She raised a hand to her heart, genuinely shocked.

"We are at war, Miss Stewart," he said tersely. "I knew

when I agreed to take on special assignments that there would be times when I would not be given all the details."

She leaned back a little and spoke with sudden insight, "This was a spy mission." She made it a statement and not a question. "Is that why you cut your hair short? Most naval officers I have known wear a queue down their back."

There was no need for torture with Lavinia Stewart questioning. The answers would pour out, bypassing his brain entirely.

"I think the discussion must stop here." It was not the questions so much as how they were phrased. Her sympathetic curiosity would be his undoing. "You cannot be privy to all the information without compromising the outcome."

"Very well," she agreed. "I will not even mention your head wound."

He raised a hand to the bruise. "Can you see it? I had hoped it had faded."

"It has, I'm sure, and I cannot see it now, even if the moon is full." As she spoke she stepped closer to him, looking intently at his forehead, testing her point. The essence of her, fresh, warm, and vital, surrounded him.

"I first noticed it this afternoon. But I am used to the mischief of boys and am always on the lookout for injury."

Did that mean that she only thought of him in a maternal way? "I hope the head wound was a miscalculation and the admiralty does not think me expendable."

"I hope so as well."

He liked the sound of that and for the first time wondered if civility might be a cover for flirtation.

That hope faded when she continued. "Angus needs you."

She might not be interested, but he was fascinated: by her eyes, her mouth, the way she stood, even the way she looked around as if the plants had the answer she was searching for.

He cleared his throat and took a step back, trying to think of a way to end their conversation without embarrassing either one of them. "You managed to send Angus home without any limbs broken or teeth missing and with only the hint of a black eye. And he seems to have learned a great deal about washing pots as well."

"Perhaps you will not need that new lash after all."

He thought their growing rapport was about to end until he noticed that there was laughter in her eyes. "There is no new lash. It is what I always tell him when I come home."

"How awful. Do you not think a seashell or some small memento from a foreign port would be more appropriate?"

"For you, yes. For a boy that is nothing but energy and mischief, a new lash is just the thing."

She moved to face the water. Instead of bidding her good night and leaving, he joined her, standing close, his hands on the cement balustrade of the terrace. She was not looking at him, but out at the lake. He followed her gaze but could see no movement on the water.

"Angus was not that poorly behaved, Captain."

"Dolley says otherwise."

"Oh, and Dolley was such a help. He was in charge of quieting them at night. He would tell them stories."

"He always has been a capital story teller."

"He told us of your heroism when you were on the *Leopard.*"

She turned toward him, pushing her hair off her shoulder and down her back. The admiration shining from her eyes made him uncomfortable.

"He told us about the time you took one of the small boats, the jolly boat I think he called it, and rescued all the enemy sailors who survived the battle even though it meant going very near to the burning ship."

"Indeed."

"Yes, indeed," she said pointedly.

He faced her again, but she only shook her head and continued. "I always meant to ask Dolley, was that not a foolish command to give? Was there not real danger that the ship's magazine would explode?"

Her puzzlement created two small lines between her eyes. He wanted to reach up and smooth them away. He clenched his fists at his side instead. "Yes, but a lieutenant does not refuse an order." *Even from a monster like Keppel.* "And luck was on our side. The powder was wet and not a hazard after all."

She nodded, her admiration accompanied by a smile. "Dolley said that during your first command you were able to capture an enemy garrison by putting the marines ashore and ordering them to attack from behind while keeping the ship just outside the range of the battery."

He smiled a little himself. He had done a drawing of that nighttime confrontation: the sky alight with the fire coming from the battery. And his ship, his first ship, the *Barbara*, riding the waves as if she were unaware of the action aimed at her.

"That was very clever, Captain."

"Honesty compels me to admit that I am hardly the first to use that ploy."

"Oh," she said, her animation fading. "I hear very little of the war even if we are only a few miles from Portsmouth." After a long silence she added, "I suppose that Dolley's stories were as much entertainment as history."

"As with all storytellers. And I am happy to know that the boys were not the only ones who enjoyed them."

"Our lives are very quiet here at Talford." He had killed her enthusiasm and he missed it already. He wished he had held his tongue and let her see him as any manner of hero her imagination would suggest.

Even worse, she was leaving. She left the balcony and entered the darkened chamber of the boathouse.

He spoke to her back, "Dolley only told you of the adventures. I would wager he left out the days, even months, in failing wind and broiling heat. In truth, it is weeks and months fighting boredom punctuated with a few hours of battle."

She stopped before the outer doorway. He followed her across the echoing and empty room.

"Dolley told us about the time you came upon a ghost ship and have never to this day determined why it was completely abandoned."

She had recovered some of her enthusiasm, but walked with him out the door and onto the grass that grew up to the edge of the building.

"The ghost ship. That was a strange experience." It did not sound much better than "indeed," but it was enough to have her pause their slow walk toward Talford Vale.

"Captain," she was as mischievous as the boys, "I thought that story would keep the boys awake for hours, but they devised several blood-curdling explanations and fell asleep in the midst of arguing over which was the most likely."

The moon cast the boathouse in shadow and he had to move very close to see that she was shaking her head.

"I would find toy soldiers, checkers, and marbles lost in the bedclothes and wondered how they could sleep, but somehow those did not keep them awake either."

*You kept me awake,* he thought, glancing at her pink shoes, *even before you decided to be "civil."*

Instead of continuing on the path home she moved to the water's edge. He was sure she would have waded into the water if she had been barefoot.

"Your quick action here at the lake earlier today was impressive, Miss Stewart. I do not know many men who would have assessed the situation and handled it as efficiently."

"I have learned to be prepared for anything where those two boys are concerned." She shrugged it off like any real hero, as if the act were nothing. "Their imaginations are more than doubled when they are together. At least today they found a target other than Sara."

"I do not think they are quite ready for the French if their attack on a mother duck failed."

She laughed again, deep and sincere.

"Tomorrow Sara will travel to her godmother's for a month. It is something that has been promised since she was ten. After a fortnight with Harry and Angus, the actual invitation could not have been better timed."

"It will make your life easier, but you will miss her."

"Yes, I will," she said as though surprised at his understanding.

"It is how I feel when I am underway without Angus."

Next he would be telling her how much he missed Carroll.

Something jumped out of the water, drawing both of their attentions.

"This is as perfect an evening as possible, is it not?"

William considered the change of subject. She was reduced to talking about the weather, not yet ready to say good night. Neither was he.

"The full moon is as much mystery as act of nature, is it not?" She raised her eyes to the night sky and he did his best not to be entranced by this night-worshipping goddess.

"Indeed." He grimaced and hurried on. "The shadows remind me of the paper transparencies that one of my messmates would fashion. The gray, pearly white, the almost black of the woods makes me realize how accurate his work was."

"I've never cared for the transparencies. Could not believe that there was any place that really was nothing more than shades of white and gray. I have been in England a year now and I can see where the inspiration came from." She turned to him, the water at her back. "You see, I was born and raised in Jamaica."

Dolley had told him that, but William pretended it was news. "I was there when I was a midshipman." He still had the drawings.

"I love the blue green of the water on a sunny day"—she stared at the grass, her voice a little dreamy with the memory—"and the way the palms click in the breeze."

She moved to the footpath that would take her home.

"Did you learn to swim there?"

They stopped by the trees that marked the Talford Vale property, the house within sight. Even if he accompanied her to the door they were only a few steps from good night.

"Yes, I learned when I was five. My uncle insisted, right after my parents died." She drew a breath. "You see, they drowned. Within sight of land."

"It was wise of him to have you taught, rather than let you become afraid of it." He himself had seen such deaths too many times to dwell on it. "And did your uncle allow you to go without shoes?"

"Oh, no. That was my own decision after I came to Talford. And, Captain," she rushed on, "I never do it anywhere but here at home and only in the summer."

"It would not do at all in London."

"But in Town it is more than propriety. To walk on grass is one thing, paved streets would not be nearly as pleasant."

"Shoes it is."

"Oh, but I have no expectation of visiting Town. I am to remain here with the children."

"Don't all young ladies go to London?"

"Not all." She moved with some purpose toward the Vale.

Why was she not going to London? If he had not first met her in dishabille he would have thought her like every other young lady who passed him by in London or Portsmouth. But he had seen her barefoot, had watched her swim, and was chatting with her as though midnight was her preferred time for a call.

Was she that naive? Or an original well on her way to being eccentric? Or could it be that she was lonely and longing for a flirtation?

"Could we not be friends and neighbors, Captain?"

"I think friendship is unlikely, Miss Stewart," he spoke with caution.

"But why? We have managed to move from contentious to civil to cordial in one conversation. This was so lovely. Or is it because you will be traveling more?"

Not nearly enough, he thought, convinced that she was an innocent. "Friendship is impossible because you are a woman and I am a man."

She laughed, but this time it was laced with self-mockery. "A woman not pretty enough for a Season with no prospects and less money."

"Nonsense. If you are not beautiful and entirely alluring, why is it that now that we are beyond civil and onto courteous I can think of nothing but kissing you?"

"Indeed," she said and laughed, all flirtation.

Her amusement seduced him as surely as an embrace.

"Oh, I see, Captain. You use 'indeed' when you cannot think of what to say."

He drew her into his arms, desperate to know which she was: flirt or innocent, certain that one kiss would tell.

At first her body was stiff. With surprise? But her lips were cool and soft. He could feel her relax against him as her first reaction faded, giving way to a tentative response.

Her hands pressed against his chest but were not pushing him away. Could she feel the slam of his heart through the linen of his shirt? Thought, consideration, and calculation drifted away, thoroughly erased by the delight that filled him. He pulled her closer, her body soft and arousing, the fit of her perfect.

He moved his mouth to the corner of hers and would have kissed her fully again, but this time she did use her hands to push him from her and end the kiss.

His curiosity was answered. He stepped back and waited for the slap.

It did not come. Instead, she raised a hand to her lips and spoke in a voice tinged with anger, "Why did you do that? Why did you spoil everything?"

She spun around and hurried, almost ran, away. He watched her to the door, wondering the same.

# Chapter 11

Lavinia grappled with the pillow as though it were a hat that had never quite fit. She needed to sleep. Sara was leaving tomorrow. Harry and Angus would, no doubt, find new mischief and Mrs. Wilcox had suggested that they approach the gardener about varying the plantings in the fall kitchen garden.

Despite her best efforts, the heart of her sleeplessness worked its way through commonplace musings.

Why had he kissed her?

She could not possibly be that irresistible a creature in her everyday dress, with her hair straggling down her back. It was more likely that he was so long without female attention that anyone with the right shape would do.

It had not been her first kiss, but it had been totally different from the unschooled efforts of the governor's son. William Chartwell knew exactly what he was doing.

She lay without moving and admitted that, whatever the reason, the kiss had warmed her to her toes. And it was hardly an insult. Sweet, decorous even, and she had the feeling that keeping it that way had taken every ounce of his self-control. She curled her toes and smiled.

Honesty did not make sleep come any more easily. After beating her pillow into submission, she finally threw it on the floor.

The full moon filled her room with light and she rose to

close the curtains, but found herself staring out the window at the gently moving trees and the cloudless night sky.

She had asked if they could be friends. What a ridiculous wish. But she had so few here. Actually, she had none. And letters from Jamaica were a long time coming, even when she answered them promptly.

Lavinia walked back to her bed, bent to pick up the pillow, and smoothed it with her hand as if apologizing to it for her previous abuse, or as one would when stroking a man's back.

He had friends. He'd spent a lifetime with men and she could readily imagine the fellowship that shipboard life created. He had friends, indeed he did, but he did not have *women* friends. Given his lifestyle she knew that he thought of women in one way only.

She might be on the shelf. She might be no more than an unpaid governess. She might walk barefoot and swim when she could find the privacy, but she was not the kind of woman who would give her virtue to the nearest neighbor. If she were, she would be part of Desmond's world. She had made the choice to refuse that life, to remain the lady she was raised to be, even if she knew that high-minded morals would be her only comfort at night.

Lavinia pulled the duvet from the bed and stretched out on the window seat. The bench was long enough for her to lie on and wide enough to hold her if she did not demand too much space. She faced the moonlit landscape, tucked her hand under her cheek, and finally fell asleep.

The next day was no easier than the night had been. Sara was excited about the trip to Kent, but began crying the moment her godmother's carriage and maid arrived. She screamed at Harry and Angus when they teased her about the tears and threw herself into her aunt's arms as if the parting were forever.

Lavinia would not allow herself the same sensibility, as

much as she might wish it. She took all the time necessary to send Sara off with a smile—a watery one, but a smile nonetheless.

She waved, and made Angus and Harry wave, until the carriage was out of sight, and then walked back into the house and down to the kitchen, where she found Dolley taking tea with Mrs. Wilcox.

Tea? Where had they found tea? It had been weeks since she had had any herself.

Dolley jumped up. "Please, miss, sit down. I brought some tea for Mrs. Wilcox and she insists that it be shared with the household."

"With you, Miss Lavinia. Not the rest of them." The cook brought out one of the plain, serviceable cups they used when Desmond was away. "Would not be right for me to have tea when you do not."

"That's very generous of you, Mrs. Wilcox." Lavinia sat down next to Dolley. "And quite clever of you, Dolley. For one can hardly take tea without something delicious to go with it."

Dolley shook his head as if denying the contrivance, but it was impossible to dispute it with the evidence of crumbs before him and the warm buns piled on the plate between them.

"We drink coffee at Talford Rise, but I know everyone here favors tea."

Everyone here being Mrs. Wilcox, Lavinia decided, and for the first time wondered if this might be a courtship. The thought brought a sinking feeling. If Mrs. Wilcox left, there was no hope of finding someone competent to replace her.

She sipped her tea and found its comforting taste did not do much to ease her self-pity.

Dolley leaned down, picked up a package from the floor, and handed it to her.

"This one's for you, miss."

"For me?" She considered the clumsily wrapped parcel. "From you?"

"Oh no, Miss Lavinia." This from a shocked Mrs. Wilcox. "That would not be right at all."

"No, ma'am, this is from the captain."

Lavinia stared at the package. A gift from Captain Chartwell was no more appropriate than one from Dolley would be.

"What is it?"

"No tellin', Miss Stewart. He handed it to me as you see it and told me to deliver it."

"He could not deliver it himself?"

"He left for London at first light."

"Oh."

"It won't be for long," Dolley added quickly as if her "oh" was disappointment and not surprise. "Angus will be staying at the Rise and coming for lessons regularlike. The captain does not expect to be away for more than a few days this time."

Lavinia pressed her lips together. He would be gone just long enough to pass on his information to the admiralty and find someone else to kiss.

"Arthur—" Mrs. Wilcox drew his attention quite deliberately—"will you please come help me collect some of the vegetables that the gardener puts on the step?"

Taking the hint, Dolley stood up and the two of them left Lavinia with her package.

There was a note tucked under the piece of string and she considered whether to open it or the package first. The package, she decided.

She unwrapped it carefully in case it was fragile, recalling his words, "a shell might be appropriate for you."

It was indeed shaped like a shell, though it had never done anything as modest as protect a mollusk. Some sculptor, a true artist, had taken a piece of stone, jasper perhaps, and worked it into a delicate scallop shape that fit nicely in the palm of her hand. It was as fine as bone china, in rippling shades of its natural state, rosy orange and cream. The edge of the bowl had been adorned with three small handles of silver encrusted with pearls.

"Oh, it's exquisite," she announced to the empty room.

She placed it gently on the table, a silver base enabling the shell shape to rest flat on a surface. Very carefully she spread open the note as though its value was equal to that of the gift it accompanied.

> *Miss Stewart,*
>
> *Please accept this as a token of my appreciation for the kindness you have shown Angus. I have the honor to remain, your most obedient and humble servant,*
>
> *Captain William Chartwell*

She smiled at the signature and laughed at the closing, worded as though the note were some official report.

Picking up the bowl, she marveled at the shimmering color and the way you could feel the luster with a stroke of your hand. It was crafted by a master and was not some careless gift, casually purchased.

She should never accept it.

The formal signature and stiff wording of the note itself eased her conscience, but only a little.

Lavinia examined the silver handles, wrought and curled around the pearls, mimicking waves. The irregular baroque pearls were set at the crest of the handles and a piece of crystal *(surely that was not a diamond?)* gleamed on the outer edge.

Did she *have* to return it? She looked around the room as if she could find the answer on the hob or with the cutlery.

It was not the first gift she had received in England. Desmond had surprised her with gowns from London. But they had been totally inappropriate for a lady. Just as this gift was.

Mrs. Wilcox's giggle told her that she and Dolley were coming back. Their relationship must be a courtship, Lavinia decided. She had not known that Mrs. Wilcox even knew how to do something as girlish as giggle.

Lavinia remained seated, staring at the elegant bowl until the two came closer.

"Oh, miss, isn't that cunning? It looks like something you could put raisins in or maybe lemons for fish."

Lavinia almost laughed out loud. Not nearly as intimate as her idea, that it should sit on her dressing table and hold her earrings.

"The captain meant it for Miss Lavinia, Maude, not for the house."

"Oooh yes, Arthur." Mrs. Wilcox took no offense at the correction. "You must take it upstairs to your room, miss. If I were to use it in the dining room Mr. Stewart might think it was his."

Considering Mrs. Wilcox and Dolley permission enough, Lavinia decided that she was going to keep it. Who would ever know besides the three of them? Yes, it was inappropriate, but she was going to keep the beautiful thing and let it remind her of happier times in Jamaica. Was that what he had intended?

She picked up the gift and the cloth wrapping and moved toward the stairs when Patty, one of the more energetic of the housemaids, came racing down the steps.

"He's coming!"

For a silly moment Lavinia thought it was William who was coming, but the maid babbled on, turning Lavinia's confusion into anxiety.

"A messenger just came from town and Mr. Stewart and his friends will be here tomorrow after dinner."

Patty's enthusiasm was not reciprocated. Lavinia's whole

attention shifted from the gift in her hands to the ordeal ahead. Mrs. Wilcox patted Dolley on his arm and scooped up the new tea chest. "Soon as I put this away in my room I'll begin working on the menus, miss."

"It's like watching a ship prepare for battle," Angus said.

Harry and Angus were sitting on the floor of the main room of the folly, rain keeping them from the terrace and the hammock outside. Angus threw a ball against the wall, never mind the elegant mural he was pounding, and Harry caught it on one bounce, angling it back to Angus. They were up to twenty throws without a miss. It wasn't a record, but they were close.

"It's like this every time Papa comes," Harry explained. "Those stupid maids sleep all day and do nothing but laugh in that stupid way girls do. The only time they work is when they know he will be coming with his friends."

"How come you have to go away?"

"'Cause Aunt Lavinia says Papa's house parties are not the place for children." He shrugged. "We used to go to Mrs. Wilcox's sister's place at the home farm, but staying at the Rise will be even more fun."

"What about Miss Stewart?" Angus did not mean to sound quite so worried, but if the maids were sluts and she stayed with them, then what would happen to her?

"She'll do what she always does. Stay behind and lock the schoolroom door until they leave. Mrs. Wilcox won't let her starve."

"How come she does that?"

"'Cause there's not enough room at the home farm for her to have her own bed."

"But this time she could come to the Rise with us."

Harry shook his head. "No ladies live there. No one to be a chaperone. Too bad Mr. Arbuscam doesn't wear skirts."

They both snickered at the mental image of their tutor in a dress.

"It won't be so bad," Angus insisted. "I like the geography and we start reading Caesar next week."

He did not so much as glance at Harry. There was no point in pretending he did not like learning since they sat side by side each day.

"I count thirty throws at least," Harry said.

"Do you think we can do a hundred?"

"If no one finds us. And everyone is too busy."

They concentrated on their record in silence for a few moments.

"Harry, don't you want to see your father?"

"No."

Harry said it with such vehemence that Angus was sure he was lying.

"Does he beat you?"

"No, he's friendly and laughs a lot, but that's 'cause he's almost always drunk."

Harry threw the ball so hard that Angus's hand stung when he caught it.

"But I guess it's better than not having one. Do you still miss yours?"

Angus nodded. "The captain says that we'll both miss him forever." He worried the ball in his hand and then tossed it very gently.

"Do you have a picture of him?"

"The captain drew one for me, but I only take it out when I begin to forget what he looks like." Not even for his very own sailboat would he admit that looking at it made him cry.

"Captain Chartwell can draw that well?"

"Oh, Harry, you should see what he can draw. He says it's what entertained him when he had no books in the orphanage."

"Do you think you could really forget your father?"

"No. Sometimes the captain will stay up late and tell me

stories of their days together before I was born. No. I'll never forget him. The captain won't let me."

"What about your mother?"

"She died when I was no more 'n six. It's like I never had a mother. At least not until Miss Stewart."

"Me too. She's better than a mother even. How many mothers know how to swim?"

Angus had no idea. "And she tells us whenever Mrs. Wilcox is trying a new biscuit or sweet."

"She lets us play in the garden after dark."

"And lets us talk all night."

"Most of the time."

They were both silent. Then Harry said very quietly, "She keeps us safe."

"And kisses us goodnight," Angus added, but the moment he said it he knew that, truth or not, he had gone too far. He twisted his mouth in a grimace, trying for disgust. Harry shuddered. "Her hugs are even worse."

They went back to their game, each satisfied that their true feelings were well disguised.

# Chapter 12

Lavinia wrapped two meat pies and found a place for them inside the cabinet that was built into the wall of the schoolroom. She knew from experience that this was the best place to keep the food that Miss Wilcox brought up to her. She wrapped the fruit and put it there as well.

Walking back into her bedroom, she wondered if she had time to hunt up the knitting she did when all the mending was finished. Knitting would occupy her even if her door were locked for weeks.

Too late to find the needles and wool, for her brother was standing at her dressing table, reaching for the bejeweled bowl. He spun around when he heard her, but showed no embarrassment at this invasion of her privacy.

"Hello, sister." He bowed to her. His smile was contagious, but she was not inclined to return it. He shrugged off her lack of welcome. "Pretty piece, this."

He dumped her hairpins onto her dressing table and fingered the pearls and the one stone worked into the silver handles. "By some Italian?"

"It is mine, Desmond," Lavinia said firmly, walked over, and took it right out of his hand.

"From an admirer?"

"No." She could hardly name the captain an admirer when he had called her a shrew. The kiss did confuse things a bit.

Desmond raised a finger and shook it in reprimand. "No

lies, Lavinia." He came a little closer. "What did you do to win that treasure? Something very creative, I hope." He leaned so close that she could smell the whiskey that was a permanent part of his aura. He whispered a ribald joke and laughed.

"Desmond!" She twirled away from him and walked to the other side of her bed, putting the bowl on the window seat behind her. She stood straight, her arms folded, wanting only that he would leave.

"Ever the lady, eh?" He laughed. She remained silent, but he did not take the hint and end the conversation. Instead, he sat heavily on the small chair in front of her dressing table. He leaned against the gilt back. Lavinia heard it crack. "I would be impressed at how upright you are, dear sister, but I imagine there are hardly any temptations here, are there?"

Had Desmond never met William Chartwell? She was certainly not going to ask.

"Hold on to your virtue then. At least until Harry is off to school next year."

"You are sending Harry to Eton? But he is not nearly ready."

"He will be ready when I say he is ready."

She wanted to remind him that he had not seen his son in two years, would not be able to pick him out in crowd, but she was afraid enough for Harry that she held her tongue.

"Do you want to know a secret?" Desmond put his hands on his knees.

"No." She shook her head. "I want you to leave."

He waved away her request. "I will tell you anyway, so that you have something to dream about." He leaned forward to share the confidence. "Brocklin finds your innocence very appealing. You remember him, do you not? Tall and well built, especially where it matters." He picked up a bottle of perfume and inhaled deeply. "He would make a good husband and take endless pleasure in teaching an innocent wife all he knows."

The amazing thing was that he actually thought it a reasonable plan. She shook her head again, frozen in place, her future growing darker by the minute.

"You are uncertain, but you will change your mind. Are you not curious about what goes on between a man and a woman?"

She did not even shake her head at this impertinence.

"In time. In time, Lavinia, you will learn it all." He smiled. Standing, he put the green perfume bottle back on her dressing table and moved to the door. "Be sure to lock up."

He gave the order as though it was his idea.

She did as he wished, but only because it was her wish too. Then she walked back, picked up her sea treasure, and sat on the window seat.

Several carriages were turning in at the gatehouse and she stayed, watching the activity below. She recognized Brocklin as the driver. He made a graceful jump down from the seat and then stumbled on the ground. One of the others who had tumbled from the coach handed him a flask and they all laughed, clearly having enjoyed its contents all the way from London.

Brocklin's charm was all calculation, as if he was measuring its effect and what it could gain him. She would work as a housemaid before she would ever consider marriage to him.

With her back to the window, she pulled her knees up and rested her head on them. She was not curious about what went on between a man and a woman because she knew. Her governess had been a widow herself and very conscientious. She had promised that with the right man it would be a tolerable experience.

"But how do you know the right man?" a much younger Lavinia had pleaded. She recalled a shadowy sitting room, the house quiet as it always was in the afternoon.

"There are several elements, my dear." Her governess' practical voice helped make the sensitive subject easier to discuss. "First and foremost, he will be a man you can trust."

These days her world was so small that it was easy to number the men she could trust: the vicar, Mr. Arbuscam, certainly Dolley and, yes, Captain Chartwell.

"A man you can respect."

That left Mr. Arbuscam off the list and a good thing as she could no more imagine lying with him than Brocklin, if for completely different reasons.

"Of your own class."

Dolley dropped off, but she had never remotely thought of him as anything more than a servant.

"Marriageable, of course."

Not the vicar. He was a good, kind man, but married.

"He should be able to keep you in comfort."

Wealth? According to Dolley, the captain was one of the richest men in the area. She'd heard the story of the Spanish transport filled with silver and gold that had been captured. It happened before Dolley was serving with the captain, but the story was legend. Captain Chartwell had been a midshipman and even then his part of the prize had been an impressive eight hundred guineas. And there were more prizes after that, his share growing as he rose in rank.

William Chartwell could certainly afford to keep a wife in comfort.

"That you should enjoy his family is helpful, though not an insurmountable requirement."

The captain insisted he had no family. Lord Morgan Braedon thought differently, but whether it was true or not, there was no father or brother or sister that was a part of his life.

No, it was Angus and Dolley and the rest of his household with whom she would have to come to terms. She loved Angus and, indeed, liked the servants she had met.

"And finally, my dear," she had said, "the real telling is in his kiss."

The problem was that her governess had never explained exactly what you could tell from a kiss. Surely it should be pleasurable. But did one look for gentleness? Or should you feel passion? She thought of their midnight embrace. Or could one kiss show both?

Or could it be that at the first touch one knew that this kiss was more than the meeting of lips? More than physical conquest? When the right man kissed you, it was an invitation from one heart to another.

In that case, Captain Chartwell could be erased from the list as well. By his own admission it was lust that had made him unable to resist kissing her. Her response was not quite as unbridled, but that one moment when she had lost awareness of time and place had come from an answering hunger.

Given that his interest was purely carnal, she had liked the kiss more than was wise. Did that show weakness in her character? She rubbed the smooth stone of the pearl-trimmed bowl. Was she more like Desmond than she had ever been willing to admit?

Lavinia stared out the window again, searching for the answer in the quiet of the empty drive. It was the first time in weeks that she had no chores to do and nowhere to go. She might constantly wish for some time by herself, without the constant demand of the children and the house, but this was too much and would be for too long. She missed the boys already.


William counted five before him—Angus, Harry, Dolley, and, by the stars, Mrs. Wilcox and Mr. Arbuscam. They had paraded into the library together, as unorthodox a crew as he had ever commanded, but it was clear that they were looking to him for leadership, if not a solution.

"Mr. Stewart'll be sorry. That new cook is no more a cook

than the gardener is." Mrs. Wilcox spoke the words with a vindictive relish. "She's taken over, Captain Chartwell. He says I'm to tell her all the dishes he likes best, that she is in charge." Mrs. Wilcox drew a deep breath. "I have a place to go"—she glanced at Dolley—"but what will Miss Lavinia do without me for support?"

"I must honestly say that I do not think young Master Harry is at all ready to go on to Eton." Mr. Arbuscam spoke in a sonorously slow voice better suited to inducing sleep than teaching. "We have only begun Caesar and his work with mathematics is improving, but, I'm sorry to say, will not impress any tutor."

Harry nodded eagerly as though Arbuscam had just given him the greatest of compliments. "And Angus has not finished his swimming lessons."

"You want me to go to Talford Vale and bring Miss Stewart here?" William leaned back against his desk, sitting on the edge, his arms folded in front of him.

"Yes, sir. We want you to rescue her." This from Dolley.

"But how has it become my responsibility?" He held his hands out inviting explanation. "She can walk out of that house at any time of her choosing."

"But she has never had anywhere to go," Mrs. Wilcox said, wringing her hands, glancing from him to Dolley.

"And where will she go now?"

They had no answer until Angus spoke. "Why, she must come here, Captain." The boy was surprised, as though he should not have to state the obvious.

"Indeed?" He folded his arms again and let his gaze travel from one to the other. No one disagreed.

"Yes, sir," Dolley said. "We can be her chaperone until it is safe for her to go home."

"Is that why she has always stayed at Talford Vale? Because there was no one who would take her in?"

"That's the way of it, sir," Mrs. Wilcox said.

"Sir," Dolley said, stepping forward, "Miss Stewart is trapped as surely as Mr. MacDonald was that time Captain Kelso had him locked up."

And William had been the one to let him out. Moments before a cannonball had made a shambles of the place.

"You must save her, sir." Mrs. Wilcox put her hand to her heart and sank into a chair.

"From that den of iniquity," Mr. Arbuscam added.

"We are ready to help," Angus said, but both boys stepped forward.

This already had all the elements of a farce. Adding two boys to the boarding team would cap it. If he was going to take it on, and it appeared he was, then it would be done his way.

"Thank you, boys, but I think this should be handled as quietly as possible."

There were several sighs of relief and Mrs. Wilcox began to weep a little.

"You did not think I would help?"

"We were not sure, sir." Mrs. Wilcox spoke with obvious discomfort. "You and Miss Lavinia do not always agree."

"Only when it comes to punishing us," Harry spoke with an air of long suffering.

"Yes, well, I hardly agree with the French either, but would never abandon them after a battle if rescue is possible." He straightened as he spoke and stepped closer to them, his arms at his side, one raised a little as if it would aid his explanation.

"That's what I thought, sir," Dolley said.

He focused on the boys. "You two can best help by going back to your studies and putting an end to the mischief." William went to his desk, sat down, and pulled out some paper.

Angus understood the dismissal even if his friend did not. He punched Harry on the arm before the boy could do more than open his mouth in protest. Mr. Arbuscam rose and the three left the room with impressive speed.

William set aside his pen and the blank paper. "Mrs.

Wilcox, explain to me how you gain entry when you need to speak with Miss Stewart or bring her food."

"It's a special knock we devised." Mrs. Wilcox demonstrated the irregular pattern and William imitated it.

"But, beggin' your pardon, sir, shouldn't I go with you?"

"No, you are needed here. I want you to direct the preparation of rooms for a chaperone and Miss Stewart. No. Make it three rooms as I am sure Mrs. Newcomb will want to have her sister nearby."

Mrs. Wilcox showed some hesitation.

"I know that is not part of your usual duties, but in this situation we must all do what we can."

"It's like battle, Maude," Dolley explained. "Even the cook helps wherever he can and never questions a command."

With Dolley's explanation William could see resolution replace doubt.

"Come with me, Maude. I'll show you where the linens are. I know the houses are the same, but we have made some changes."

"Very good, Dolley," William said. "But come right back. I have an errand for you. You know Mrs. Newcomb, do you not?"

"Aye, sir. The lady who called when you first settled. The one whose son died at the Nile."

William nodded. One of Dolley's true gifts was his good memory. "I want you to take a note to her as soon as Mrs. Wilcox is situated."

"Aye, sir."

William picked up the pen but did not put it to paper. He dare not command Mrs. Newcomb to appear. The lady was old enough to be his mother and should be approached with respect. In the end he opted for the style he would use when reporting to a senior officer who was also a friend. It took three efforts and by then Dolley was in front of him again, waiting in silence.

William handed his butler the sealed note. "Have someone

go with you." William rose from his chair. "Someone who will wait and escort her and her sister back here."

"Yes, sir."

With a satisfied nod, William left the library and made his way to the stairs. At the first landing he leaned over the railing. "Dolley, do one other errand for me before you leave. Tell Gibson that his cooking days are over. I have managed a spot for him and his brother aboard the *Challenge*."

"Then Miss Wilcox has a place here, sir?"

"If you can convince her."

Dolley was all smiles and made a beeline for the back of the house.

"Deliver the note to Mrs. Newcomb with due speed, Dolley. It is essential that she be here before I come back with Miss Stewart."

"Aye, sir," Dolley called back even as he pushed through the swinging door that separated the main house from the servants' area.

In his room, William stripped out of his traveling clothes and reached for his uniform. He was stepping into the white breeches when he rethought his dress. He did not want to call attention to himself. This was more a covert rescue than a mission to search and destroy.

He wanted to bring Miss Stewart here without any damage to her reputation. It would be better for all if he went through the kitchen rather than start at the front door. He tossed the breeches on a chair and reached for his at-home apparel: buckskins and a linen shirt with a dark brown jacket and a casually tied cravat. No one would mistake him for part of the house party in this dress.

The conventions were too much, damn it. He tied his cravat and realized that he could actually agree with Miss Stewart on that. And going barefoot was the least of it. This was the worst: the only way to protect her virtue was to lock herself in her room. How ridiculous that comfort was not an option if it meant a room in an all-male establishment.

William checked that he had buttoned the jacket correctly. He could hear Mrs. Wilcox in the hallway, dithering about which sheets to use, but doing her best to rise to the occasion.

What had Dolley said? "In a battle everyone helps where he can, whenever he can."

But they were not aboard ship. That was made clear in one significant way: he had not given the order, his crew had.

He shook his head. What would it be like to have her in his house, so close, twenty-four hours a day? Heaven, or hell? Or a little of both? Pushing his own uncertainty to a far corner of his mind, he headed down the steps.

His crew had ordered him to rescue Miss Stewart and he would obey.

# Chapter 13

He was not familiar with the back of the house either at Talford Rise or Talford Vale. After a quick reconnoiter he found a side door that led into a narrow hall and then into the kitchen where the new cook was doing precisely what she had been hired to do.

The gentleman who was receiving her attentions was not the slightest bit embarrassed at the interruption. "Go find your own, unless you are interested in an activity for three."

William made his way up the back stairs. At the first landing he came out onto the hallway and practically fell into the arms of a woman who made the most of her charms by showing them off through a sheer bodice that left very little to the imagination.

"And who are you?" she cooed.

He almost gave her his name, but stopped himself and shook his head instead.

"A shy one? I can help you with that." She reached out and trailed a hand down his shirt and farther down so that he stepped back, annoyed more by his embarrassment at the fondling than her aggressiveness.

"No, madam. I have another assignation and will not keep the lady waiting. Step aside."

"Who do you think you are to give me an order?"

He cursed to himself. It was one thing to dress like a land steward, another to assume the attitude.

A man came out of the nearest room and spared William the effort of smoothing over his mistake. From behind her, the man wrapped his arms possessively around the woman, his fingers brushing the tips of her barely covered breasts.

She twisted into his arms and William seized the chance to escape, this time opting for the front stairs rather than the servants'. He took them by twos, eager to be away from the debauchery.

This floor was blessedly quiet. He knew the four doors on the west side of the house led to rooms that were all part of the children's wing. He tried the door to the schoolroom. As expected, it was locked.

The rhythmic series of knocks Mrs. Wilcox had demonstrated drew no response. He pressed his ear against the door and heard no sound from the other side. He tested the knob again, bent down for a closer look. He could pick it easily but had not thought to bring tools.

He tried the coded knock again. Still no answer. He turned away toward what he thought was Harry's room. Certainly the boy would have something he could use to pick the lock. At that very moment he heard the lock being loosened. The door opened a crack and before he could face her again, he heard a gasp, followed by her attempt to slam the door shut.

He pushed his body against it calling, "Miss Stewart," even as he did so.

The door gave way. He fell into the room and onto the floor in time to see a swirl of skirts disappear through a door to an adjoining room.

"Miss Stewart! Lavinia! Wait."

He stood up, but stayed where he was. The connecting door remained ajar and he expected that he had not seen the last of her. A moment later she reappeared.

No mermaid today. An Amazon, dressed in dark gray, her hair in a braid down her back, her feet bare. Her eyes set with an expression he knew. Primed for battle if needs be. Determined to win.

She held a sword with her two hands, and had raised it as though to slice off his head, or arm, or whatever part of him she could reach.

She recognized him then but did not put the sword aside. No, she held it at the ready even as hostility drained from her face and surprise took its place.

"Captain Chartwell?" She spoke in some disbelief, as if she did not believe the evidence of her eyes.

"At your service." He bowed, but stepped no closer. "You are amazing. Resourceful, brave, stoic. I swear on Nelson's grave that I would welcome you as part of my crew anytime."

She lowered the sword and put it on the child-sized table next to her.

"Gather your things, Miss Stewart. I am to take you to Talford Rise."

"You've come to rescue me?" she asked.

Incredulous was the only way he could describe her tone.

"I hardly expected you to swoon in my arms, but some sense of relief would be welcome. Something a little more appreciative than exasperation."

"But it's absurd."

"Yes, I thought so from the first. Tell Dolley, tell all of them. They ordered me to do it"—he spread his arms wide—"and here I am."

"They ordered *you*?"

"Yes, I see you recognize that oddity quickly enough."

"Captain, I do not need rescue." She sank down onto the edge of a window seat and he was glad there was no urgency to be gone. She might take some convincing. "Why do they think I do?"

"Because Mrs. Wilcox has been replaced and is worrying over who will feed you. Because Angus must learn to swim and Harry is not at all ready to go to Eton. Because, by the stars, this is not a fairy tale. There is no excuse for you to be held prisoner in your own home."

"This is hardly the first time that I have felt the need to lock myself in. I tell you I am perfectly safe."

"Are you?"

He stalked closer and she stood up and took a step back. He watched her make a conscious effort to stop her retreat and hold her ground.

"Are you safe, Lavinia? If you are, then why do you feel compelled to answer your door with a sword at hand? Why did you feel such panic before you recognized me? Why are you shaking?"

She wrapped her arms tightly around her body as if that would still her nervousness, but shook her head, denying it.

"You know, Miss Stewart, I have some experience at this sort of recovery and I will tell you it is the first time anyone has ever questioned their good fortune."

"I hardly think wickedness in the library is reason enough to call His Majesty's navy to the rescue."

"Actually, it was debauchery in the kitchen and a trollop on the landing." He was sorry he had corrected her when he saw her blush of embarrassment.

"None of which are threats to me, Captain. They will be gone in a day or two. I can bear it."

"But there is no need to."

She shook her head.

"Is it the proprieties that concern you? I've arranged for Mrs. Newcomb and her sister to come and act as chaperones."

"Mrs. Newcomb? She speaks to me, but we barely know each other."

"But she knows me. I served with her son for a time. She and I are the best of friends and she will do as I ask without one single question. You could learn something from her in that regard."

"I will tell you this, Captain. I have learned in a hard school to question those who think they know what is best for me. Would you like me to tell you my experience the one and only time I agreed to attend one of Desmond's house parties?"

"You have no need to. There are empty bottles and the smell of liquor is everywhere. That is explanation enough. I do understand that while this is little more than an inconvenience for me, it is a matter of reputation and respect for you."

She gave a curt nod and he could see that emotion kept her from speaking.

"Would it reassure you to know that Mrs. Wilcox has already claimed the kitchen at the Rise? The house will be a veritable hen party."

"Hen party?" She laughed a little. "Is that supposed to encourage me? That and the suggestion that I am an inconvenience?"

"Lavinia," he stopped and spoke as gently as he could, "pack your essentials and come with me."

She considered the request, staring at the floor as if the decision could be found in the pattern of the carpet. He could see that she had yet to be convinced.

"Say please, Captain." She enunciated the first two words as if they were in some foreign tongue.

"Now you are the one being absurd. What does please have to do with the matter at hand?"

"It is a simple courtesy of which the navy must be unaware." She folded her arms as if the one word were a non-negotiable condition of a treaty.

"My men would think me crazy if "please" and "thank you" became a habit. They are not words that suit command."

"I am not one of your men, nor am I under your command."

"Obviously. And I am rethinking inviting you to join my crew. You are too inclined to mutiny." His attempt at humor drew no answering smile. They stood at a stalemate until he realized that she would not budge until he did as she bade him.

He made an elegant bow. "Would you please allow me to escort you to Talford Rise?"

She gave him a curtsy. The first time she had ever used that gesture to him. "Yes, thank you. I appreciate the offer."

She disappeared into the other room, her bedroom he assumed, and he settled on the window seat to wait. He waited. And waited. And waited. It was true that there was no reason to hurry, indeed the evening would aid the secrecy of their departure, but the quiet from the other room grew so pronounced that he wondered if she had escaped without him.

Venturing to the door, he stopped short when he saw her seated at her dressing table, struggling with her hair, still in a braid, but a mass of tangles.

She turned to him, already defensive. "If I am going to meet Mrs. Newcomb then I must do my hair. I will not appear on your doorstep looking like a hag."

"You could never look like a hag, but you are absolutely right about appearances."

"I am?"

"Yes, it is why a clean uniform is so important." He walked over to her. "You forgot the combs." He untangled one and slipped it into his pocket, and the second one as well.

She watched him in the mirror's reflection, but he gave his complete attention to her hair. He made himself undo the queue slowly so as not to hurt her. Handling the silken strands was a fine torture.

"Yes, indeed." He cleared his throat. "Appearance makes your first impression for you. Bearing and appearance are everything to carrying off any proposition."

He held his hand over her shoulder. "Give me your brush." He looked from her hair to her face, like his, reflected in the mirror and added, "please." His courtesy lessened her trapped look, but the tension was palpable.

She handed him the brush even as she said, "I can brush it."

"I know," he said, and began with the ends, moving up an inch at a time, lifting her hair, combing it over his hand until it was smooth and no longer tangled. He finished and ran a hand over the smooth dark length of it as a reward for his service. She shivered and he stepped away, no doubt in his mind that the shiver was from awareness and not insult.

She had her hair done in a severe chignon so quickly that he could hardly follow her fingers. Three hairpins held it in place and she stood up.

He stepped back, but did not leave the room. In case she should need more help, he told himself.

The first thing she picked up was the jasper cup he had sent over with Dolley. She emptied the hairpins from it. Though she had a shawl in hand, she held the cup out to him rather than wrapping it.

"This is quite lovely, but I cannot accept it."

"But you have been using it." He waved at the hairpins in an untidy pile on her dressing table.

"Our circumstances are changed." She thrust it at him so that he had to take it or let it fall to the floor. "Besides, it is much too extravagant a gift for an unmarried gentleman to give to a lady. Surely you know that."

He shook his head.

She refused to discuss it further, turned from him, found her shoes, donned them quickly, and then gathered her clothes from the press. These she wrapped in a large shawl. She reached for her bonnet, the plain straw with the blue ribbon she had worn for that first formal call.

He lifted her excuse for baggage and followed her into the schoolroom. Picking up the sword, she went back into her room and came out without it. She closed a window and checked to make sure the room was in order.

They made their way in silence down the servants' back stairs. William prayed all the while that the maid and her gentleman were finished with their dalliance. It was an immense relief to find the cavernous room empty.

They left through a different door, this one leading them into the kitchen garden. They went through the creaking gate and were only two steps along when a voice came out of the dark. "Who is it? What are you stealing? The food belongs to me, it does."

An old man was hurrying after them, his cudgel raised, ready to strike.

William handed her the shawl-wrapped clothes. "Go ahead. I will be along in a moment." He was surprised when Lavinia obeyed without argument.

The man came at him with the club, but William disarmed him with the ease of much practice. And then threatened him with it. "You will not use that on any woman again."

"Yes, sir." The man cowered at his feet. "If you say so, sir."

"If you feel the need to beat something, then sit here and wait for the night animals. They are the ones stealing your vegetables."

After a brief contest of will, the man lowered his eyes and tugged his forelock and William handed him his cudgel. With it in hand, the gardener began a narrow-eyed patrol.

William found Lavinia not too much farther along the path. He took the bundle from her and they walked on in silence.

"That was a rescue, Captain. I could show you bruises from that cudgel . . ." Her voice trailed off as did her laughter. "If it were not for the children I would be happy to never set foot in this place again."

He swallowed his "indeed" and as they walked from Talford Vale to Talford Rise, William considered her options.

# Chapter 14

This was the fairy tale, Lavinia thought. Surrounded by a chorus of welcome and warm embraces. Harry and Angus all but knocked her off her feet with their hugs. Mrs. Wilcox kept brushing at her eyes with the edge of her apron. Even Mrs. Newcomb and her sister were smiling, nodding approval.

Her own laughter was edged with more unguarded emotion than she had permitted herself in a year. For all her insistence that she was not in danger, it did feel as though she had been saved from a heinous situation.

She looked around, determined to thank her rescuer, to make sure everyone understood that she was here because William Chartwell had cared enough to respond to their pleas. But he was not among the small crowd.

Dolley saw her searching the room and came over to whisper, "He'll be back in a skip, miss."

He raised his voice. "The captain will join the ladies for tea in the blue salon. The young gentlemen are to bed." When she made to escort the boys, Dolley stopped her.

"I will see to them tonight, miss."

Good nights took a few more minutes. The boys grumbled when she hugged and kissed them. Clearly her embrace was an entirely different gesture from their wild greeting.

As Harry and Angus raced up the stairs, one of the staff, the one who wore a black scarf around his throat, escorted all three of the ladies across the hall.

Lavinia followed, allowing Mrs. Newcomb to lead as she was the senior lady present. It was awkward and more, for Lavinia was not at all sure how the older woman would receive her.

The few times they had met in the village had been civil enough, but the widow had never done more than exchange the most conventional of greetings. The younger of the two was virtually a twin, but lived to disagree with her sister. Lavinia did not know whether that would work in her favor or not.

The servant opened the door and stepped back. They moved across the threshold and stopped short.

"Why, this room is gorgeous!" Lavinia said in real surprise.

"I hardly knew what to expect, but never this," Mrs. Newcomb agreed. "Who would ever imagine such an elegant feminine room in this household?"

Her sister appeared unimpressed. "Not as large as the ladies' salon at Petworth."

"Not large, but lovely." Lavinia stepped farther into the room. "There is nothing like this at the Vale. This room is," she thought a moment, "a billiard room with a card table."

"You can easily see which of the two houses started as a bachelor establishment," Mrs. Newcomb said with a sniff.

Lavinia nodded, admiring one of the floral murals that was almost a match for the flowered material that covered the two dainty sofas near the fireplace. "It's rather like finding a French doll in the boy's toy chest."

"Indeed," said a voice from the door. "You can understand why I have never entertained in here before, though I do believe that I have reached the age where I can appreciate the beauty of a French doll."

The captain had changed his clothes. Was that why he had disappeared so quickly? A faultless dress coat in bottle green had replaced his casual country clothes. Breeches and a meticulously tied cravat completed his look. Yet another "costume" to help him carry off this unconventional proposition?

Her dark gray dress was hardly fashionable, but Mrs. Newcomb and her sister were dressed similarly, so she refused to feel self-conscious.

It was awkward, none of them certain which lady was hostess and which lady was guest. William escorted Mrs. Newcomb to the seat nearest the tea table and invited her sister to sit on the sofa next to him. Lavinia took the only remaining seat in the grouping, next to Mrs. Newcomb.

"Tea with good company." Mrs. Newcomb smoothed her skirt. "What a lovely end to a busy day."

She straightened with real offense when her sister and Lavinia laughed. Even the captain smiled.

"Really!" Mrs. Newcomb said, raising a hand to her pink cheeks. "It was not meant to be funny."

"Oh, but, sister, it is. Each of our worlds is all confusion." The younger of the two went on, "Miss Stewart rescued. The captain's quiet house filled with ladies and children. Mrs. Wilcox let go from the Vale, hired here at the Rise. And you and I invited to be part of the adventure."

Mrs. Newcomb accepted the chastisement with a strained smile. "I suppose you are right, but good manners dictate that we not dwell on the upset." She addressed the captain. "Though I expect that this must be tame when compared to most of your experiences."

Lavinia could not resist adding, "And I imagine very few of your missions end with tea in the blue salon."

He bowed to them from his seat. "Much better than brandy alone in the library, dear ladies."

The smile he gave the older woman made Lavinia stare. Sweet. It was nothing less than sweet. With a familial fondness she had not thought him capable of. In that moment she realized that while Dolley had told endless stories of sea life, she still knew nothing of his childhood, his mother, his family.

"None of this would be possible without your presence here, Mrs. Newcomb." He glanced at Lavinia. "Thank you."

"You are more than welcome, Captain."

The tea came and Mrs. Newcomb poured. Once they were each settled with cups, the older lady spoke again.

"You know how welcome you are in the community, Captain. It is so unfortunate that you have not done more to cultivate the right people. If you had it would help you overcome the awkwardness of this situation."

"Indeed."

Lavinia had been staring at her tea, but now gave him her attention. His countenance was as bland as his single word. Lavinia could not tell if he thought himself insulted or well advised.

"But it is not too late." Mrs. Newcomb stirred some more sugar into her tea and set the spoon down. "Do you have domestic uniforms for your staff, Captain?"

"No."

"How unfortunate." She made it sound an error akin to serving bad fish. "Uniforms will have to be ordered."

"If you think it necessary."

"The man who showed us in here wears a scarf around his neck. He must remove it. One's staff should endeavor to look the same and the scarf marks him too individually."

"No, Mrs. Newcomb." The captain was smiling slightly, but there was no doubting the firmness of his refusal. "Chasen wears the scarf to cover a disfiguring burn. The scarf stays as long as he wishes it."

It was her turn to nod.

"Then why does your butler not have a wooden arm so his loss is not so . . ." she hesitated, "um, so obvious?"

"Because Dolley considers his wound a badge of honor. As it is."

The captain had not touched his tea. Lavinia wondered if he was rethinking brandy in the library.

"Whether your staff is dressed properly or not, the very first step is to invite the vicar and his wife to dinner."

"No." He glanced again at Lavinia. "I will call on him personally."

"Very good, but not enough," Mrs. Newcomb began.

Lavinia bit her lip to keep from laughing again and refused to look at Mrs. Newcomb's sister who was making sounds that could be no less than restrained giggles. Their audience of two found the Chartwell/Newcomb struggle for authority vastly entertaining.

Mrs. Newcomb set her cup down. "Captain Chartwell, this is as much a campaign as any planned battle at sea. For Miss Stewart and her reputation, it is every bit as important as the Battle at Trafalgar. In your note you asked for more than my advice. If I recall correctly, you asked for my help."

She waited.

Finally, the captain nodded. "Yes, Mrs. Newcomb, I did ask for your help." His carefully neutral look gave way to something that was irony or maybe chagrin. "What I did not fully understand is that you are, in fact, an admiral in disguise."

"An admiral? Nonsense," her sister insisted. "Surely no higher than a commodore."

It broke the tension and they all laughed a little.

"I learned long ago never to pretend expertise," William said. "And where society is concerned I know less than a girl in her first Season. But I want your promise, dear lady, that when you are at sea you will no more question my orders than I will question yours."

"Agreed." Mrs. Newcomb began again, "You will call on the vicar and invite him, and his wife, to dinner. As soon as possible. Remember, it is not a social occasion. It is an element of our battle plan."

"Thank the stars we have Mrs. Wilcox."

"Part of the reason that this is exactly what to do. I know people who would pay to eat anything she would wish to feed them."

"A veritable treasure." The captain's smile became a grin and Lavinia could guess what he was thinking. *A treasure and soon to be a permanent part of his staff.*

"As soon as the house is under control"—even Lavinia was terrified at what that implied—"I will take Miss Stewart to pick out fabric for new gowns. Two at least." She looked at Lavinia. "You have been in mourning quite long enough."

"Yes. An excellent idea." The captain spoke with such enthusiasm that Lavinia wondered if he was relieved to have the gun aimed elsewhere, or if her dress was truly awful.

"And I will make it clear that I am paying for them." Mrs. Newcomb spoke directly to Lavinia. "No one would believe that you have the money. They know your brother too well. And we cannot risk the speculation that they are a gift from the captain."

"Thank you, Mrs. Newcomb." It was impossible for her to be embarrassed when the older lady was so practical, though she was determined to find a way to pay her back.

"It is all part of our campaign," she repeated. "Captain, you are to spend all your time in your library or, better yet, go to London."

"But I have only just returned."

"You can go again. The road does run both ways. But not before the vicar comes."

For the first time the captain showed disappointment, but he did not argue. He had learned to accept commands in a far harder school than this. "London it is. Is there anything you ladies would like from Town?"

"I will make a list." Mrs. Newcomb stood up then. The tea party was over. "I will do all I can to make this arrangement acceptable for as long as it must last, but I can only wonder what the gossips will make of it."

None of them could deny that. Lavinia hoped their imaginations were not as fertile as hers.

Within three days, the captain had called on the vicar. He and his wife had been to dinner and the stories came to find them at Talford Rise.

Lavinia, Mrs. Newcomb, and her sister were to go shopping that very day, after noon, when the captain called her to the library.

He was sitting at his desk, but rose when she came into the room. Angus and Harry stood in the middle of the room, dirty and bruised.

"Have you two been fighting?" She walked around them, wincing at Harry's swollen lip. "Well, that is stating the obvious, is it not? But why? You two are the best of friends and I can see that this is beyond a squabble."

"Not us, Aunt Lavinia. We were defending you."

"And the captain," Angus said as he rubbed his bruised and bleeding knuckles.

"From whom?"

"That lying pig, Culver, and his friends."

The fight was not over if she were to judge by the vehemence of Angus's words.

"Culver? The surgeon's son?"

"Him and three of his stupid friends." Harry's split lip gave him a lisp but she understood him. "They look worse than we do."

"I think I broke his nose." Angus spoke with real satisfaction.

"Oh, Angus."

"He was saying the worst things, Aunt Lavinia."

"What sort of things?"

She addressed the captain and he shrugged. "They have yet to be specific."

"Insults about why the captain rescued you."

"And how much he paid Mrs. Newcomb to pretend to be a chaperone."

"And how you are no better than your brother."

"And how the captain will turn you out when he is done with you."

The captain held up both hands. "That is enough, I think. We understand."

Lavinia knew she was blushing even though it was no worse than she expected.

"How can you be so calm?" This from an outraged Harry, near tears and too upset to try to stop them.

"Because it is not true." Lavinia wanted to sit down and draw him down beside her, but he was almost twelve, and would say he was too old for that sort of comfort.

"It is no more than the speculation of idle minds." The captain came around from his desk, took Angus's hands and examined his knuckles. The boy leaned closer to him and the captain ran a hand over the boy's tousled hair. "Angus, you met the vicar and his wife when they came to dinner."

"Yes, sir," Angus said.

"They have heard the story and believe it is the truth." The captain lifted Harry's chin and examined the bloody lip. He shook his head. "I know that hurts."

Harry shrugged. The tears were gone. The captain squeezed the boy's shoulder and came back to the desk.

"I understand that you felt you had no choice but to defend us."

The boys were relieved, though Angus's nod was far more guarded than Harry's vigorous one.

"And because I would have done the same, I want you to know there will be no punishment from either one of us."

"You did not start it," she agreed with him completely on this. "It would be vastly unfair to punish you for a fight that you did not seek out."

# Take a Trip Back to the Romantic Regency Era of the Early 1800's

**4 FREE BOOKS ARE YOURS!**

## 4 FREE
### Zebra Regency Romances!
(A $19.96 VALUE!)

**Plus You'll Save Every Month With Convenient Home Delivery!**

## We'd Like to Invite You to Subscribe to Zebra's Regency Romance Book Club and Send You 4 Free Books as Your Introduction! (Worth $19.96!)

If you're a Regency lover, imagine the joy of getting 4 FREE Zebra Regency Romances and then the chance to have these lovely stories delivered to your home each month at the lowest price available! Well, that's our offer to you and here's how you benefit by becoming a Regency Romance subscriber:

- *4 FREE Introductory Regency Romances are delivered to your doorstep (you only pay for shipping & handling)*
- *4 BRAND NEW Regencies are then delivered each month (usually before they're available in bookstores)*
- *Subscribers save almost $4.00 off the cover price every month*
- *You also receive a FREE monthly newsletter, which features author profiles, discounts, subscriber benefits, book previews and more*
- *There's no risks or obligations...in other words, you can cancel whenever you wish with no questions asked*

Join the thousands of readers who enjoy the savings and convenience offered to Regency Romance subscribers. After your initial introductory shipment, you'll receive 4 brand-new Zebra Regency Romances each month to examine for 10 days. Then, if you decide to keep the books, you pay the preferred subscriber's price, plus shipping and handling.

### It's a no-lose proposition, so return the FREE BOOK CERTIFICATE today!

A $19.96 value – **FREE** No obligation to buy anything – ever.
**4 FREE BOOKS** are waiting for you! Just mail in the certificate below!

# FREE BOOK CERTIFICATE

*YES!* Please rush me 4 FREE Zebra Regency Romances (I only pay $1.99 for shipping and handling).I understand that each month thereafter I will be able to preview 4 brand-new Regency Romances FREE for 10 days. Then, if I should decide to keep them, I will pay the money-saving preferred subscriber's price for all 4… (that's a savings of 20% off the retail price), plus shipping and handling. I may return any shipment within 10 days and owe nothing, and I may cancel this subscription at any time.

Name _____

Address _____ Apt. ____

City _____ State _____ Zip _____

Telephone (___) _____

Signature _____

(If under 18, parent or guardian must sign)

Offer limited to one per household and not to current subscribers. Terms, offer and prices subject to change. Orders subject to acceptance by Regency Romance Book Club. Offer Valid in the U.S. only.

RN094A

*Treat yourself to 4 FREE Regency Romances!*
*A $19.96 VALUE… FREE!*
*No obligation to buy anything ever!*

**REGENCY ROMANCE BOOK CLUB**
Zebra Home Subscription Service, Inc.
P.O. Box 5214
Clifton NJ 07015-5214

"Exactly," the captain said.

Angus's great relief was evident. Did he think that the captain was going to use the switch on him?

"I want you both to go upstairs, clean up, and change your clothes." Lavinia came closer and considered the ill-used garments. "I think these can be salvaged if only for tree climbing."

The captain walked to the door and opened it. "Have Dolley look at the cuts. And have Chasen give you some of the salve he uses. The surgeon gave him enough to share. It seems to cure almost anything."

The boys left, taking any inclination to conversation with them. William watched her and she looked everywhere but at him.

"We must discuss this," he said finally.

Lavinia knew he was right, but his words sounded so much like an order that she ignored the seat he offered and moved across the room to the door.

With her hand on the doorknob she turned back to him. He was leaning against the desk, his arms folded across his chest. "Are you going to call Mrs. Newcomb or her sister to attend us?" He straightened as he spoke.

"You know very well I am not."

"I will do whatever makes you comfortable, Miss Stewart, but we must discuss this." He took a few steps closer and waited for her answer.

"I think I am perfectly safe here with you." She took in the books lining the shelves, the desk with its clean top, and the captain who was waiting for her with a bland, if not patient, look in his eyes. "After all, we have been only the two of us at the lake at midnight. You have been in my bedroom and there was the time I went after the boys when their boat overturned—" She stopped. Why was she prattling on so? It would be wiser not to remind him of that moment in his arms with her clothes soaked through.

He came over to where she was standing and reached for her. She took a startled step back, and then flushed red when she realized that he was merely reaching for the doorknob.

"No chaperone, then." He bowed to her and closed the door.

She walked back across the floor and flopped into the chair, feeling as though she had been tricked into this discussion. "You think we should discuss this? Captain, I would rather be washing clothes with lye soap."

"Yes, it is uncomfortable and I regret it as much as you do." The captain spoke the perfunctory words as he returned to his desk and took his seat behind it, across from her.

He appeared every inch a landed gentleman, but his air of command was an even more permanent part of him. He was confident and in control and suddenly she found it more of a comfort than an annoyance. It went a long way to convincing her that he had a plan that would resolve the whole.

"Miss Stewart, neither of us is responsible for the boys' fight or for any of what has brought us to this moment. It is your brother and his unconscionable behavior that is at fault." His voice had an edge to it.

"You sound as though you would take the cat to him."

"If he comes near here, I will."

"He does not even know I am gone." She did not mean to dismiss his anger. "Desmond cares more about his cattle than he does about me."

"It may be as you say, but I have some experience with unwanted family attentions and I assure you he will never be welcome here."

She was shocked at his vehemence. Was he talking about that visit from Lord Morgan Braedon? No matter what his reason for this strongly held view, she appreciated his support. "Thank you."

"It is unforgivable that your brother's indulgences should force you into behavior that is not what you would want."

"So far it has not come to that."

"But it has." His smile was an apology, as though he was sorry that he had to tell her. "You are here because those who love you insisted, not because you chose to come."

"Oh, yes. I see. But it is far easier to accept their demands than Desmond's. I know that the children and Mrs. Wilcox truly care for me. Their only motive is my safety."

He nodded, as though that was exactly what he thought she would say. "And that was the reason that I was able to convince you to make the choice and come to Talford Rise?"

"Yes." He said nothing, so she went on, realizing tension as much as innate command held him straight in his chair. "But my decision was more complicated than that. The children trusted you to do what was right and so did I."

"Good." He said it with relief, but he did not relax. "I value your trust, Miss Stewart, and hope never to abuse it."

"I cannot imagine how that could happen. We live in very different worlds. Our lives are entangled for the moment, by my current situation and how close our estates are," she paused and then added the last, "and the children." Perhaps the ties would be more difficult to lose than she at first thought.

He was quiet so long that she wondered if he was worried about the same thing. She waited, for though he might be silent, she knew this conversation was not finished. In those few moments he made his own decision and relaxed back into his chair. His eyes were less intense but no less focused on her.

"There is a belief among men of the sea, Miss Stewart. A certainty that if you want a mermaid to stay with you, then you must steal something of hers. Usually it is a brush or mirror, since they do spend an inordinate amount of time caring for their hair. As long as that item is in the man's possession, the mermaid has no choice but to stay." He opened his desk drawer and took out a comb.

Lavinia recognized it as one of her ivory hair combs, one of a pair that her uncle had given her after some trip.

The captain reached across the desk and placed it within easy reach.

She did not take it, held still by his expression, trying to fathom the reason for this abrupt change of subject. His eyes searched hers, his own guarded as though he would touch her soul but protect his own.

"Lavinia, there is one way to solve this gossip. Put an end to the rumor and unseemly speculation."

"Yes, of course. I can return home in a day or two. Desmond will soon tire of the country. He always does."

"Yes, but what will you do the next time Stewart decides to bring friends to Talford? And it will hardly stop the gossip already started."

"You know of a more permanent solution?"

"Yes." He folded his hands on top of the desk and leaned over them. "Marry me."

# Chapter 15

"Marry you! Is that an order?" Lavinia stood up and grabbed the comb from the edge of the desk. "How absurd. You cannot be serious."

"I thought you more sensible than most women." He wasn't surprised at her reaction, but he was disappointed.

She eyed him with suspicion. Did she not think it a compliment? He plunged ahead. "I was hoping you would see this as a practical solution to a bothersome problem."

"Bothersome problem?" The sound she made was a cross between humor and disbelief. She put the comb back down on the desk, circled the room once, going nowhere near the door, and then came back to stand in front of him.

"Marriage seems an extreme solution to a problem no more than 'bothersome.'" She looked down at the blotter and then at him. "You would be willing to sacrifice your freedom and allow me into your home?"

"Yes." His disappointment ebbed, swamped by surprise. Was she considering it?

"You do understand that I would not leave Harry or Sara?"

"Of course not—they are welcome here."

"You know that my brother must agree?"

"I am sure I can convince him."

Lavinia shook her head. "Despite his indifference, he does have plans for me."

"Plans?"

"Yes. One of his friends, a man named Brocklin, has expressed an interest in marriage."

"And do you share that interest?" He did his best to keep his voice level.

"Not at all. He is vulgar and cruel. It is only that Desmond might not be agreeable to another plan."

"Oh, I think I can convince him."

Her gaze flitted to his hands, one fisted in the other, and he made himself relax them. "Now *you* are being absurd. I will not use brute force, I promise you. Stewart has earned it, but you deserve better than scandal. It is what I am trying to avoid."

"You know that I would make changes."

"Yes. What woman would not? After dealing with Mrs. Newcomb's ideas, I feel I am prepared."

"And is that why you are proposing? To rid yourself of Mrs. Newcomb? Is she as much a 'bothersome problem' as the gossip?"

"This is not a teasing matter, Lavinia." He suspected that those two words—bothersome problem—would haunt him forever. "I want to marry you. I want you to marry me."

"But how can you want that? The last time we were alone together you called me a shrew."

"No, the last time we were alone you held a sword and you were ready to use it. At that moment I finally understood how difficult your life has been. How your brother has forsworn his most basic responsibility: to keep you safe. How every man is a threat to you. Even me."

Lavinia fingered the comb again but left it on the desk. "I would remove that painting immediately." She pointed to the one with the brace of birds that she had referred to on her first visit.

He stood up and took it from the wall. Setting it on the floor, he put the image of the dead animals against the wall so they would not disturb her again.

When he turned back to her, she was seated. Her head was bent, but he could see tears on her cheeks.

When she raised her face to him he saw both embarrassment and irritation. "Ignore them." She gave an unladylike sniff and the tears slowed.

"Ignore the tears?" He gave her his handkerchief and sat next to her so that the desk was no longer between them. "Asking me to ignore your tears is like ordering me to overtake a ship of the line in a rowboat. Impossible."

"It is only that moving that picture was such a lovely gesture."

"So lovely that it has moved you to tears?" he asked, unable to hide his puzzlement.

"Oh, it is not you who have caused the tears. It is not you at all. Do you not understand that tears are the only recourse of the powerless?"

"Then I wonder how you define power, Miss Stewart."

"You see, Captain, I have insisted for so long that I am not without power. But the truth is that I am totally at the mercy of my brother's whims, as much a dependent as the children."

"Now that I know what those whims entail, I can see how his notion of power would distress you."

"Yes, precisely," Lavinia said. "Your proposal makes me realize that being powerless will be my lot in life. I have only been lying to myself if I think otherwise."

"You think my proposal would be nothing more than trading one kind of control for another?"

"Yes, and not at all necessary if only I had my own money and the control of it. But I have no money and a single woman is rarely allowed control. But if I did, I could manage, for I assure you I am not helpless. Not feeble. Not weak." She had leaned a little closer with each "not." She leaned back again. "I am only powerless."

He shook his head. "It would be a great mistake were anyone to mistake you for weak, feeble, or helpless. I saw you with a weapon in hand, ready to murder to protect yourself. That was power, Lavinia."

"It was? Yes, I suppose it was even if born of desperation." She considered it and a little smile worked its way through the upset. "I like the idea that I can take care of myself and that at least one person believes it of me."

She drew a deep breath and after a thoughtful silence she spoke. "When I first met you, I thought Angus and even Dolley were in the same position as the children and me. Or even worse, for you used a switch on Angus. You used a whip on a child." She shuddered a little. "I hated you for using your power that way."

She stood again and put some distance between them. Was she restless or nervous? Or was it fear?

"In time I came to see that none of your staff feels threatened. They obey your commands without question, but they do not feel threatened," she repeated. "And Angus loves you like a father."

The edge of wonder in her voice told him that this still confused her.

"Your power is as complete as Desmond's, but far less selfish, almost totally unselfish."

He winced. She was making him into a model of goodness. He had only to think of his reason for marriage to know that "unselfish" was far down on his list of admirable qualities.

"You do not agree, Captain? Then I ask you, if you are not generous, why do you have a household staff unaccustomed to shore life and an energetic boy in residence?"

He chuckled. "Yes, they do not seem essential to a officer's life, do they?"

"You use your power for good while Desmond uses it as a convenience for indulgence, gratification."

He did not reply. For him, marriage would be convenient and very gratifying.

"A marriage in name only would relieve you of the burden of managing Talford Rise." She stopped her pacing. "Why do you not hire a housekeeper?"

"Because I am not interested in a marriage in name only."

"Oh." She blushed and dropped her gaze. "Of course not. You would expect us to sleep together." She made it a statement.

"Yes." He took a step nearer. "There. You see? I am not the hero you imagine. Holding you and lying with you is the reward for my generosity."

She was standing by the desk and picked up the comb again. "I had always hoped to find some romance in a courtship."

"I am sorry, Lavinia, but this is not about love. I do believe we can deal well enough together, but if you expect undying devotion from me . . ." He let his voice trail off, afraid that he was sabotaging his own proposal.

She tucked the comb into her hair and shook her head firmly. "I would be selling myself."

"Yes, you would." When she was surprised at his frank agreement he went on. "What do you think you would be doing if you went to London? Parading your admirable self in hopes of attracting someone who will give exactly what I am offering."

She shook her head and turned from him.

"In many ways you are better prepared for a decision than you would be in London."

"Because?" she asked, looking over her shoulder briefly.

"We have seen each other at our worst and our best. That knowledge came unobstructed by the facade and fripperies the ton lives by."

She remained silent, which made him think that he was making headway with this argument.

"Here we have come to know each other without the constraints of the Season. It has been unconventional, but even

Mrs. Newcomb would agree that it is a courtship nonetheless."

Lavinia walked to the window seat and sat down in the middle of it, her face turned from him so that he could only see her profile. He joined her on the seat and she moved a little so that he could fit in the space next to her. Their bodies barely touched and he judged it acceptable to her since she did not move away.

"Lavinia Stewart, I will give you a home where you are safe, where you will never be abused, where you never need worry about how to pay the butcher's bill."

She pressed her lips together and stared at him so intently that he could see into her heart. "A husband and children," he whispered. "Family in every sense of the word." He waited a beat. "Respectability."

"Family." She said the word as though it was her dearest wish.

"It is all possible, Lavinia." He felt a surge of guilt for using her longing for family this way. For all of a moment he felt more selfish than Desmond Stewart on a bad day. "You do understand that there will be responsibilities as well as comforts? Your husband will be gone for months on end."

"You would leave?" She asked the question as though he had roused her from a dream.

"Yes, I am a post captain and hope to live to be an admiral. I will take whatever command the Admiralty offers." He could not tell if this was welcome news or not. "In fact, you may well be a wealthy widow before your first anniversary."

"Stop." She spoke with asperity, raising her hand as if she could physically restrain him. "You will not make light of that. Not ever."

"Not if it troubles you," he agreed, "but even if I live to be one hundred there will be times when you will have to manage without me."

"Running a house? Caring for children? I have done that

for more than a year with only the meanest of support." She relaxed and her eyes lost some of their severity. "But what if we do not find each other appealing?"

"Oh, we hardly need worry about that." He tried to keep his elation from showing. "Attraction can be so easily tested."

She did not ask, but her look was question enough.

"A kiss, Lavinia. One kiss is all we need."

He was close to her, very close. He gathered her into his arms, drew her not-yet-yielding body to him and pressed his lips to hers. He could feel her shiver of response. Her arousal echoed through him and he lowered her to the soft cushion of the window seat, his body as much a caress as his lips.

He used his mouth to entice her and his hands to woo her. Within seconds, any plan he might have had to beguile her with the promise of pleasure was forgotten as he was seduced by the softness of her breasts, the generosity of her response, the warmth of her.

He touched the edge of her lips with his tongue and her small gasp gave him the entry he wanted. Teasing her tongue with his, he felt her whole body melt into his. When she sighed in surrender, he raised his head to look into her eyes.

His longing was made bearable by the promise of triumph, but the languid yearning in her eyes faded as she stared at him. She moved her hands from around his neck to the front of his shirt. She lay very still beneath him. "You must promise that you will never use a whip on me."

"Use a whip on you? No, never." He sat up and she did too, edging away from him until she was crowded into the corner of the window seat looking more trapped than entranced.

"Where did you hear of that, Lavinia? Is it something Desmond told you?" He took her hand, but moved back to give her more space.

"No. Why would Desmond tell me?" Her hand was restless in his and he let it go. "I have heard stories of it from Dolley. You used it on Angus that first day we met."

"Oh, that sort of whip." He adjusted his own understanding to match hers. "I already promised never to abuse you, Lavinia. My word is my best and only pledge. You will be my wife and always deserving of my respect."

"But can you control yourself?" She seemed uncertain. "It has been the way punishment is given for almost your whole life."

He laughed, short and hard. "By the stars, Lavinia, control is one thing I excel at. I have spent a lifetime learning to control myself in every way you can imagine and some you cannot."

She lowered her head. "Yes, I suppose that must be true."

"Besides, a gentleman would never punish his wife."

"Even if she is a shrew?"

He kept his silence until she looked at him.

"Not even if she is a shrew." He raised her hand and, before he kissed it, he promised. "I will never force you. I promise I will never use a whip on you." He waited until she nodded and added. "Unless you ask me too."

"Unless I ask you? To whip me?"

Her dismay made him wonder why he was teasing her like this.

"Some find it a way to increase pleasure."

"Pleasure?" Her blush told him the minute that she took his meaning. "Do you . . . ?"

He shook his head and leaned closer and kissed her again. This time she was at least as willing as she was curious.

He touched the corner of her mouth, moved to the sweet spot below her ear and then found her lips with his. The tantalizing touches drew a deeper, more fervent response than he had expected. She was not so passive and he smiled against her mouth when she ran her hands down his back and then under the wool of his jacket.

He let her taste and explore until she stopped with a sudden movement that brought him back to time and place in a maddening instant.

"How can anyone need more than kisses?" she asked, her breathing a little ragged, her mouth as red as any rouge could make it.

"Oh, I promise you, Lavinia, in time you will beg for more."

She straightened and stood up, looking down at him. "But never a whip." She pressed her lips together.

"Never, I promise you."

"Captain?" She already had his undivided attention, but she waited a moment before she went on. "What will you beg for?"

She blushed a little once the question was out, but she waited for his answer. This was not some coquettish tease, but a serious question.

"I am begging now, Lavinia." He knew he did not sound at all lover-like. He rubbed his forehead, annoyed and not nearly as certain as he had been before their kisses. "And, my dear, I have never begged for anything in my life."

"Then perhaps I will marry you." She turned and hurried across the room, as if he would run after her. "I will consider it." She was out the door on the last word.

He let her go, suddenly not as determined to draw an answer from her at this moment. The passion in their kisses might have made her consider his suit, but it had pushed him in the opposite direction. Was marriage the wisest course of action?

He had a house and a boy, the beginning of a family that had come to him in an unorthodox way. He needed a wife to share his bed, keep his house, and make his life more simple.

He stood up, went to his desk, and sat down.

The last thing he needed was a wife who would complicate it and, worse yet, a woman whose welcoming arms would make it difficult to leave for months at a time.

He put his elbows on the desk and rested his forehead on his folded hands, considering the problem.

No, he decided, straightening again. Once they were married, once they were together every day and in every way the frustration would be over—familiarity would make parting easier—because this was not about love. It was an offer designed to give two people what they wanted. Family for her and for him. Though they both would define that need differently, it was what they both wanted.

It was only that their last kiss had ended too soon, leaving him frustrated. It was some consolation that she was as enthralled as he was. That could make for some long, delightful hours of lovemaking.

If she said yes. When she said yes.

He leaned back and opened his desk drawer and stared at the second of the two combs he had slipped in his pocket that evening when he helped untangle her hair.

# Chapter 16

London had not changed and never would. The weather was kind for August, but the town was empty of the ton. William preferred it that way. He could make his way through St. James without being harassed by dandies and their curricles. There was no crowd at the bookstore or perusing Rowlandson's latest cartoons. His rooms at the Falcon were as always, but the hotel was blessedly quiet.

He would have preferred to stay in Sussex, but Mrs. Newcomb would not permit it. The temptation to mutiny against her oppressive control was strong, but two considerations stopped him: What if she took offense and left? What would happen to Lavinia?

Then news came to him through Mrs. Wilcox's sister at the home farm that Desmond Stewart had left for London. Despite the fact that several of his houseguests remained in residence, word was they would be leaving within a sennight. Stewart had no plans to return to Talford anytime soon. There had been some discussion of a trip to Brighton. Of a sudden, London was exactly where William wanted to be.

He left for Town on the heels of Mrs. Wilcox's news, with a list of tasks from near everyone in his household and some of his own that would mean being away for at least a week.

First was a call on the Admiralty to make sure they had not forgotten him. He was well received, which eliminated any lingering doubts he might have regarding his failed mission to France earlier in the summer. No one had heard from Garrett and most thought they never would.

Next, he sent a message round to Stewart's townhouse requesting a meeting. His plan was simple: ask for permission to court Lavinia, slightly after the fact, and make sure that Stewart would stay away from them all.

While waiting for an answer, he addressed the errands, which took him from Greenwich to Richmond and into the depths of a draper's shop on Bond Street. Despite the fact he was no more than an errand boy, this task was easily the most intimidating of all.

There had been a response from Lavinia's brother waiting for him when William had returned to the Falcon and he had hurried out almost immediately to meet Stewart.

Two hours after that  meeting he was at Hatchards, staring at a row of books, his mind miles away with Lavinia and his future.

His conversation with Desmond Stewart had been every bit as easy as he had hoped. Money was the key. Give the man a thousand guineas and he would allow Satan to court his sister. Give him another thousand and he would sell his children as well. Money was one commodity that William had in abundance; he had just exchanged a bit of it for family in abundance.

The only unexpected element had been Stewart's one question: "Why do you want to marry the chit?"

He had answered with perfect honesty. "Because I have need of a wife. I have a ward who needs discipline, a house that needs attention, and a staff that is willing but unschooled."

Stewart had regarded him with a long, calculating stare. "You've had some fun with her already, have you?"

"No."

Stewart waved his word away. "More fool you. Have you seen her barefoot? Or better yet, swimming?"

"You are treading on dangerous ground here, Stewart. Your sister is a model of virtue."

"Virtue? All right, I'll grant you that, but not a model of propriety. Hardly."

"She is unconventional," William corrected him pointedly, "and that suits a man in my position and with my commitments."

"Give her a brat or two and she will forget you exist."

The thought had occurred to him as well, that a child would fill her days while he was away, but William did not like the way Stewart had phrased it. That was hardly surprising since there was nothing about the man he found at all likeable.

Finally William presented Stewart with his demands. He had spent the better part of a week buying up every one of Stewart's markers. With them in hand, William ordered Stewart to never contact his sister again. If he did intrude on their lives, William promised he would insist on payment of the debts and have no qualms about sending Stewart to debtors' prison.

Stewart blustered and stammered, more about the threat of imprisonment than the commitment never to see Lavinia, but in the end he had no choice but to agree.

Last of all, William made Stewart swear that he would never tell Lavinia of their dealings. Less a fool than most drunkards, he nodded without comment and the two parted, William satisfied and Stewart significantly more plump in the pocket.

Lavinia would not hear of this meeting from him either. With a family and a home to manage and his attentions at night, she would forget her predatory brother in no more time than it took to turn the hourglass.

He considered the books at hand. She was the only person at Talford Rise who had not asked for something from Town. Even Angus had begged for a surprise. William had found two small wooden boats that the boys could race on the lake. He was determined to find Lavinia a gift as well.

The clerk suggested *Sense and Sensibility*, but after he explained the story William shook his head. The family failing at the root of the Dashwood sisters' change of circumstances would strike too close to home.

He had heard that Lieutenant Marryat had written a book. *Post Commander* would be a novel they could read aloud together, but he was told that the publishing date had been delayed.

When the clerk held out an elegant leatherbound book entitled *The Lady of the Lake,* William needed no more than those five words to know it was meant for his mermaid. It took three volumes to tell the story and he wondered if Lavinia would think it too extravagant a gift. Would she reject it as she had the jasper sea shell? He could always save it for a wedding present.

"Captain Chartwell?"

The words were spoken very quietly, but with certainty.

When he turned away from the books he found himself facing a well-dressed woman, her dark brown cloak thrown back to show a gown the color of the Mediterranean Sea. Her eyes were brown and her dark hair was half hidden under what he was sure was a very fashionable bonnet. After the briefest of moments he recognized Mariel Whitlow—Mariel Braedon Whitlow.

"Madam." He bowed to her.

"Thank you." She curtseyed but kept her eyes on his. "Thank you for not turning your back on me."

"Mrs. Whitlow, I insulted you once and have no wish to leave you crying again." It had been an embarrassment for all of them, that meeting at a private card party where he had refused to be introduced to her.

"I am remarried and am Mrs. Hadley now."

"My best wishes to you both." He bowed again.

"If you will be in Town for some days, my husband and I would like to invite you to dinner."

"I leave this evening." He would go to Portsmouth or China, anything to make the dinner impossible.

"Then would you come with me now? Please?"

"It is too late in the day for a call, Mrs. Hadley."

She agreed with a slight nod but appeared determined nonetheless.

He wanted to say no and walk away. His mouth formed the words, but he decided on a different approach. "If you are going to discuss my connection with your family then I must refuse."

"You mean the fact that you are my brother? My legitimate brother? Totally unknown to us until two years ago? Is that what you will not discuss?"

"Yes."

"Excellent. Since that is not at all what we wish to talk with you about. You have made your sentiments on that abundantly clear. You have no wish to be a part of the Braedons. I want to speak to you and seek your expertise on an entirely different matter."

"Indeed?" What was this? An attempt to draw him close like a ship flying false colors and then bring out the guns once he was trapped?

"Please come. I promise you I will not mention the Braedons or brothers even once."

Her clear, direct eyes were as honest as they were brown and he found himself hurrying his purchase and ordering his carriage to follow hers home.

As the coachman urged the cattle toward the Hadley townhouse, William wished he had asked for some idea of the subject they were to discuss so he could prepare himself. As it was, he could only guess, his imagination settling on one unappealing possibility after another.

Her new husband was waiting in the foyer and showed only a little surprise at an unexpected guest so late in the day.

William remembered him well. Edward Hadley was a favorite of the ton and almost everyone else in London. They had played cards together several times.

"Happy to meet you again, Chartwell." Hadley, known for his good humor, was all affability. He greeted his wife with a kiss. William found the intimate gesture in front of another embarrassing. Hadley must have noticed.

"Excuse us, we are newlyweds and you *are* family."

"Shh, Edward. I promised that we would not discuss the connection."

"As long as we do not need to pretend it is a secret. At this point the whole ton knows."

They did? Chartwell tried for a bland expression. It was just as well he had no plans to bring Lavinia up to Town once they were married.

"You remember Gerald Lockwood, Chartwell?"

"I do," William said, recalling Lockwood was one of Hadley's best friends.

"He wants a rematch, you know."

"A rematch of that ridiculous card-playing marathon?" William asked.

"Yes. Exactly."

"But he *won* the marathon, Hadley. What is the point of a rematch?"

"He feels the win was compromised by the fact that you were called away. He wants to prove himself at some time and place when the Admiralty will not interfere."

William shook his head. "Hadley, the ton at play is a puzzle to any sensible man. Tell Lockwood that my commitments do not allow for a prolonged stay in Town." Another thought struck him. "Is this why you invited me here?" The two of them were nothing more than a sober Desmond Stewart.

"Of course not, Captain." Mariel Hadley threw a desperate glance at her husband. "Edward, you are deliberately baiting him so he will refuse to stay."

"Oh, was I that obvious?" He grinned back at her, full of amused disappointment.

"Yes, you were, and you know this is important to me."

"My pardon, dear," he said, sobering.

William considered their conversation. He could learn something here. Something about marriage. This was one sample of it. Two people not quite bickering, but each trying to best the other. But then there was that kiss of greeting. Hardly typical and completely sincere.

"Please sit down, Captain." Mrs. Hadley's words bore the air of a monumental request. And it was. Sitting meant he would have to hear them through. But he was interested enough in the way they dealt with each other to take a seat and listen.

Mrs. Hadley sat and he followed her action. He waited for her to speak but it was her still-standing husband who began.

"I must be honest here, Captain Chartwell. My wife has wanted your opinion for a while and I have not. But since you have settled the matter by coming to us, then I will bow to her interests. She would say it is God's will. I could argue the point and call it the action of some imp of Satan, but love has blinded me."

"I can hardly tell if you are trying to aggravate me or simply test your wife." William kept his seat but his voice was anything but cordial. "In either case you are close to insult. Do you ever go to Jackson's?"

"To box? Every ten days or so." Hadley ran his tongue around his teeth, but a laugh managed to escape.

His wife clapped her hands, as though she was twenty years their senior.

"Oh, stop it, both of you." She looked from one to the other to be sure she had their attention. She was not angry, but Hadley seemed to know that he dared not go any further. William wondered how long it had taken this man to understand the limit of his wife's patience. And what were the consequences of going too far?

"Very well, Mariel, but he is so easy to annoy. The temptation is irresistible."

"Resist it, Edward." She sat down again. "You two do not deserve tea." She spoke to her husband, "Would you please pour some wine?"

Hadley did as he was directed, presented it, and this time took a seat next to his wife. He put his arm along the back of her seat and William noticed that she did not move away from the gesture. In fact, her mouth softened and she smiled a little.

The Hadleys were obviously in love. He had only to pay attention to see it. Here in London he numbered at least eight marriages he could learn from, and he had to find this couple. A man so besotted with his wife that he allowed her to run his life as well as her own.

If he wanted to prolong exile and make Mrs. Newcomb happy he could stay in Town and make a study of the subject, but he was missing Talford Rise already. He missed the boys yelling. He missed the hammock at the boathouse. He even missed Mrs. Newcomb harrying his staff and Dolley's pleading looks.

He did not miss Lavinia because he could recall at will the feel of her body, her lips, the very breath of her.

"Captain Chartwell?"

He pulled his thoughts away from home and back to this comfortable salon and the two people who had finally decided to tell him what they wanted. "I beg your pardon, ma'am. I was woolgathering."

"Yes, and your smile makes me want to apologize for interrupting."

He did not answer and to her credit she did not press him but began, "My husband and I are engaged in various small charities."

They smiled at each other, as though this was something new and special they shared. "We are interested in enlarging our scope and would like to do something for the men who have served His Majesty in the navy. But we are uncertain what to do. We were hoping that you could advise us."

"You are going to give money away? And you need me to tell you how?" He wanted to stand, cross his arms, and take command of the situation.

"Yes. We need your help." She smiled encouragingly as if he were a none-too-bright child who had grasped a complex idea. "We would like this charity to have some naval connection."

"Yes, but why?" They might be in charge, but they were not wearing uniforms. He could demand an explanation.

She stared down at her hands for a little while. "Because I want to make amends in some little way for a great wrong."

"If this is about my father's rejection, his decision to send me away, send me to sea, why not just give the money to me?"

"Because that is too easy. For both of us. And because you do not need money."

"I need nothing from you." He made to rise from his seat. "This is a waste of time. I have more pressing problems to deal with."

Mrs. Hadley spoke as though he was not set on leaving. "No, you do not need anything from us, Captain, but there are others who do. Would you deny them?"

He sat down again, a little more in sympathy with Hadley. When she spoke with such earnest appeal it was hard to deny her. She wanted him to name a charity? All right, he'd give them one that would test their interest. "A French orphanage."

"I beg your pardon?"

"Give the money to a French orphanage." He felt a twinge of guilt for calling their bluff by naming something so impossible. "The orphanages are no longer run by the church.

Half the nuns and priests went to the guillotine. The one I grew up in was disbanded. That is the reason I was sent from France to my father."

She raised a hand to her throat. "But what happened to the other children?"

"I have no idea. I was not much more than a child myself. But I do know that I was one of the lucky ones."

"You realize that until Napoleon is gone, sending money or people to France is impossible?" This came from Hadley.

William was not going to allow them that easy an escape. He thought of Angus and the hundreds of boys like him. "Then fund an orphanage here for the children of seamen." He thought of one more impossibly expensive suggestion. "Create a society that will provide for officers' widows."

It was Hadley who radiated interest. He spoke while looking at his wife who nodded as he did. His behavior reminded William of a lap dog, eager for approval.

"We will do both, fund an orphanage for the children of seaman and give each new widow of an officer fifty pounds."

"You will take this on? But it will cost a fortune."

"Yes," agreed Hadley cheerfully, "and I am lucky enough to have a substantial one."

Which his wife seemed hell-bent on spending.

# Chapter 17

He should take his leave. It was enough that he had given them an idea. He placed his wine glass carefully on the table at hand, but did not move from his seat, reconsidering in an instant. It was too amazing an offer to let fail.

"Not all officers' widows are in need." He paused and then added, "It all has to do with the chance to take prizes. Some men are luckier than others."

Mariel Hadley gave her husband a triumphant look and he gave her a small nod of acceptance.

"You, apparently, are one of the lucky ones, Captain," she said, "but how are we to know?"

He considered the question. "I would suggest that you give a hundred pounds to the widow of any married lieutenant who has not yet had command. That would be enough to see her through a year or more and most of them remarry quickly."

"And you think lieutenants who have not had command would be a more realistic group to deal with?" Hadley stood up and went to a small desk where he began to make notes.

"Yes. And easy to identify."

"Once they have command they will have accrued enough prize money to be able to keep a family?" Mariel Hadley asked.

"It is not always true, but it seems the most manageable way to arrange it."

They did not seem inclined to agree. "We could examine them individually," Mrs. Hadley said.

"You may have enough money, but you cannot have enough time unless you wish to hire a staff to examine each situation. Of course, that would be another way to spend your fortune."

"Do I detect disapproval, Captain?" Hadley asked.

"To allow your wife to spend in this way is a ludicrous indulgence."

They both laughed. "He is truly your brother, my girl. How could I have ever doubted it?" Hadley spoke to him directly. "This was a hobby of mine since well before we were married. At first, Mariel felt much as you do."

"A hobby? This is not the first time you have done this?"

"No, but before Edward and I married, he gave smaller gifts to individuals."

"But how can it be that this is not the talk of the ton?"

"Because," Hadley said, "it has always been random and anonymous."

"Anonymous?"

"For the fun of it."

"You find amusement in others' misfortune?" They were worse than Desmond Stewart. At least he did not mask his entertainments as good works.

"No, we do not," Mariel Hadley insisted. "But misfortune exists and we find pleasure in easing someone else's burden."

"It is the height of self-indulgence." William knew he sounded like a prig and did not care.

"And where is it written that giving has to be trimmed with righteousness?" Mariel asked. "Why is it wrong for us to find some pleasure in a generous gesture?"

He was about to debate the point when he thought of his proposal to Lavinia. He was determined to give her his name to save her from a miserable future, to give her the family life she longed for, but he had every intention of finding pleasure in the gift.

"When we married I convinced Edward that we should consider a more organized approach to giving."

"But more important than the history of our efforts, Chartwell, is the fact that no one knows of this. You are the first. And we wish to keep it that way."

"It's completely understandable. If it were common knowledge you would be deluged with requests." He drank the last of his wine. "I assure you that I have kept confidences more vital than this one."

"Good, we should prefer to keep this in the family. I do hope that you will be willing to continue to advise us."

He heard the words and realized the trap. "This was quite a neat bit of subterfuge. You two are like a commander who paints his whole ship to change its appearance and fool the enemy." He put his wine glass down with a clink and shook his head. "Is this nothing more than a contrivance to draw me into the Braedon family circle?"

"Absolutely not." She spoke firmly but it was not enough.

"I do not believe you." He knew the anger edging his words made it an insult, but he was furious with them and with himself for being so taken in.

"I mean to make a difference in people's lives."

"How admirable. But I have no need of you in mine, Mrs. Hadley."

He stood up and so did Hadley.

"I want no further contact with you. Not every man is as easily led as your husband, madam."

He was certain that his comment would cause Hadley to mention Jackson's again. Had said it deliberately, in fact, hoping for it.

But Hadley surprised him. "I warned her, Chartwell. I tried to make her understand."

Chartwell walked to the door. Hadley kept on speaking.

"But some women are so fixed on family that they are willing to risk all manner of insult."

William spoke to them one more time from the doorway. "If you wish no more insult, then do not seek me out again."

As the coach made its way through the late-day traffic, he calmed. He blamed them, but he was the one who had agreed to the meeting and had been tempted by their charity. He had broken his primary rule regarding the Braedons: avoid them at all costs.

By the time he had returned to his rooms, packed his clothes, and was seated in the carriage, headed for Sussex, William saw one thing more quite clearly. Before Lavinia accepted his proposal he would have to tell her something of his family. The truth.

And make it perfectly clear that he forbade any contact with them. If she was not willing to obey him in this, then they had no future.

He might have managed to observe only one couple on this trip to London, but it was clear that living with a woman would be an entirely new experience.

But hadn't shipboard life taught him to rub along well enough with men of endlessly different sensibilities? He could apply that expertise to marriage.

And in the course of his seagoing life he had learned how to share his authority. Yes, he was used to command. Too used to it to give it up. But no one man could run a ship, or a home, without help. Lavinia would be in charge of the house and the staff. She'd already proven she had the makings of a fine first lieutenant. Beyond that and the children, he would be honest but careful in what he shared with her.

He pulled out the sketchpad that was always tucked beside the seat. Even though the rocking carriage made a poor easel, he entertained himself drawing quick, short sketches of Lavinia at the lake, with the boys, in the hammock.

It could all be managed quite simply. As long as she understood he was the one in charge and no amount of cajoling would change that.

Lavinia had not the slightest idea what to expect in marriage. Her parents had died when she was too young to notice anything more than that they were hers and Mama always smelled wonderful. Her uncle had been a bachelor, her brother a widower.

Lavinia wriggled a little in the hammock and it began a gentle swing. Angus and Harry would be here in a few minutes and her peace would be over. For a little while longer she was alone with the sun, warm and drowsy.

She knew what being married entailed: an intimate relationship with a man, eventually children, a house to maintain, and staff to direct. It all was manageable, familiar even, or at least most of it was.

The intimate relationship with a man was terrifying. She smiled a little. Not terrifying perhaps, but, well, embarrassing. To lie with someone, to join together in that way. Her brother insisted that one could find pleasure in it. It must be true or mankind would have ceased to be long ago.

His kiss. No, *their* kiss. Could it be that was only a glimpse of the feelings in store? Was he right when he said it was proof enough that they would be able to please each other?

Her governess had said that it was rarely that way for a woman, that the most she could hope for was to find contentment in the closeness. But the captain had said that they would both find pleasure. That she would beg for it.

She smiled again, her thoughts enough to pinken her cheeks even though she was by herself. Did he know? Did he have so much experience with women that he knew from a few kisses that she longed for more?

He might have experience with women. But what did he know of marriage? Less than she did?

The sun shone, still warmed her, but her pleasure in the moment dimmed a little. Yes, it was possible, likely, that he knew less than she did of what it was like to live as man and wife. His life had been in an orphanage and at sea.

Could she find confidence in the fact that when it came to the children they were like-minded? So in agreement that one could finish the other's thoughts? Surely that could be applied to other aspects of married life. They would learn together. They would make their own way.

Did that mean that the rule-conscious beau monde would be even less inclined to accept them?

Not that it mattered to her anymore, but there were the children to consider. Harry, Angus, and Sara. And any children she and the captain might have. She wanted them to be well received in the world. Would do anything to ensure it.

Including marrying a man she hardly knew?

He was well-to-do and established. The world might think that recommendation enough, but there was more to it for her.

She remembered the lovely stone shell she had given back to him in that absurd gesture of propriety. He was generous. Angus and Dolley were proof of a different kind of generosity.

He was loyal. She knew that from Dolley's stories of his life at sea. She'd also learned that he would never abandon those for whom he was responsible. His friends knew they could depend on him, as Lieutenant Carroll had when he left Angus in his care.

What else mattered? Honesty, she decided. Was he honest? How could one ever test that? How did one know truth from lie?

Generous, loyal, and honest. She would not say yes until she was certain that all three of those qualities were as important to him as they were to her. Desmond was gone and his friends with him. That would give her months and months to decide.

How lucky for her that the captain had gone away, given

her time so she could see that even the most passionate kiss was a poor foundation for a lifelong commitment.

She heard one of the boys coming through the anteroom. Sweet of them to be quiet so she could sleep longer. Sweet, too, of Dolley to insist that she rest every afternoon, that she had two years of sleep to make up for. On days like this, with a blue sky and a perfect world, she could only agree.

She could feel the boy watching her and smiled. "Angus, can two people fit in a hammock?"

"Only if they want to be very, very close."

Instead of four feet of mischievous boy she opened her eyes to six feet of man. Blinded by the bright light she thought at first that it was William, but knew as quickly that it was not. Desmond's friend Brocklin stood next to where she lay.

Stretched out in the hammock, she felt utterly vulnerable. It rocked wildly as she moved to climb from it. He stopped its swinging with his hand, moving his body closer so that the hammock and her hip bumped against his thigh.

"Why are you here?" She sounded petulant when anger was the truest emotion. "I thought everyone had left."

"Not quite. But I was willing to tolerate the boredom in hopes of seeing you. I've been watching out for you. God knows it's taken you long enough to shake off your duenna."

"The boys are coming. At any moment they will be here."

He ignored the warning and once again bumped against the hammock with his leg. "You look quite delectable lying there, my dear." He narrowed his eye like an artist seeking perspective. "Rather like a tray of sweets begging to be touched, taken, tasted." He reached over and took one of her bare feet in his hand. He bent closer and raised it. Before she knew what he planned, Brocklin lowered his mouth.

The feel of his lips on her toes made Lavinia physically ill. She shuddered convulsively and jerked her foot away.

The hammock rocked again and this time she took advantage of the motion to roll out of it on the side away from him so that it was between them.

She found her feet, but her hands were shaking and her heart was pounding so hard that it was an effort to form words. "You are disgusting."

"No, not at all. Only more experienced than you are."

The hammock was not much protection from his advances and he eliminated it completely by raising it over his head and stepping under it.

She moved away, but was thoroughly trapped. The terrace balustrade dug into her back as he came closer. Brocklin stopped an arm's length away, but it was not nearly far enough.

"I could show you pleasure without ever breaching your maidenhead."

She stared at him, quite unable to visualize what he had in mind. There had to be some way out of this. Even without a weapon.

"Move away and do not touch me." The harsh voice that roused instant attention from the boys only made him laugh. She raised her hands and pushed against his chest, but he merely took her hands in his. With a painful brute strength he lowered them and twisted them behind her back, pressing her body intimately close to his.

He lowered his mouth to the curve of her breast where it showed modestly above her gown. Her legs gave way, not from pleasure but from fear. Terror.

He mistook the half faint and laughed. "I can show you so much more than that fool of a naval officer."

He pushed his leg between hers so that she was forced to straddle him and could not use her legs or her knee to defend herself.

Tears started and he leaned forward and tasted them with his tongue. She knew she would be sick and did not hesitate a moment to use it as a defense. Lavinia vomited all over his coat of dark green superfine.

Brocklin jumped away, fell backward over the hammock, and landed on his shoulder. He lay stunned and out of breath just as Angus and Harry came through the door.

Angus looked at Brocklin, then at Lavinia, and raced from the room. She could hear the boy calling out as he ran.

Harry hurried over to her. "Are you sick, Aunt Lavinia?"

She tried to say "yes," but could not manage to speak.

With a groan followed by words Lavinia had never heard before, Brocklin stood up, pulled off his ruined coat, and used it to brush at his waistcoat. He rolled his coat up, called her a stupid bitch, gave the boy a venomous look, and left the boathouse.

Harry watched Brocklin leave and concentrated his attention on his aunt. "Was he hurting you?" he asked, his eyes narrowed in suspicion.

"No."

"Should I go after him? Make him pay for insulting you?"

"No!" God only knew what he would do to a boy who ran after him demanding satisfaction. "Is that water, Harry?"

He nodded and handed her the leather skin he was carrying.

She let the cool liquid trickle over her hot cheeks and then rinsed her mouth out. She had only just handed it back to him when Angus came out onto the porch again, this time with the captain.

"Go to the house, boys," the captain spoke without looking away from her. "We'll be along in a moment." She had no idea what he saw in her eyes, but there was anger and fear in his.

The boys did not say a word, not even the usual, "aye, sir" from Angus. The moment they were gone he stepped toward her and asked, "It was Brocklin?"

"Yes." The word came out a strangled sound as she struggled to reclaim some composure.

"Did he hurt you?"

She shook her head and then nodded too. "He touched my foot." Tears began and she hated herself for the weakness. "He would have kissed me." She hesitated. "And more, I think."

He reached for her then and she fell into his arms. She allowed herself sobs that took her breath away and he did no more than hold her and rock her as though she were a child. She felt her tears soak through his jacket.

"I cannot stand it anymore." She needed this security more than she needed to know of his background, his family, her much-touted three required virtues. "Please, please marry me, Captain. Keep me safe."

# Chapter 18

Keep her safe? The best he could do right now was hold her, as tight and close as he dared. It seemed to be enough. She burrowed closer as if she could hide inside his jacket.

"Tell me what happened. Did you come here with him?"

"Come here with him? No! Never."

She made a half-hearted effort to pull away from him. He let her move, but not completely out of his arms.

"I do not want to talk about it."

"It will help you to speak of it." He pulled her close again. "Why do you think we tell sea stories over and over again? To help us deal with the unthinkable." He hoped that in this way at least women were a little like men.

"But this was not a battle . . ." She did not finish the sentence and he did not need to tell her that indeed it was.

"I was in the hammock. Resting." Her voice was little more than a whisper. "Enjoying the warmth and the sound of the water. I was expecting the boys to come down and have a swimming lesson. When someone came onto the terrace, so very quietly, I thought it was Angus. I asked him if two people could fit in a hammock." She sniffed. "But it wasn't Angus or Harry."

Could two people fit in a hammock? Someday he would show her how well it worked.

"He took my foot and touched it with his mouth." She

whispered the words and he hoped it was only because she was embarrassed and not because of any further insult.

"He did not . . ." He was at a loss for words. Clearly there had been no rape, but there were other kinds of violation.

"He pushed his knee into me."

Rage poured through him and he felt her stiffen and try to push away again.

"I did nothing to encourage him. I swear." She shuddered. "But neither could I think what to do."

"Scream?"

She stiffened again. "I did not think of it."

He could feel a different kind of tension in her. "I did not want his attentions, Captain." She sounded doubtful and went on explaining to herself as much as to him. "I could not believe at first that I could not make him leave. I was sure I could find a way to best him."

She began to cry again. She drew a deep breath and stopped before more than a tear or two had soaked into his jacket. He knew she would call them the tears of the powerless.

"But you did best him, Lavinia. How did you manage it?"

"I threw up all over him," she said and added, "quite on purpose."

He laughed, but only a little. "Perfect."

"Then the boys came and he left." She shuddered. "I will never go barefoot or lie in the hammock again. I promise."

"Stop, Lavinia." He spoke gently while stroking her hair. "It is not you I'm angry with. And there is no such thing as a mermaid who wears shoes when she does not have to."

"Captain, mermaids do not have feet." She remained curled as close to him as a clam in a shell, but her voice sounded stronger, less ravaged.

"Mine does." He kissed the top of her head.

She pressed against his arms and he let her go. Stepping back, he could see anger taking over from shock.

"Is my body the only thing men want?" She looked away,

down at the hammock, and out to the lake as if nature had the answer to that. "It appears to be the only thing of value I have to offer."

"No, Lavinia."

"No? Why are you marrying me? You say you want to keep me safe, but you insist that I be your wife in every way. You are more a gentleman than Brocklin, but you want the same thing."

"Never class me with that man, Lavinia. It's an insult."

"Then we have both been insulted today." Her countenance was so set and on the edge of anger that he knew he needed to say something more.

"I assure you that if all I wanted was to sleep with you I would not have proposed."

"You would have seduced me."

"No, Lavinia." It was an effort to stay calm and reasoned when she so obviously wanted to argue. "You are an innocent. I would have respected that."

"Oh, yes, your valued self-control."

"Which is being sorely tested."

She ignored the warning. "What am I bringing to this marriage? What do you want from me besides sex?"

He wanted to throttle her. He spoke through his rising annoyance, not caring if he sounded more pedantic than amiable. "Angus needs discipline when I am away. I have a house that needs attention and a staff that is willing but unschooled." It was the same list he had given Stewart and as true in this instant as it was then, even if protection had moved up a notch or two.

She accepted the answer, but did not meet his eyes. It did not appear to be the response she was hoping for.

"Come back to the house, Lavinia, and let Mrs. Wilcox make you some tea."

"I accept your proposal."

If his explanation had been pompous, her words were more confrontation than agreement.

"No, I will not accept your answer tonight. You are upset and afraid at the moment."

"Yes"—her eyes flashed—"because I have had a very crude lesson in how vulnerable I am and how much I do need the protection of a man's name. And you are refusing."

"No! I am not." His frayed control snapped. "In the navy we would call this coercion, damn it. I want you to think about it a while longer. Until you can freely choose."

"Freely choose? Captain, what other choice do I have?"

She left him then, her hair trailing down her back and the ribbons on her dress askew as she hurried from the boathouse. She broke into a run when she reached the grass.

He moved as if to follow her, but then stopped himself. He was almost as angry as she was, but only because she had so deliberately provoked him. He understood even if she did not that the anger was another way to release fear.

There might not be love between them, but he knew with sudden insight that love was not the only emotion that influenced a couple.

He rubbed his hand across his forehead, overwhelmed by the realization. If he thought that his married life would be as much in his control as life aboard ship, he was more deluded than a rum-soaked seaman. Even discounting love, there would be a dozen other sensibilities Lavinia would embrace.

Her anger—he was well acquainted with that—skepticism and mistrust, as was just demonstrated. Jealousy would come. Any man who was away for months must contend with that. But, he assured himself, if he were lucky there would be laughter, passion, sweetness, and constancy.

But probably not tonight.


Lavinia came to the schoolroom door. She heard voices and expected to see Angus and Harry. It was later, and the afternoon sun lit the room fully, making candles unnecessary until well into twilight. But despite the generous light she could see no one.

She moved toward the door to the bedchamber that the boys shared.

"It was a great fight." Angus's voice was filled with enthusiasm.

She whirled around, expecting he would be behind her. There was no one there.

"Jolly good," Harry agreed.

He, too, sounded near enough to hug, but the room was empty. This was odd. The space was the same as the schoolroom at Talford Vale, even down to the window seat. She continued to scan the room trying to find a spot where they might be hiding.

"Plenty of blood, too. Hand-to-hand is the best kind of fighting," Angus insisted.

What battle were they talking about? They had their favorites from Dolley's many stories and endlessly recounted them, playing different roles and always arguing over which one of them would be the captain.

She saw the curtains fluttering and realized the window was open. They could not be sitting on the roof, could they?

Of course they could. Angus ran up and down trees like they were a staircase and Harry was a fine student where climbing was concerned.

And she herself had hid outside this same window, though that had been in Desmond's house, when once she had wanted to avoid him. It was safe, rather like a small balcony, enclosed on three sides with the wall about three feet high. There would be no danger, unless they were sitting on the wall.

It did not matter where they were sitting. They should not be out there. She hurried to the window, determined to pull them in from the ledge.

"Brocklin got the worst of it."

She froze. *Brocklin?* This was no naval battle they were discussing.

"I would rather have seen swords than fists. The captain is very good with a sword." Angus's pride was obvious as his appreciation of a good brawl.

"Or guns. I would have liked to see a duel," said Harry wistfully, "but they're illegal."

"And you heard the captain tell Brocklin that he was 'not worth a bullet.'"

"Yes, it was a capital insult," Harry said. "I wrote it down so I would not forget it."

"And that he would not have Aunt Lavinia's name made common by issuing a formal challenge."

They were both silent a minute, neither claiming that bit of speech. They had yet to reach an age when they thought a woman's reputation of more merit than a fight.

"The best part was when he pulled Brocklin off the ground and the bastard cried like a baby."

"No, it was when the captain took his handkerchief out and wiped his hands and walked away from the son of a bitch."

She wanted to hear more, every single detail, but this was degenerating into a contest to see who could use the worst language and that she did not need to hear.

"Dolley, where are the boys?" she called out and then pretended that he answered. "Outside playing? All right. I think I had better close this window since the air will cool once the sun sets and the breeze freshens. I suppose I had best lock it as well." She walked closer to the window as she spoke.

"What did you say?" She tiptoed to the door. "I'm coming," she called out and waited, pressing her lips together to keep from laughing at her own playacting.

A minute later two boys came tumbling through the window.

"That was a near thing, Harry. We might have had to break the glass."

Angus was brushing off his shirt and did not see her as he

spoke. Harry did. He nudged his friend and Angus straightened, his eyes widening when he saw her standing with her back against the closed schoolroom door.

"I wonder if the captain brought a new switch from London?" she mused, as if talking to herself. "I think I will find him and ask."

She left without another word, fully expecting that the anticipation of discipline would spoil their dinner. And she knew that Mrs. Wilcox planned to make their favorite pie with the first apples. That would be punishment enough. There was no need to bring William into it. And yes, she admitted to herself, she had every intention of avoiding him until dinner.

She wandered down to the kitchen to see if Mrs. Wilcox knew anything. Yes, she did, and the cook was more than willing to tell her all about it.

"It was real fight, miss. Right in the drive, it was."

Lavinia stood at the worktable opposite Mrs. Wilcox who was working on a dough. Picking up an apple and a small paring knife, she began peeling. It was all the invitation that Miss Wilcox needed.

"The captain caught up with Brocklin not two ticks before he hopped into his carriage. Can't say where he was going but he's all for London now." She said the last with a nod of satisfaction and began fitting the dough into a pan.

"Brocklin tried to laugh it off, treat the captain as one of his cronies, but the captain was having none of it. He let Brocklin say his piece and then took him apart like he was made of paper."

Lavinia paused, a long dangle of peel suspended. "I've never seen the captain that angry."

"No, miss. Dolley said he's only seen it twice before his own self. Once when some youngster was being bullied bad by a junior lieutenant and the captain found the young one making to jump overboard to kill hisself."

"How awful." Lavinia picked up the next apple and began peeling. "And the other?"

"When someone called his mother a whore."

"Really?" The peel broke, Lavinia pushed it aside, and started up again. "But I thought he was raised in an orphanage and never knew his mother."

"Miss, it's an insult no man can tolerate, even if his mother is not a lady. Leastways that's what Dolley told me."

Lavinia filed that bit of information away. It only added to her growing curiosity about the captain's family. "Are you certain that the captain was not hurt?" The boys had made no mention of it but Brocklin seemed strong enough. It certainly had felt that way to her when it was no more than the two of them on the boathouse terrace.

"I don't think so." Mrs. Wilcox stopped rolling out the crust and reconsidered. "But Dolley did go right up to his room with some of the salve that Chasen swears by."

Lavinia only then remembered that she was annoyed with the captain. "It serves him right. How foolish to fight. It never solves anything."

"Yes, it does, miss. You can bet money that Mr. Brocklin will not set foot here again. And the captain was so angry he needed to hit someone. That man deserved every punch."

"I never thought of you as bloodthirsty, Mrs. Wilcox." She finished the last of the apples and began slicing them.

Mrs. Wilcox watched her a moment. "A little thinner, if you please, miss."

Lavinia reached for a different knife. "You did see Brocklin leave? He is gone for good?"

"Oh, miss, no. I did not actually see it myself. Dolley had the story from my sister's husband who heard about it from the butler at the Vale."

"How awful!" Lavinia stopped slicing the apples. "It will be all over the village before nightfall."

"I think not." Mrs. Wilcox shook her head. "The captain

would not like that at all. And after seeing what he does when he's angry, well, miss, no one is like to test it."

Lavinia wished she were as sure. She worried about it for the next three hours and even more when Dolley brought word to them at table that the captain was too busy to stop for dinner.

Mrs. Newcomb was disappointed. "It is his first day back."

Lavinia forbore to mention that she had complained only a few hours ago that the captain had returned too soon.

"Did you have a nice afternoon, dear?" Mrs. Newcomb asked.

Lavinia almost choked on the soup. "Yes," she answered cautiously.

"Good" was all the interest she showed and then began a monologue on the fabric that the captain had brought back from London, exactly what she had described but there was not quite enough for a gown with a matching spenser. A pelisse would be all they could hope to make from the material.

Lavinia relaxed for the first time since her afternoon rest was interrupted. Maybe the servants were more discreet than she expected. Could it be that the gossip would go no farther than between the two houses? She smiled and gave her attention to Mrs. Newcomb, all the while thanking heaven for small graces.

# Chapter 19

The long summer evenings were giving way to darkness a few minutes earlier each day, but there was a good hour or so of light after dinner. The boys had begged to use the last of the daylight to run to the home farm to see some new puppies. Lavinia walked with them beyond the boathouse and watched until they were out of sight, on the far side of her brother's house.

Could she go back to Talford Vale? She did not even try to answer the question, but hurried toward the far more welcoming home she'd found at Talford Rise.

She was passing the boathouse when she made herself stop. For almost two years she had considered this small building and the lake it guarded her escape from misery. Cast in the sharp, strong light of the early evening, she studied the arched entrance and the floral stonework in the pediment and wondered how long it would be before she was comfortable here again.

With an effort, which took more deliberation than she thought reasonable, she walked toward the entrance, then veered to the left and to the edge of the water instead. She bent down and took off her slippers, giving in to the lure of the water. She raised the hem of her dress and stepped in, just deep enough to allow the laplets to wash over her feet.

It felt like warm liquid satin and she waded out two steps farther, letting it bathe her ankles. She watched the fish rise to feed on the bugs of this evening's hatch. The surface was dimpled everywhere. She did not move and soon she was as much a part of the lake as the water, the fish, and the high-growing grass on the far bank. She did not step back onto the bank until she was pulled from her contemplation by a fish splashing mightily as he leapt for some dinner.

She began to walk purposefully toward the boathouse. She was not going to let Brocklin ruin it for her. The main room was deeply shadowed and she hurried onto the terrace. The hammock was not empty and she gasped.

The small sound was enough to wake the captain. "Lavinia." He smiled at her and reached out to set down the bottle he had been holding.

"Good evening." His voice was filled with triumph. "Hurrah for you. I was sure you would come. Knew you were too sensible to allow that fool to spoil this place for you."

Was he drunk? The bottle was only half empty, but he was rarely this talkative or so relaxed.

"Ah, I can read your mind. I have only had a few drops of medicinal brandy." He lifted the bottle from the floor and set it on the far narrower balustrade as if to prove his point.

"Then you *were* hurt this afternoon." She came closer, but could not tell if it was the shadow-filled light that made his jaw look bruised.

"Never a bit. Brocklin tried a kick. It missed its intended target but caught me right on an old wound that annoys me occasionally." He pointed to the bottle. "This is all the doctor I need."

"And some of Chasen's salve."

"And who did you learn that from?" He narrowed his eyes, his face losing its lazy look.

She leaned back a little. "Only Mrs. Wilcox, and I insisted she tell me." She paused a moment and then went on. "You should not have, Captain."

"Yes, I should have. Brocklin deserved worse. What I

should not have done was choose such a public spot for his thrashing." He sighed. "Too late."

"Mrs. Newcomb knew nothing of it at dinner."

"Indeed." He considered that and put his hands behind his head. "If you are not going to sit down then I should stand up."

"Please do stay just as you are." He was so relaxed that Lavinia decided that he must be just a little inebriated.

"Very poor manners. What would Mrs. Newcomb say? Of course I do have a solution."

"The last time you used that phrase you proposed to me." She rather wished she had not brought up the subject but all he did was nod.

"Do you still want to know if a hammock can hold two, Lavinia?"

As he spoke he reached out and pulled her just enough so that she lost her balance and fell into the canvas basket.

Her body pressed against his, but movement was a pointless effort. It was inevitable that in a hammock, with no support, all the weight should fall to the center.

"Stop fidgeting, or we will have a nasty fall," he whispered, and she did settle, but only because he was right. The swinging slowed.

"We really should stand up, Captain." She lay stiffly beside him, pretending that she could not feel every one of his muscles from his shoulder all the way to his knee.

"And so we will, but not quite yet." He seemed to feel no awkwardness. "Unless you are afraid?"

She shook her head, bemused by concern in his eyes. "Though we are rather snug."

"Yes, very close." He was quiet a moment. "But not unpleasantly so."

It was almost a question and she smiled her answer even though he could not see it.

"We can be even more comfortable."

At first she thought he meant to kiss her or touch her, but he did not. He moved ever so easily and in a minute her head was in the hollow of his shoulder and her body was in the shelter of his arm. His shirt smelled of sun and salt and him. She hoped she smelled half as good.

They were silent a rather long time. He began stroking her hair.

"Hmm," she said. The last of her fear of Brocklin, of this place, of men, disappeared as she let herself be calmed by his gentle caress. "What if Mrs. Newcomb comes?"

"Has she ever?"

"No," she answered honestly. "She prefers to walk in the garden and she insists the evening air is full of bad humors, but she may wonder where I am."

"She knows I wish to be private with you. We will just tell her the truth."

"The truth?"

"That we were at the boathouse waiting for the boys to come back from the home farm."

She opened her eyes but did not move lest he stop his very slow, very gentle caress. "The devil being in the details?"

He did not answer and the silence drew out once again. This one not as comfortable as the first. She watched a bat swoop down low over the lake and listened to the water racing down from the upper lake.

"What happened in London, Captain?"

He did not answer at first, but she could feel him playing with the ends of her hair. "In London? Nothing untoward."

"I'm happy to hear that. Then everything went as you wished?"

"Yes."

She waited in silence, willing him to answer more fully. He did as he began the soothing caress again.

"I talked to your brother. He is more than willing to permit the courtship. We have agreed on everything. The children will stay with us and he will make no demands on any of us."

She stared at the buttons on his shirt, and then up at the twilight-laden sky wondering why that had been so hard for him to say. It struck her after a moment's thought. "How much did you have to pay him?" When he remained silent, she went on. "I know he did not agree out of the goodness of his heart."

"It was a mere fraction of what you're worth," he finally admitted.

"It is very good of you to try to spare me the hurt, but it is only the last in a long list of cruelties. With your support, Desmond's lack of family feeling does not even tempt me to tears."

"Indeed."

She smiled at the word. Why was it that sometimes it drove her mad and other times it was endearing?

So he had spoken to Desmond. That meant that the decision was fully hers. Loyalty, generosity, and honesty. With this afternoon's discomfort so thoroughly behind her, she found those three virtues did matter to her.

"Will you tell me about your family, Captain? Please."

The sky lost light as the sun finally fell behind the Downs.

He stopped playing with her hair and she was annoyed with herself for spoiling their reverie.

"Oh, Lavinia." He said her name as though she was more torment than temptation. "You are worse than a siren. I suppose I must tell you. I owe you that much."

"You owe me nothing, but it would help me." Help her what, she wondered? Understand him better? Help her decide whether to marry him? She was relieved when he did not press her for an explanation.

She angled her head so she could see him. "It is not a question of legitimacy, Captain. You have made a fine reputation for yourself no matter what the accident of your birth. It is hardly a deciding factor for me."

"I am legitimate, Lavinia."

"All right." She would admit very quietly and to herself that it was some relief. She nestled back on his shoulder, hoping he could speak more easily if she was not looking at him.

"My mother." He spoke the two words and then said nothing more.

"I suppose you cannot remember her at all?"

She felt him shake his head.

"No. I've never even seen a picture of her. She was married to Straemore. He was an earl in those days. He was raised to marquis early in this century. No matter his title he was wealthy and considered a great catch." He was quiet and she knew he would take a drink of the brandy only he had no hand free nor could he reach it if he did.

"They were married for five years. She had one son already but she abandoned him and her husband and ran away to France with a music master who had come to the neighborhood."

He began stroking her hair again but now she thought he was the one finding some comfort in it.

"I know very little of why she ran away. If Straemore was cruel to her or she was that inconstant, but the fact that she left wealth and privilege for the insecurity of life with a musician tells me that she must have been very unhappy."

Lavinia nodded against his chest.

"What she did not know when she left for France is that she was with child and that Straemore was the father. She died giving birth to me."

"Oh, how awful."

"Indeed."

"Awful in every way. For you, for her, for your family in England, for her lover."

"Yes, well, her lover went on to put me in an orphanage. One of the better ones for what that was worth."

"But why did he not send you back to England?"

"I have no idea. But most likely because he doubted my father would believe that I was truly his."

"There is no doubt, now?

"None. I look almost identical to my brother, Viscount Crandall, who is himself a younger version of our father."

"But who is Lord Morgan Braedon, then? The man who was here that first time I called? He does not look like you at all."

"My half brother. My father remarried and had three more children."

"I see." Were there any sisters, she wondered?

"Events in France transpired along with the death of my mother's lover and I was sent back to England when I was ten. Left on the doorstep at Braemoor and sent away almost as quickly."

"To sea?" She felt him nod. "But why? They did not want you? How could that be?"

"Lavinia, family is not as important to everyone as it is to you."

"Desmond taught me that."

"Then how can you be surprised by the Braedons?"

"Is family disloyalty the norm in England?" She could feel her temper rise. "I was twenty-four when I came to live with Desmond and even then his insult was painful. I cannot imagine what it would be like to be a boy and have your father send you away."

"My father's second wife did not want him to. I remember—" He stopped and then started again on a different track. "The marquis sent me to Captain Bessborough on the *Chartwell*. He could have done worse, much worse. Bessborough became a father to me in every way. I served as his cabin boy until I was old enough to be called midshipman."

"And you changed your name."

"Yes."

"It is a terrible story. Is your father alive? Will your brothers recognize you if you approach them? Do you have any sisters?"

If it was possible to distance yourself from someone when pressed into less than twenty inches of space, the captain did it. "I do not want your pity, Lavinia. I want your help in my household. I want the comfort of your body.

"You will not contact them. I do not want or need a family that has never once thought of me until some right of succession reared its head. They are a selfish lot. I have no use for them at all and will not receive them. Not ever. Is that perfectly understood?"

"Yes." It was as close to a burst of temper as she had ever heard from him. She was not afraid of the anger, understood that it was a cover for pain, a hurt so long buried, so old that she could not expect to change it. At least not yet.

"Before, when you said that I was worse than a siren, what did you mean?" She was teasing him or inviting him to tease her, but he was not laughing when he answered her.

"Because unlike a siren you would leave me alive, even minister kindly to me and only ask that I bare my soul."

It was her turn to soothe. She reached up and rested her hand on his cheek and kissed the other one.

"It's a long, difficult story, Captain. Thank you for telling me so completely."

She felt him nod and the two of them held silent, letting the pain of the old story be eased by the night and the breeze and gentle sway of the hammock. She hoped this silence would convince him that she would respect his wishes. That she meant comfort and never pity.

"Do you have any other questions, Lavinia?"

"No," she said, though she did try to think of one or two more as she was very sure what was coming.

"Then are you ready to answer mine?"

"Yes." This was it. How unfair to be compelled to decide when they were so close, his body so arousing. And when he had just revealed, if unknowingly, that he needed family as much as she did.

She thought back to last night when she had been alone and lonely despite the boys and Mrs. Wilcox and the chattering of Mrs. Newcomb. How much she had missed him sitting nearby. "I will marry you, Captain, if you will marry me."

She twisted in his arms so that their bodies were pressed together. She felt the hard length of him against her breasts, her stomach, and her thighs, and wanted to feel the hard length of him in the most private place of all.

"My name is William, Lavinia."

Had any woman ever called him William? Not his mother, except perhaps as one of her dying words. Maybe a lover who was close enough to see beyond his rank. But no one else.

"Yes, William," she breathed against his mouth, "I will marry you."

# Chapter 20

The vicar began reading the banns within the sennight. One visit from William had satisfied him as to all the particulars.

Mrs. Newcomb heard the news of their engagement and took to preparations in a delighted frenzy, torn between ordering bride clothes and planning the wedding breakfast.

Eventually Mrs. Wilcox convinced her that she need not worry about the food. Mrs. Newcomb's sister put it bluntly: "If you do not stop pestering Mrs. Wilcox *you* will be the one cooking breakfast."

Sara returned from her stay with her godmother and burst into tears when she heard the news—from happiness, she insisted. "Pure joy at the idea that my dearest aunt has found love so close to home." Lavinia did not correct her. Girls of fourteen were endlessly romantic.

The letter Sara's godmother sent with the child clarified the situation. Lavinia read it with some amusement. "Sara needs to hear the way of men and women and I am too old to play her mother." That and the inclination to tears convinced Lavinia that in one short month Sara had left childhood behind. Despite her own distraction, Lavinia resolved to make time to talk with her before the week was out.

The boys had taken the news with cautious interest, curious only as to how it would change their lives. Not much, she assured them. They nodded and went back to the giant wooden sailing ship they were building under the supervision of Walcott, a ship's carpenter who was ashore, blind in one eye. Their casual approval was enough.

Some things did not change. As it had for the two years before, the onset of cooler weather slowed Lavinia. While Mrs. Newcomb bustled and Mrs. Wilcox cooked, Lavinia lingered in bed. She was long past sleep, but too comfortable to push the covers back and start her day with bare feet on a cold floor.

By the time there was a frost she would be used to the chill once again, but the first cold days took her by surprise. Her life was more her own to order now and she allowed herself to stay in bed until the fire had warmed her room.

It was such an excellent place to worry.

Was William having second thoughts? Despite his avowed interest in a full and complete marriage, he had been quite aloof since she accepted his proposal.

There had been nothing restrained about him that night at the boathouse, their kisses warm and passionate. But in the month since he had more than made up for his ardor with a distance that was unexpected and troublesome.

He spent most of his time in his library, dealing with letters from London and even a messenger or two.

They saw each other at dinner, but there were always others present and the conversation centered on subjects of Mrs. Newcomb's choosing. Lavinia even went to the boathouse one evening and waited in the too-cool night air, but he did not come. Finally, she stood before the library door and knocked, but there was no invitation to enter. She went away in tears.

He had gone to London once and Portsmouth twice. Those trips grew from the meddlesome Mrs. Newcomb's insistence that an engagement made his presence under the same roof even less appropriate than it was before.

When Mrs. Newcomb finally finished her lecture, William had bowed graciously, but refused to consider her suggestion that Lavinia remove to Talford Vale. He was away for London the next morning.

He'd left Lavinia a gift, an engagement present. Even that had not come to her personally. He had left it with her new lady's maid, Malton, who had given it to her an hour after he left.

Lavinia tried to find comfort in it. Scott's *Lady of the Lake* made her smile, but the note that accompanied it was so stilted that her delight in the gift evaporated.

She lay in bed, the covers pulled up to her eyes, nestled in three pillows, and trying to sort out the meaning of this estrangement.

Was this what all men did? Once they won the hand of their intended bride did they lose interest like this? Or did he regret his proposal?

She jumped from bed, not willing to tolerate uncertainty one day longer. Malton was learning quite nicely and was at the door not a minute later. They made a hurried toilette despite their usual inclination to linger over it, trying new hairstyles or discussing a fashion magazine.

Malton was all for cutting her mistress's hair to a fashionable length, but Lavinia said no. One of her cherished memories was that long evening in the hammock with William. She would leave her hair to her waist forever if it meant that he would hold her like that again.Though she was beginning to think that it was entirely possible he would not.

She was moving purposefully down the staircase when a commotion from above stopped her.

Angus and Harry came charging down from the schoolroom, each one holding one of Sara's dolls by its hair.

Sara came racing after them shrieking, "Give them back! Give them back!"

The boys skidded to a halt when they saw Lavinia. Harry looked over his shoulder and Angus began mumbling an apology for running.

"Boys, do you have a reason for aggravating Sara?"

"No, Aunt Lavinia," Harry said, dropping the china doll he was holding as if it had suddenly become too hot to handle.

"But she doesn't want them anymore," Angus tried to explain, "and all our toys are left behind and the captain will not let us set foot in Talford Vale."

"So you've taken to dolls?"

"We were pretending that they were ladies who needed rescue." He shook his head, mortally embarrassed that he had even attempted that explanation.

"I do too want my dolls," Sara wailed.

"You never play with them," Angus pointed out reasonably.

"That does not mean that I do not love them, you stupid boy." She bent down and lifted the one Harry had dropped and cradled it in her arms. Angus handed her the other.

She grabbed both dolls and ran down the stairs and into the blue salon.

Lavinia shook her head. "I thought Mr. Arbuscam was taking you to talk with the apothecary today."

"He is, but he had to change into his best coat and he has been an age. We were bored."

"Bored? How awful," she said with rare sarcasm. "Come down and wait for him in the hall. Sit in the chairs on either side of the table. Sit in silence until he comes."

"But he could be an hour," Harry whined.

"Oh, really? Then that will give you some idea of what it really means to be bored."

The boys followed her and took their seats. She placed them so they could not see each other and assured them that she would leave the door to the blue salon open so she would hear if they disobeyed her.

Once she was sure they understood the punishment, she considered Sara. She was anxious to see William, but this was the ideal quiet moment to talk to her. Lavinia had not been delaying the conversation precisely, but this particular week had convinced her that she had no understanding of men at all. She had hoped to delay the discussion of men and women until she had been married for a while.

She went into the blue salon, her mind clear, knowing exactly where she would start with this girl who was more daughter than niece. The room was as comforting as always, its feminine charm further warmed by the fire that Dolley kept kindled from first light.

Sara was seated on the sofa, her dolls prettily arranged next to her. She was using her finger to clean the dirt and dust from Flora, the oldest of the two.

"They must have dragged her in the dirt, Aunt Lavinia. She is filthy."

"Hmm," was all Lavinia said. How many months had it been since Sara had touched them? Lavinia held her silence, sure that a reasonable explanation was not in order here.

"Will those boys ever grow up?"

"They grow in mind and body every day, darling."

"But they still play with toys!"

"But do you see that they are building toys these days, not just playing with them? The boat that Walcott is helping them with will be very like the ones that Captain sails, only smaller. Even Mr. Arbuscam thinks it a good learning experience."

"They are just so different."

"Yes, they are. And they always have been. It is only since your trip that you are beginning to understand how very different."

"Did Aunt Peterkin tell you in the letter?"

"Yes."

"I was going to tell you. Really, but . . ."

"You were embarrassed?"

"Uh-huh," she said, blushing.

Lavinia sat beside her and gathered her into her arms. "It makes you a woman, Sara, and you are about to begin a great new adventure."

"You mean learning to dance?"

"Yes." Lavinia smiled and kissed the top of her head. "Learning to dance. And much more."

Sara straightened so she could see her aunt fully.

"You see, Sara, becoming a woman and learning to be a lady are two different things entirely. You become a woman quite naturally with no help from anyone. It is a gift from God and to be treasured. It means that someday you can be a mother."

Sara considered what Lavinia said and nodded slowly, not convinced, but apparently willing to consider it. "Will you be a mother? I mean, once you and the captain are married?"

"Of course." Lavinia tried to sound cheerful and practical, determined not to let Sara see that she was even a little nervous about the weeks ahead.

"It is a truth that in our society being a lady is far more work than becoming a woman." Lavinia changed the subject even though she could tell that Sara was curious. *Not yet, my dear. Give me a chance to come to terms with it myself.* "To my mind one can be a lady without a minute of training. It is not as natural a state as being a woman is, but comes from some place of goodness deep inside. Why, Mrs. Wilcox is every inch a lady and she has no idea how or when to make a morning call. Do you understand?"

"Mrs. Newcomb only tries to be a lady," Sara said, trying to puzzle out the oddities of the ton.

"And Mrs. Newcomb is a lady," Lavinia explained, "only she is somewhat distracted by society's dictates. But she is right in many ways. As a lady you must learn to go about in society. Dancing and conversation are part of it, but there is a much less definable element: propriety."

Sara straightened, put her hands together in her lap, and made the tips of her toes touch the floor.

"Yes, like that, but also in how you behave when you are with other people. Things that your governess will teach you."

"I am going to have a governess?" True excitement laced her voice.

"Yes, I must speak to the captain, but it is time. She will be a far better teacher than I can be."

"But you are a lady, are you not?"

"Yes," Lavinia replied firmly, "but I was not raised here."

"Is that why you are barefoot in the summer?"

"Yes." The one word was so much easier than explaining that swimming and feeling the grass beneath her feet were as much about her being a woman as they were defiance of convention.

"Sara, I want you to tell me if you ever feel as though society is asking too much of you. Or not enough."

"I will." Sara spoke with caution and Lavinia knew the girl remained child enough to have no idea how even their small social world would influence her.

"And I want you to treat the boys with respect. Remind yourself that they are growing as you are and someday they too will stop using the word stupid to describe anyone they do not understand."

That drew only a grudging nod. Sara gathered up her dolls and then put them down again. Coming closer, she hugged her aunt. "I love you, Aunt Lavinia."

"And I love you, dearest."

The girl gathered the dolls once again and moved to the door. Lavinia stood in the middle of the room staring at the rose and blue pattern on the fine old carpet, wondering why heartaching affection came so readily with Sara and the boys, but not with the man in her life.

Oh, her heart ached when she thought of him, but the heartache came from nerves and uncertainty.

She heard Mr. Arbuscam come down to the hall, delighted and more than a little surprised to find the boys waiting so patiently. They were gone on their trip to the village without further delay and Lavinia walked into the empty entry hall, then walked a few feet farther to knock on the library door.

She was prepared to pound until William allowed her in. This time he called "enter" only a moment after her insistent rap.

He was standing by the window and she walked over to where he stood watching Sara walk down the drive and then onto the gravel path leading to the boathouse. "Oh dear," Lavinia said. "Here I have only just been talking to her about proper ladylike behavior and off she goes without anyone with her."

The captain stood with his arms across his chest and shook his head. "Dolley is at the boathouse supervising the winter storage of the boats there. If she is looking for a place to be private she will be back in a moment. If not, Dolley will be guardian enough."

"Did you notice how Sara has changed since she came back?"

He nodded and she pretended it was with interest.

"She spends hardly any time with the boys."

"But she still manages to bait them at every opportunity."

He sounded as annoyed as Angus and Harry. She reached deep for the "lady" in her. "I think she will stop that soon enough."

"Good, even I find her constant superiority wearing."

"I would not long for it too heartily, sir. She will stop because she has outgrown the boys and will begin to notice men."

"Indeed."

"Indeed." For once Lavinia heard emotion in the word, a wealth of uncertainty. "She is turned fourteen. She should have had a governess before this, but Desmond would not spend the money for one. It is not too late and it will give her confidence to have the advice of someone familiar with the ton." She had tried to make it an order but it sounded like a long ramble and much too tentative.

"Whatever you think, Lavinia."

He had agreed, but Lavinia hurried on, defending her request. "She must needs learn a great deal before she is introduced even to local society."

"Lavinia, do not prose on. I have told you to do as you wish."

She had had quite enough of this, not at all mollified by his easy generosity.

He moved away from the window, but before she could ask if he truly did wish to marry her, he pointed at the chair on the other side of his desk. "Sit down."

# Chapter 21

*Please sit down*, she thought, but was made uncertain enough by his terseness that she left the word unspoken. She looked over her shoulder to judge his feeling, but he was standing by his desk with his back to her, waiting to seat himself as soon as she sat.

She regarded his back as though there were some message written on it, but it was nothing more than stiff, broad shoulders covered by dark wool with the hint of a starched white cravat at the back of his neck.

She waited. Still he did not turn back to her, which edged up her annoyance, so she moved away from the window and around the desk. She could see his face and it was no more revealing than his back had been.

Ignoring the chair, she remained standing, unwilling to give him any more command over her than he naturally had.

Again he spoke before she could ask about their engagement.

"I am called to Portsmouth."

"Called to Portsmouth?" Anxiety swept all other feeling aside. "For another consultation?"

He shook his head slowly and spoke deliberately. "To take command of the *Splendid*."

She tried to appear happy for him while her mind shouted an instinctive, "no!" She almost screamed it, but forced a calm that bottled the anxiety inside her, making her stomach knot.

"I am to report in three weeks. I should go sooner, but I have an excellent first lieutenant who can supervise."

The window was behind him and the light cast an aura that made it hard to read his face. If it ever was easy.

"If you wish to delay our wedding you have only to say so," she said.

"What?"

The word was almost as annoying as his "indeed," and the irritation it generated gave her the courage to press her point. "If you prefer, I will cry off and leave you free . . ." her words faded as he leaned across his desk. She could see that he was more puzzled than relieved.

"I have no desire to end our engagement," he spoke with some urgency. He opened his desk drawer, glanced down, and then closed the drawer without taking anything from it. "In fact, I was going to ask you if you would consider a license from the bishop. Under the circumstances I could arrange for one."

He spoke in such a businesslike way that she was only a little convinced. "Then you do wish to marry me?"

"Yes." He came around the desk as he spoke. She turned toward him as he came closer. "Of course I do, Lavinia."

Hardly a declaration of anything, or at least nothing more than that he would honor his obligation.

"It is only that you have been so distant lately." They were both in front of his desk. She saw that he was watching her with equal intensity.

"We have spent no time together except at meals when everyone is present." She let her eyes fall to her hands. "I thought that you had lost interest once I said yes."

He lifted her chin so that she had to look at him. There was nothing distant about him now. The touch of his finger on her face was like a crumb of bread for someone starving.

Hunger made her raise her mouth to his and the spiral of arousal made the kiss a feast. She put her lips on his and the feel of him, the taste of him, was so satisfying that she gave him all of herself, full and unguarded.

He did not even pretend to resist but pulled her to him, held her as though she would try to escape. He took her with him beyond passion to some darker place where he demanded surrender.

William was the one who ended the kiss. "Lost interest? Not want you?" He put her from him firmly as though she had been the one gripping him tight enough to bruise. "Damn that interfering woman!" He raised a hand to his forehead. "Mrs. Newcomb would go on and on about propriety until I was afraid that even being in the same room with you would cause gossip."

*Only Mrs. Newcomb,* Lavinia thought with such relief that she could actually forgive the woman.

The captain took one step nearer. His words were laced with frustration, even anger. "But no matter whether I am here or a hundred miles away, you haunt my nights and tempt me every day. Not want you? I can barely sleep for thinking of you beside me."

He kissed her again and this time it was short—so quick and tantalizing it was almost brutal. "To think I would have to leave without making you mine is the worst nightmare I could imagine." He had his hands on her arms again. "I lied, Lavinia. I hardly care if you want me to go for a license or not. I have already scheduled an appointment with the bishop."

She was stunned and a little shaken by his intensity. If this was not love, then it must be something close to it or so far removed that she should run from it as from a nightmare. "You have? I'm not sure, Captain." She hesitated, but she did not have to say another word.

He moved away from her and rubbed his forehead with three fingers again. "Lavinia, I apologize. I do not mean to frighten you." He came back, took her hand, and kissed it very gently.

She did no more than nod and smile a little at his embarrassment. He must be upset, she thought. And, oddly enough, that calmed her.

He was not angry. No, this distress was a cover for another emotion. Disappointment? Frustration? And she was sure he had a headache starting. That would happen whenever he was seething with feelings he was doing his best to hide.

"It is only that I had hoped that for once the Admiralty's timing would be a little better," he said. "To test me by making me choose between two things that are important to me is more challenge than I want."

"But there is no choice in this, William. I will be here when you come back." She realized she had left one important question unasked and turned practical. It was what he needed most from her. Not temper or tears. "How long will you be away? Do you even know?"

"It's only escort duty," he said with evident relief. "I'm to meet three ships coming from the East Indies when they come into port for supplies."

She noted that he did not say precisely what port.

"*Splendid* will escort them the rest of the way. Very prosaic."

"It is a routine assignment?" she asked, holding her hands tight, one within the other. "Not like your previous one?"

He nodded and she sank into the nearest chair relieved, very relieved.

"I should not even tell you this much, but I think no more than five months."

"Five months is not even half a year."

"I thought I would be the one comforting you."

"I suppose that if this were a love match there would be temper and tears, but our marriage is more conventional than that, is it not?" She did not look away.

"Conventional, yes. Based on needs," he agreed.

"I need the security of your name, you need a mistress for this home and a maternal eye on Angus." She spoke the words giving up the last little wish that his passion was about something more.

"You have the license?" She folded her hands in her lap.

"I will within a sennight."

Lavinia took a deep breath. "I think we should be married as soon as it is granted. That way we will have two weeks together."

"I know I sound desperate, but I will bow to your wishes, Lavinia," he said, as in control as she was.

"Marriage is the only way I can remain here, William. The vicar has been very understanding but that will not last forever."

"We can wait until I return to sleep together."

He had closed his eyes as he spoke and she knew it was as generous an offer as he had ever made. She laughed and stood up.

"William." She said his name with some asperity. "Do you think this is a contest? Which one of us can make the most generous offer?"

His expression was all confusion.

"If so, then you win." Bridging the distance between them, she tucked her hands inside his jacket. Slowly, slowly, slowly she moved her hands along the fine thin linen of his shirt, feeling his heartbeat, his breathing. She pressed her body to him so he could feel hers. "Wait until you return?" Before she kissed him she whispered, "I think not."

# Chapter 22

The license was granted by a sympathetic bishop, one who understood the vagaries of the Admiralty and the wishes of the bride and groom—the Admiralty, because he had a brother in Mahon serving as aide to the admiral, and the wishes of the bride and groom because he had been a groom himself not once, but twice.

Twice, William thought. A man willingly went through this more than once? He was standing with the vicar at the altar, making a supreme effort to appear calm. He felt a bead of sweat trickle down his neck as Lavinia made her way down the aisle.

They had all come to the church together only a bit ago, but it seemed like a century. Who was this elegant woman? Had she been wearing that blue satin dress with the white lace when they left the house? Surely she had not been wearing that veil that was tucked under the knot at the top of her head? She seemed a complete stranger and was not fifty feet away from taking his name.

He should not go through with this. She deserved so much better. Not a man like him who knew infinitely more about life below deck than he did a family. His epaulets felt as though they weighed a hundred pounds and it took all of his strength to stand straight.

Four pews from the front of the church his bride glanced to her left and smiled at the boys.

When she faced the front again she looked directly at him, a smile on her lips and in her eyes. The smile grew slowly until it was almost a grin and William recognized his Lavinia. His barefoot mermaid dressed today as an elegant lady, but every bit the woman he could hardly wait to hold.

It was too late to call a halt. His palms were sweating inside his gloves, but what man wouldn't be nervous when his life was about to change forever? His nerves gave way to the conviction that he was the luckiest man in the world. He'd found a woman whose needs matched his own, whose common sense made marriage a reasonable choice, and whose beauty made her a prize as valuable as any he'd ever taken at sea.

She was only a few feet from him and then he could do nothing but look at her. He tried a smile and hoped it conveyed half the pride he felt.

They approached the vicar together and knelt down. The opening words of the ceremony were called out in the vicar's best voice of command.

William was sorry that there were so few to witness this: the vicar and his wife, Mrs. Newcomb and her sister, and the children.

Lavinia had no special guests to add to the list, at least none living in England. She encouraged him to invite his own friends, but they were all at sea and not available. She seemed neither relieved nor disappointed at the small group.

He could have invited the messenger he'd left waiting for him at the Rise. Not one of the *Splendid's,* but some runner from the Admiralty. He could have invited him, but had told the man he would be back in less than an hour and sent him to the kitchen to be spoiled by whatever wedding breakfast tidbits Mrs. Wilcox would let him sample.

It might happen one time only, but today he was going to put his own needs before that of the royal navy.

William gave the ceremony his complete attention as the

vicar began to read the vows. Lavinia repeated hers in a steady voice—clear, but not overly loud, as though she was saying them for him alone.

And then the vicar spoke to him.

"Do you, William Chartwell, born Braedon, take this woman to be your lawful wedded wife?"

He felt Lavinia look at him, but could not meet her gaze. Though the bishop had only suggested he include the Braedon reference, William knew an order when he heard one. He could think of only one or two commands he had acted on with as much dislike and now that it was done he hoped never to refer to it again.

Then it was over. They signed the numbered, ruled pages of the parish register, and accepted the congratulations of the vicar, Angus, Mrs. Newcomb, her sister, Harry, and Sara, who were closer to family than they had been an hour ago. They all proceeded out into the sunlight.

The entire village was there.

Lavinia laughed as they cheered. "It is because they hold you in such high esteem," she said.

"It is because so little of interest happens here. The way spotting a whale at sea draws the crew to the deck." He grimaced, realizing how ungracious that sounded. "No, Mrs. Chartwell, the real reason they came is to catch a glimpse of the most elegant bride in Sussex."

She smiled and he felt as though he had corrected that misstep.

They rode back in the carriage. Angus had begged to climb up with them. William was about to say yes, thinking this might be a welcome distraction. Why did they not have weddings at four in the afternoon? Exactly why did the church insist that all weddings be completed before noon? So that the couple would have a chance to let their nerves worsen to the breaking point?

Sara had grabbed Angus's arm. "It's a wedding, you stupid boy. No one takes children up with them at a wedding."

Lavinia's agreement was not so acerbic, but it was firm, accompanied by a fond smile that took away any sting.

William told Harry and Angus that today they must walk, grateful to a merciful God that he had not obviously classed himself as a "stupid boy" by allowing their company. Not wed an hour and he could already see that marriage was laden with possible missteps.

The boys' antics as they raced beside them filled the few moments' drive back to Talford Rise. He had thought ahead. Their wedding breakfast awaited them and then perhaps they would take a walk in the park.

He'd all but forgotten the messenger until Dolley reminded him. Once he'd read the waiting letter, the question of how to fill the time before he took his bride to bed was no longer his biggest concern. Events outside Talford Rise conspired to send his worry in an entirely different direction.

Despite his preoccupation, their wedding breakfast was far more entertainment than he had expected.

His bride—his wife—had been the center of attention and for good reason. In those few hours at the table she was a loving mother, a caring wife, and a true lady. There was more laughter than he had ever heard at the Rise.

He did not know if that was because of the champagne or a surfeit of happiness. He wished that he could take to the role of husband as effortlessly as she wore the mantle of wife.

By evening, Mrs. Newcomb and her sister had left for their home in the village. The children had gone to bed. The night was lit by candles and the constant fire in the blue salon.

The *Splendid* was all but screaming for his attention. He fully expected his first lieutenant would arrive within a day if he did not come to Portsmouth immediately. His new orders were bent on disrupting his life once again, a most perverse wedding gift from the Admiralty.

With a deep sigh, Lavinia rose from her chair. William had been sitting across from her, the growing quiet deafening. He must tell her that he would have to leave in the morning. He had almost told her three times but had kept his counsel.

He stood up and before he opened the door for her he asked, "Will you please come to my bedroom after you have changed for bed, Mrs. Chartwell?" He could not help the smile when he said her new name.

She was surprised, and it was not pleased surprised.

"Should you not be coming to my room?" she asked.

Was she being coy? No, she looked more puzzled than shy.

"Not tonight, Lavinia. It has been a long and tiring day. I only wish to talk with you of our plans for tomorrow."

"All right." She was puzzled but, thank heaven, not inclined to argue.

She did not keep him waiting. Did she have any idea how he valued that? Almost as much as he appreciated the more conventional things that would appeal to a man.

When she came into his room all of the practical reasons for this late-night rendezvous evaporated from his blood-starved brain.

Her robe was heavy green velvet, pale as Chinese jade, the color of the Caribbean when it is close to the shore. Over it she wore an elaborate lace shawl that framed her face and her dark hair. He could not see anything beneath and tortured himself with the fantasy that she was naked under the sweet confection of her robe.

When she took the winged-back chair he offered, she tucked her bare feet up under her, the material of her robe puddling on the floor. His mermaid sat before him.

She accepted the glass of champagne he handed her, but he noted that she did not immediately taste it.

He raised his glass. "To marriage, Mrs. Chartwell."

They both drank to the toast, Lavinia watching him over the rim of the glass. He could have been drinking saltwater.

Her hair was undone from the more formal arrangement that she had worn for the wedding. As soon as she set the glass down, she began to braid it.

"Leave it."

She raised her eyebrows and kept on with the braiding.

"Please, leave it for a few moments."

With a slight smile she combed the first few plaits out with her fingers.

By the stars, did she know how that affected him? He shifted in his own chair and wished for a blanket. Better to look like an old man than to shock her.

He stood up and took an object down from the mantelpiece, setting it on the small table beside her. "I hope that you will accept this permanently. As a wedding present."

It was the jasper stone cup that he had tried to give her once before and her obvious delight in it convinced him that he had, at least, done this right.

"It really is so lovely. Like something the gods would use to scoop water from the sea."

"A mermaid. Something a mermaid would use."

"You are too much a man of the sea, Captain." She shook her head. "I am hardly a mermaid, but I shall treasure this nonetheless."

She rose, went to the door that connected their rooms, and was back in a moment, holding a small package that she handed to him.

He opened it and looked up at her.

"You will be gone so long and I do not wish you to forget me or the children."

He nodded, too moved to speak. It was not one but four miniatures: Lavinia, Angus, Harry, and Sara. His odd little family. As if he would ever forget them.

"It's a perfect gift, Lavinia. Thank you." He came over to where she sat, knelt on one knee, and took her hand. "Lavinia, new orders have come from London."

She shook her head and tried to pull her hand away. He would not let it go.

"I must leave for Portsmouth tomorrow. As soon as the stores are loaded *Splendid* will be underway."

"No." Her hand curled around his, holding it with surprising strength. "You said we would have two weeks."

"I thought we would, but they have decided that *Splendid* is to go ahead and await the convoy's arrival so that the escort duty can be completed without delay."

"Must you leave tomorrow? Will it not take days to load the ship?"

"Yes, but Lieutenant Tenley tells me that the captain of the port is being difficult. My presence is needed to convince him that we have priority."

She stood up, picked up her glass of champagne, and threw the contents on the fire. When she faced him again, her eyes were narrowed with anger and shiny with tears. "Then we have nothing to celebrate, do we?" She stayed facing the fire, setting the glass on the mantelpiece.

A very small selfish part of him was glad that she was angry, that his early departure was more burden than boon.

He came up behind her and put his hands on her shoulders. Her unbound hair moved over his hands as she lowered her head. It felt like silk. No, heavier than that. Like satin. "There was no easy way to tell you. I have tried to find a way for hours, since the message came."

"A message?"

"Yes, I am sorry, Lavinia, so sorry, but you knew when you agreed to this that my life was not my own to order."

He felt her shrug.

"Yes, I did agree to it, but what I did not fully understand is that my life would not be my own either. I did agree, Captain, but . . ." her voice trailed off.

"Call me William, Lavinia. Especially in private." He had asked her once before. This felt suspiciously like begging.

"I will, but at the moment you are more captain than husband."

He could make her see him differently, but he had told her that he would not rush her, that she would have time to grow used to the idea of sleeping with him. "Go to bed, then. We can say goodbye tomorrow. I will not leave until late in the morning."

"Go to bed? Alone?"

"Lavinia, I promised you that I would give you time." Was he mad? Why was he playing the gentleman? What was he afraid of?

"Yes, but five months is longer than even the most frightened bride would need. And William, I am not at all afraid." She considered him for a moment. "But if that is what you truly wish . . ." She smiled an impish smile that drew a cautious smile from him. Instead of walking away she came up to him and took his face in her hands.

"Good night, William." She kissed him lightly. "Sleep well, William." She kissed him even more lightly. "Have the sweetest dreams, William." This time she did little more than breathe on his lips.

She pressed her lips together as he knew she was wont to do and he realized that she wanted to stay. He said nothing, trying to listen to the debate screaming in his head.

Lavinia mistook his silence, or perhaps she perfectly understood it.

She moved away from him, lowered her head, and walked to the door. He watched her until she had her hand on the doorknob. He already felt cold despite the steadily burning fire. This misstep was more than a stumble. It was a fall down an open hatch, amidships.

"Lavinia." He followed her to the door and made to open it for her, but stayed her with a hand on her arm. "I would not have you with child so soon without me here."

She kept watching him, in silence.

"It would be the height of selfishness, Lavinia."

She walked by him to the bed and with her back to him began to unfasten her night robe. "It is very cold in here, even with the fire burning."

He came over to her, swept her off her feet, and laid her on the bed. "How fortunate then that I know the perfect way to keep you warm."

She drew him to her onto the bed. "Then come, William, and let us be selfish together."


The next day was a muddle of tears, kisses, and farewells. The next week was a brutal effort to load the ship and prepare to sail. The next month and the ones after were filled with long hours sailing in an unfriendly wind, the boredom broken only by the daily exercise of the great guns with no enemy in sight. Through it all he carried her miniature in his inside coat pocket, close to his heart—so close to him that even if the ship were to sink he would not lose it.

Whenever his duties permitted the indulgence, he would sketch, sometimes on deck, usually in the solitude of the great cabin. His favorite was the drawing he had done of his wife in the early morning of their one night together. She was curled on her side toward the middle of the bed. Her hair spread across his pillow and her shoulder, sound asleep, but smiling.

The sketch captured the look of her well enough, the fulfillment, the satisfaction. But her generosity and the joy of discovery: those were impossible for his limited talent to put on paper. He would carry them in his memory until they were together again.

It was their only night together, but a night he could dream about forever. He wrote to her, sending three letters from the same port with a merchantman bound direct for London. With each letter the certainty of his affection grew. He never mentioned it, barely acknowledged it to himself except in the quiet hours before dawn. In time, he came to understand his hesitation on their wedding night. Taking what she so sweetly offered was admitting love, when lust had been all he wanted to feel.

# Chapter 23

Even Dolley was worried. William had been gone for eight months. There had been no word in all that time, from him or from the Admiralty.

A month ago when she had first allowed herself to question, Dolley had convinced her that five months or eight was almost the same at sea. The water had its own way of counting the minutes and the ship was a slave to it and to the wind.

This morning she could stand it no longer and had called Dolley to the captain's study and he had tried to distract her with stories of drawn out cruises. She hardly listened and finally stopped him by simply saying his name.

He remained standing when she took a seat in one of the chairs in front of William's desk. The two contemplated the empty seat in silence.

"I ain't never been left behind, not before this." Dolley twitched his shoulder and empty sleeve. "It's worse than scurvy."

"Yes, and women do it all the time."

"Aye, ma'am."

"You do agree then that something is wrong?"

"Seems it," he admitted grudgingly, "but we've had no word from London."

"And I can wait no longer. We must find someone to contact at the Admiralty."

"Did he leave you no letter? Nothing?"

She was about to deny it when she remembered. "He did, Dolley. He did!" She jumped up from the chair. "Almost two years ago when he went on that short trip. When Angus came to stay at Talford Vale for the first time. He left a note for Angus but there was also a message for me."

"That's good, ma'am." He hurried to the door to hold it for her and then stopped. "Is it still at the Vale?"

"It must be. In my glove drawer."

Dolley shook his head doubtfully.

"Yes, I'm sure that Malton left the gloves there when she went to pack up my clothes. They were worthless and worn."

Dolley's eyes showed a little more hope.

"I am going over there immediately."

"You need someone with you, ma'am, even with the house empty and closed up."

"I will take Angus with me. The note is for him after all. And Dolley, I will be safe. The caretaker there is well known to me."

Angus came promptly, nodding solemnly when she explained their mission and came with her to the front door in silence.

Lavinia grabbed a shawl from the back of a chair near the door and they hurried out, down the steps and across the grass.

The late May day was not particularly pretty. It had been a miserable winter—so cold and wet that even this imperfect spring was welcome. She had yet to go barefoot, but the sun was breaking through the clouds today and with it she could feel the air warm even as she walked.

She walked briskly when what she really wanted to do was run, but there was no need. The letter had been in her glove drawer for more than a year. It was not going to be any more or less legible with a few more minutes' delay. She hurried nonetheless. Holding it, touching it, reading it would bring William closer than he had been for eight months.

Angus glanced at her three times but did not speak. He was growing and it took little effort for him to match her stride.

The caretaker welcomed them as though he longed for some company and she left Angus with him while she went upstairs to her old bedchamber.

The caretaker's voice echoed up to her as she made her way through the nearly empty house.

"Any word from the captain?"

It was a constant question in the close-knit village. Lavinia longed to give him an answer different from their standard "not yet, but soon."

Her room was exactly as she had last seen it the night William had come to rescue her. Of course, the personal items were gone, and with them any inclination to feel sentimental about this place that had been anything but a happy home.

She pulled open the drawer to her dressing table and lifted out the yellowing pair of gloves that were exactly where she thought they would be. The letter was beneath them. She picked it up and went to sit on the window seat, holding it close against her heart.

She remembered the moment he had given it to her. The first time she had been in his study. He had told her that opening it did not necessarily mean he was dead, only that there had been complications. He could be a prisoner, or sick, or injured, or simply delayed. Then, those options had seemed reasonable. Now they did not make her feel any better at all. She unfolded the paper and read.

It contained nothing that she did not already know: the name and direction of his prize agent and a written statement that she would be responsible for Angus until his grandparents were contacted and travel to Scotland was arranged.

Businesslike and direct: a thousand heartbeats from what she wanted from him. It did give her an idea of how to proceed, though. His agent. If his prize agent was not the exact person to contact he could at least tell her who to speak with at the Admiralty.

She stood up and faced the window, holding the sealed smaller letter close to her, staring down to the boathouse, then up at the clouds and the almost blue sky.

"Aunt Lavinia?"

Angus stood at the door. He was all boy but she could begin to see the kind of man he would become. Tall—taller than Harry would be—rugged, and not always tidy. He would endear himself to anyone with the boyish smile she knew he would never lose. And drive the love of his life mad with his inclination to leave books open everywhere and speak Latin as often as he spoke English.

Not a month after the captain left she had suggested that he call her aunt. His pleased grin was all the agreement he gave her and she knew then that he would be as much a son to her as Harry was.

He came to her. She handed him the sealed note. He took it and like her, did no more than hold it.

"He is coming back," he insisted with manly obstinacy, while the boy in him was miserable.

She pressed her lips together and gave a slight, unconvincing nod. He moved away from her and ripped the seal.

He turned back a moment later, dry-eyed with effort and handed the note to her.

She read it with infinite attention to every curve and swoop of William's written words. Why had she never noticed that his sprawling lavish hand was as generous as his heart?

Tears filled her eyes and she did not look at Angus lest they spill down her cheeks.

She read the note again, this time translating William's words into the feelings of the man she had come to know: the undying loyalty he felt for Carroll MacDonald, that loyalty now given to his son, the longing to be part of the boy's life and watch him grow to manhood. She looked at the last line again and knew with certainty that *Remember me with kindness* was his guarded version of *I love you*. To her horror, tears splashed from her eyes and onto her hand.

"Don't cry!" Angus shouted. "He is alive! I know it."

Grabbing the note from her, he raced from the room.

She made to run after him, but the tears came too freely and they were the last thing he needed to see. More than he, she needed time to come to terms with her fear. She walked down the stairs and left the house, giving the caretaker the barest of thanks.

The sun had taken over the sky but it was not nearly warm enough for her Jamaica-raised soul. She walked to the boathouse and out onto the terrace where it would heat the stone and surely warm her. She stood, staring at the quiet water of the lake.

How many other wives waved goodbye? Put on a brave smile? The prospect of years of separation was not the worst of the farewell. No, the worst was accepting what she was facing now. That he might never come back. That one night together could well be the sum and total of her married life with William Chartwell.

It might as well be one as one hundred. For even one million days and nights would not be enough.

How could women do this? She closed her eyes and found the answer in her heart. She could not speak for every wife, but she knew that she could smile and wave goodbye because she loved him. And loving him meant accepting that his place in the royal navy was an essential part of who he was, as essential to him as the sun was to the earth.

She loved him.

She stood against the balustrade for a long time, staring at the water. *Come home, please come home*, she begged, *even if you never learn to love me*.

The sun glinted on the small waves and she wondered if she could ever swim again without thinking of him. She might not be a mermaid, but he held her as surely as any man ever held a charmed creature.

She took a long route to the house, stopping by the new greenhouse that had been built precisely to the captain's specifications. The gardener showed her the progress of the newest of the plants and waxed enthusiastic over the specimens the captain was sure to be bringing back with him.

She stopped at the stables as well. Horses were of as little interest to her as they were to the captain. He had long ago explained that most seamen were indifferent horsemen at best and he was no exception. Despite that, he cared enough to have the best cattle and a groom who knew them. The groom told her that the captain would be delighted with the new foal that was the beginning of a fine stable.

Finally she made her way around the side of the house and through the new rose garden that represented her conviction that he would return. The bushes were beginning to bud, though they were weeks away from a full bloom.

By the time she reached the front of the house she was as sure as Angus, the gardener, and the groom that William would be home—that her tears were a foolish weakness grown from a newly realized love.

She heard a carriage on the drive and moved along quickly, patting her hair, which was, she could tell, less than perfect. It could be the vicar, but truly she could not think of anyone else who would come to call in more than a cart or astride a horse.

This was a grand conveyance and she realized with a great soaring joy that it must be William. She began to run, laughing and crying, neither adequate to her emotions.

The coachman jumped down and opened the door, lowering the steps. A man stepped out and looked about.

"William!" she called out, loud enough to be heard in London. "William! Welcome home!"

# Chapter 24

Lavinia was a few steps from throwing herself into her husband's arms when she realized that the man before her was not William. He had the look of him, but was only a pale copy. His skin was not bronzed. His blond hair did not have the bleached look from years in the sun. He did have the same strong jaw and gray eyes, as cautious as William's ever were.

She stumbled to a halt and the man automatically reached out a hand to steady her. His touch did nothing but hold her upright and a rush of misery eclipsed the joy. "Not William," she breathed.

Someone threw open the front door and the two boys tumbled out, followed by Dolley, Chasen, and anyone else who might have heard the carriage or her welcome.

With a brief "I beg your pardon a moment," Lavinia abandoned her guest and walked toward the group who all regarded the stranger with a mix of surprise, delight, and calls of welcome.

"My apologies, Angus, Harry. To all of you. It is not the captain."

The group's elation collapsed as completely as hers had. All but Angus, Harry, and Dolley faded into the house. The boys came toward her as she went back to her guest. Angus and Harry stood on either side of her, eyeing the stranger who stood waiting while the confusion was resolved.

"He looks like the captain," Angus said.

Lavinia put a hand on his shoulder and he leaned toward her. "Yes, he does, Angus." She tried to recall the name William had mentioned the one night he had spoken of his family. "I do believe this is Viscount Crandall."

She said no more, repressing her curiosity, trying for brusque and unwelcoming. William had been insistent. This man was a Braedon and not a welcome visitor.

She could not quite bring herself to say that part aloud.

The Braedon bowed to her. "I am Marquis Straemore now."

"I beg your pardon, my lord." She had eight months to perfect her wife-of-the-captain manners and despite untidy hair and tear-stained cheeks, her dignity was in place. She curtseyed with great formality. "My condolences then on the death of your father. We had not heard. I am Mrs. Chartwell, Captain Chartwell's wife."

He nodded and switched his attention to the boys. She bit her tongue and did not introduce them. That did not phase the marquis in the least. He moved closer to them. "You are Angus MacDonald? The captain's ward?"

"Yes, sir."

"And I am Harry Stewart. I live here too."

The marquis accepted Angus and Harry's bow and then he once again gave his full attention to the still-suspicious Angus.

"I look like the captain because he is my brother."

"He was raised in an orphanage," Angus said as if revealing a lie.

"Nevertheless, we are brothers."

He sounded exactly as her husband did when someone questioned him. Hardly surprising, she decided; they were both used to having their orders obeyed.

"Can you see my face and doubt it?" He spoke with a little more kindliness this time.

Angus's expression remained wooden.

The marquis allowed the silence for a long challenging moment and then gave his attention fully to her.

"I have news of the captain, Mrs. Chartwell."

She opened her mouth and then closed it.

"What news? Tell us." Angus spoke with such vehemence that even a grown man would obey.

"He is well and merely delayed."

The sun had been shining for hours, but this was the first time today that Lavinia's spirits lightened to match it. She laughed, only a little breath of sound, unable to contain her relief.

"The Admiralty last had word of him from Mahon. As of the middle of April he was proceeding as directed."

The boys let out a cheer. Lavinia hugged Angus who hugged her back. Angus stepped away from the embrace quickly enough though and asked, "Is that all? Do you have any more details?" He tacked on "my lord" as a hurried afterthought.

She would invite him in, she decided, giving in to impulse and Angus's questions. William's orders were not nearly as important as hearing what more news he might have. She stepped toward Dolley who was wiping a tear from his eye. "Dolley, would you have some tea brought to the captain's library?"

Lavinia tried to see beyond the marquis into the darkened carriage. "Is anyone else with you, my lord?"

"No," he said shortly and then added, "my wife is not well enough to travel. That is another reason I thought to come here without further delay."

The marquis glanced at the boys and the longing that winked out in a moment told Lavinia all that she needed to know about his wife's illness: she had lost a child. Lavinia was almost sure of it. Her coolness eased a trifle more.

"Do come in, my lord."

The boys followed the two adults into the front hall and it occurred to Lavinia that despite his rank and the good news he brought, her boys were not about to leave her with a strange man.

"The marquis and I will be in the captain's library having a private conversation. I will tell you any other news he has of the captain within the hour." They did not move away. "While you are waiting, why not take the hammock down to the boathouse? It's time for it to be put out."

Harry allowed himself to be distracted. "You want us to do it now?"

"Yes."

"Capital!" Harry nudged Angus, who abandoned his suspicious consideration of the marquis.

"Do you recall where Dolley stored it, Harry?"

"Yes, ma'am," Angus said, avoiding Harry's eyes. They took off up the stairs as though she had set a time limit. Angus paused briefly at the top and glanced down, then raced after Harry.

Lavinia was about to apologize for their rude departure, but the marquis was watching the boys with nothing less than a smile. It made him infinitely more approachable.

"I beg your pardon, my lord. They have been asking daily for permission, as if they have not spent the whole winter using the hammock in their room. The plaster in the south wall will never be the same. I suspect boys are a greater threat to a house than wood rot and mice together."

The marquis actually laughed a little. "My brother Morgan once asked me to hide some frogs in my room. I refused, of course, and he tried to kick me. He kicked the bed instead and knocked a chunk out of it that we never did find."

The exchange of small stories helped ease the constraint between them. She had already violated William's order and allowed the man into her house. She had every intention of finding out every possible detail of the marquis' visit to the Admiralty.

At Dolley's invitation, he left her to freshen up. Less than thirty minutes later James Braedon—Marquis Straemore—was with her in the library. He carried a package with him. He placed it on the floor beside him and then ignored it.

She handed him a cup of tea in her best china dish. He accepted it and then set it on the table at hand.

"Any and all details would be welcome, my lord." She hoped it did not sound like begging and then did not care if it did.

As her tea cooled next to his, he spoke.

"I am only being honest when I say that I know little more of the captain's cruise and less the plan for his return. Viscount Melville told me that the convoy had been attacked off the East coast of Africa and repairs made for a long delay. *Splendid* was put on routine patrol while they awaited the convoy. When the ships finally left the Mediterranean under *Splendid's* protection there were further problems, but all because of weather: first, the lack of wind, and then a gale. It played havoc with all the shipping."

"But the *Splendid* came through both unscathed?"

"That is what I was told and have no reason to believe otherwise." He sipped what must be cool tea. "You have had no word from him?"

She shook her head, wondering at that oddity herself. Was she so easy to dismiss from his mind when she was out of sight? Had he not thought of her every night when he was alone in his hammock? Or perhaps he had not always been alone? Too late she realized that her long silence was some indication of her distress. She straightened in her chair and tried for a matter-of-fact air that she was far from feeling. "Family is new to him, my lord."

It was not precisely an insult, but it did make the point that in this household the Braedons were not considered family. "William surrounds himself with those who are as loyal and generous as he is," she continued. "We do not need constant letters to reassure us of his affection." *But one or two would have been nice.*

The marquis' good opinion did not matter, she insisted to herself. His family knew nothing of loyalty or generosity.

"To be honest with you, Mrs. Chartwell, I did not know William even existed until three years ago."

"How could that be? You are head of the family."

"Not until two years ago when my father was declared unfit and even then I would not have known if we had not discovered some journals my stepmother kept."

Her ill will was ever so slightly eroded.

He set his cup down and sat back in his chair. For all his apparent calm, she felt him grasp at the slight easing of her distrust. "Braemoor burned to the ground and in the course of recovery, the journals were discovered."

"How awful."

"Yes, fortunately no one was hurt, but it was the first true sign of the marquis' insanity. He started that fire and not six months later attempted to destroy the dower house where we all were living."

She bit back another "how awful" and said instead, "This was the man who was William's father?"

"Yes." His curt word and even more defensive demeanor did little to comfort her. "He was always an autocratic demigod, behavior my wife says that I have learned from him. But the instability came after he suffered an attack of apoplexy."

"Yes, well it does seem that the inclination to command is a trait both you and the captain share."

"And I was trying to be charming."

He smiled and Lavinia found it quite irresistible. William had never smiled like this—part flirtation, part diffidence. Her husband's smiles were sincere and almost sober as though humor was a foreign language he was trying to learn.

"My wife tells me that her good graces have been my salvation." He seemed sad at the mention of her.

"Is she not recovering?"

"She is. She will. But she is profoundly disappointed. I have told her a hundred times that I need no heir, that I need her infinitely more but—" his voice trailed off, clearly embarrassed that he had spoken of something so personal.

Lavinia allowed the silence. He might be embarrassed, but those words told her so much more than a conventional response. She revised her first opinion. He was loyal and very much in love.

"The reason I am come, Mrs. Chartwell, is to inform the captain that he is the heir apparent. He is married," he nodded to her, "and he must be aware that his children are in the direct line. He will, of course, not have the title of Viscount Crandall as long as I am alive, since I could someday produce an heir, but it appears that he and his legitimate sons will be the ones to inherit the Straemore title and estates."

"But he does not want it," Lavinia said, overwhelmed at the prospect for herself, if not for William.

The marquis shrugged away that disclaimer as though the captain's opinion was not worthy of consideration. "You are in fact Lady William Chartwell, or Braedon, if he could be convinced to use his birth name."

He glanced at the package on the floor and then at her.

She was at a loss for words and could only repeat. "He does not want it, my lord."

Once again, the marquis ignored her. He reached over and picked up the package, he had brought into the room with him. "He may not want it, but that does not change the law. If he does inherit it, it will be as great a responsibility as any ship he might command."

"Yes, I understand. You want to ensure the well-being of all those who depend on you."

"There are hundreds, thousands even, if you consider the seats in parliament that Straemore controls."

"You grew up knowing that you would inherit, my lord.

You must understand that this will come as an immense surprise to William—to our whole family."

"Yes, but that makes it no less a fact."

"The captain did grow up with a sense of duty. I think the most you can hope for is that William will understand his responsibility. That may be possible."

"I would accept that, but my wife hopes for something more. Family is more important to her than jewels or clothes."

Lavinia considered the unknown marchioness, intrigued at the thought of someone so highly placed caring in that way. She knew he could see the curiosity and he pressed his advantage, leaning a little closer himself.

"She would fight; indeed, she has fought quite literally for the happiness of those she loves."

His words loosened the hard edge around her heart. She had not fought, and certainly not literally, but she too had found a way to protect those she loved. Her marriage to William had seen to that.

"I know exactly how he feels about the whole Braedon family, Mrs. Chartwell." He placed the package on the desk. "I have brought the journals we found. I am hoping that your husband will read them and perhaps see us differently."

"These are why you came in person?" She reached out and touched the topmost of the three irregular volumes, worn and dirty, but bound together with a clean white ribbon.

"I wanted to be certain that he understood and I was afraid he would burn a letter unread. And yes, I wanted to deliver the journals." He thought a moment before adding, "Bringing them was my wife's idea. And she may have the right of it. They made a great difference to me."

She reached out and took the three books from the table and held them in her lap. "They will be here when he returns."

The marquis smiled a little. "You might as well not fight the temptation. Give in to it and read them yourself."

She would never read them before William did. Had she

not kept the letter unopened for almost two years? It was close to an insult and she stiffened.

"My wife read them long before I did."

"She did?"

"Oh, indeed, after I specifically told her not to. It caused her any number of sleepless nights."

"Tell me more."

It was all the invitation he needed. She poured hot tea and James began. "You see, she came to Braemoor as my housekeeper . . ."


She invited the marquis to stay the night, but he would only take an early dinner, explaining that he wished to return home that day if possible.

Whether good ton or no, Lavinia invited the children and Sara's new governess to join them at table. Even though there was a family connection, a dinner *a deux* was hardly appropriate.

Before the soup was drunk the marquis had shared his news from the Admiralty and charmed them so that even Angus relaxed enough to tell some stories of the captain.

The marquis set the seal on their approval of him when he asked for Mrs. Wilcox and congratulated the blushing lady on a wonderful dinner.

"She is the best cook for fifty miles," Harry said after she had left the room.

"I do believe she is. Could I double her pay and entice her to Braemoor, do you think?"

"No," said Sara hotly, clearly unaware that the man was teasing them. "She is about to marry Dolley so you cannot steal her away. She will never leave us."

"I see." He looked profoundly disappointed. "Does she make cream cakes?" the mighty marquis asked as if willing to torture himself with what might have been.

"Yes, and marvelous lemon tarts." This from Harry.

The marquis sighed and shook his head.

The house was too quiet when he left. Lavinia went to bed early and listened as evening settled around them. She was just drifting off to sleep when she thought to wonder how the marquis had known of their marriage. No announcements had been sent. It had been overlooked in the rush of William's departure. Indeed, how had he known anything of them, much less that the captain was away and so long overdue?

# Chapter 25

William returned within a sennight. It was a long week waiting. The boys made endless mischief, Dolley was distracted by his newlywed status, and Sara was in a continual sulk brought on by her governess's refusal to allow her to learn the waltz.

In an effort to divert them all, Lavinia suggested a picnic dinner at the boathouse. Dolley brought down some old carpets and a blanket or two along with a jumble of pillows to make the hard, cold floor comfortable. The late day sun poured through the doors while they feasted on the treats that the new Mrs. Dolley thought suitable for dinning alfresco and it was almost warm enough to consider swimming.

They were on their way back to the house—the boys detouring off into the woods and then back again, Sara walking next to her aunt—when they heard and then saw a carriage come up the drive.

Lavinia tried to stay calm. It could be anyone, as her visitor the other day had proved. The boys were not so inclined and ran as fast as they could, reaching the carriage before it was more than halfway up the drive.

The coachman drew it to a stop. The captain did not wait for the steps to be lowered, but jumped down and into the welcoming arms of the two shouting boys. He gave them all his attention for a moment and then looked up and saw her.

Lavinia stopped and drank in the sight of her husband. He was home. He was safe. He was hers once more.

Reminding herself that this reunion was not yet wholly about the heart, she started toward him. He kept his eyes on her though the boys and Sara were madly chattering, each over the other.

"We are so happy to see you, William," she said.

"You have no idea how I have longed to hear you say that." He took her hand and kissed it.

"I hope for as long as I have been wanting to speak it."

He nodded, a small nod. It was his smile that captured her heart yet again. The light caress of his hand on her palm was as close to intimacy as the moment allowed.

The children had quieted during their greeting, but they did not leave, and William turned to the rest of his family after one lingering look at her mouth that was as good as a kiss.

The horses showed their restlessness and with a word to the coachman he sent them on to the house. They all moved to the grass as the carriage made its way up the drive.

The children were between them. The westering sun cast a great golden glow around William and the three children. Lavinia thought that they resembled a live tableau, the kind that the more sophisticated fairs featured. This one would be entitled "Homecoming."

She was content to watch. Her family. Her husband. They would have the whole night together and, God and the Admiralty willing, a hundred more all in a row.

"Sara, you have grown. I believe I would hardly recognize you were it not for that smile that is so like your aunt's," William said.

Sara dropped her eyes and blushed.

"Each of you tell me the most interesting thing that happened while I was away." They came closer, clustering around him. "And then I want some time with my wife."

"I have a governess," Sara began. "I have learned to play

*Für Elise* on the pianoforte. And I am taking dancing lessons. Captain, may I . . ."

Before she could go on, to ask if she could learn the waltz, Lavinia was sure, Harry stepped forward.

"That's more than one thing." He had matured enough not to ruin this homecoming with an insult, but his clenched jaw proved it an effort.

"We have built a model, Captain. A big one. Five feet long. Of a first rate and we just had a picnic in the boathouse."

"That's more than one," Sara said under her breath.

The captain did not seem to mind and waited for Angus to speak.

"Dolley was married three days ago and we launched a hot air balloon."

Harry chimed in yet again. "And the Marquis Straemore came to visit last week."

William's indulgent smile disappeared and he spoke to Lavinia. "The old man came here?"

"No," Harry answered for her, "He was not old, at least not older than you, Captain."

William nodded, understanding what that meant. He showed no sadness at the news of the death of his father. But that could be because so many other sensibilities were roiling through him.

"The marquis stayed for dinner," Harry volunteered, "and let Angus and me ride up with the coachman as far as the village."

Her own smile faded as she watched disbelief, betrayal, and hurt show in William's eyes, followed by a steely look, one he must use aboard ship when he was too angry to speak.

She gave only a graceless jerk of her chin that screamed guilt. Though before this moment she would never have thought guilt was what she would feel when he found out about the marquis' visit.

"I don't understand, Captain," Angus said. "He says he is

your brother. That you have an entire family right here in Sussex and yet you told me you were raised in an orphanage."

"Do you wonder which of us is telling the truth?" the captain asked gently, though there was an edge to his voice.

"No, sir." But it was clear he was confused.

"They both speak the truth, Angus." Lavinia tried for practical, and stilled her shaking hands by holding them folded and tightly against her. "It is a very sad story."

"Thank you, madam," William said coldly, effectively cutting off any further explanation she might have made.

"The captain and I are going to walk down to the boathouse." She was frantic, desperate to reclaim the welcoming smile that was so completely gone. "We will all have tea together in an hour."

"Not the boathouse. In my office, Mrs. Chartwell."

She was almost afraid of the coldness in his voice. "Very well," she whispered and walked slowly ahead of him with Sara beside her. The girl had enough understanding of men and women to know that with one sentence something had gone wrong.

Lavinia patted her hand where it was now tucked through hers. They both listened as the boys asked questions as they walked alongside the captain.

"Did you take any prizes, sir?"

"No."

"Did you fight any battles?"

"No."

"Did you see any French ships?"

"No."

"Any of the enemy at all?" Harry asked somewhat desperately.

"Only a great way off."

"You scared them away," Angus said with pride.

"It sounds boring," Harry said, amazed.

"It was."

"But then why did you not write us?"

"I did." He spoke with such surprise that Lavinia stopped and turned around.

"We never received any letters," she said.

"I received the ones you wrote at Christmas just this past month at Mahon." He did not smile but his mouth softened.

"I know you told us not to write because it was supposed to be such a short trip and you were uncertain if the letters would find you, but when Christmas was upon us, we decided that we would try." She knew she was babbling but kept on, hoping the rush of words would ease his anger.

"The marquis told us there was a terrible gale," Harry said.

The slight softening disappeared. "Straemore seems very well informed."

"Yes, the marquis went to the Admiralty and they told him you were safe but delayed by poor wind and then a big storm," Harry added.

"Indeed."

Lavinia winced. Harry seemed to realize, finally, that there was something amiss. He stepped closer to Angus who was watching the adults in worried silence.

"We will see you at dinner," Lavinia said as she sent the children off, relieved that William did not countermand that suggestion too.

She went into the library, but he did not follow her. She told herself he meant no insult, that he must see Dolley and the others, but as the five minutes grew to fifteen she began to debate the subject he was sure to address. By the time he joined her, she was convinced that she had done nothing wrong.

He opened his desk drawer and closed it. She remained standing and so did he.

"You allowed the Marquis Straemore into this house."

It was an accusation, not a question.

"Yes, but, William, he had—"

He cut her off. "How did Straemore know I was away? Had you written to him?"

"No! He said he came because you had married and there were some issues of inheritance that must be addressed."

"How did he know I was married? How did he know that I was so long away?"

"I have no idea, truly. I wondered myself but only thought of it after he left."

William shrugged. "He has some spy in the neighborhood. It is exactly what I would expect of him."

"You believe me?"

"That you did not write and invite him here? Yes. But you welcomed him once he came. Despite the fact that you understood that the Braedons are not wanted here, that the name was not even to be spoken."

"He came with news of you. I could not refuse—"

He raised his hand with sharp insistence. She stopped without finishing the sentence. "Angus must tell you the story of the Trojan horse, madam."

"I know the story." She could feel her cheeks heat and her breathing was ragged. "It is wrong to harbor a years-old grievance that the new marquis knew nothing about."

The captain looked down at his desk. Lavinia followed his gaze. It was polished to a shine, the inkwell exactly where he liked it, the paper there ready for his use.

He folded his arms across his chest and spoke, his eyes hard. "On board when an officer openly defies the captain it is called insubordination. And then you convinced the children to welcome him as well. That, my wife, is mutiny."

"But we are not on a ship, William."

"You overstep yourself, Mrs. Chartwell."

"You are too rigid in your beliefs. Is that what comes from eight months at sea where your word is law?"

"So he has seduced you." He paused a moment. "Seduced your mind at least."

Her cheeks flamed at the insult, her temper afire as well, but she managed to hold her tongue.

"Being Mrs. Chartwell is not enough for you? You must be 'my lady' as well?"

That insult was more than she could bear. "Are you going to have me flogged?"

"No," he said, but only after a long moment of silence. He opened his desk drawer again. This time he took something from it, holding it out in his open hand. It was the other of her combs. "Do you recall what I told you of how a man holds a mermaid?"

"Yes," she said, her heart beating uncomfortably hard.

"I no longer feel the need." He tossed the comb onto the desktop. "I would never beat you, Lavinia."

She nodded, knowing what was coming was infinitely worse.

"But I will never trust you again."

# Chapter 26

*I will never trust you again.*

He went on as if those words had not changed her life. "I will spend some time with the children, make my report to the admiralty, and wait for my next assignment."

His meaning was clear. She was no longer part of his life.

He sat down and pulled a sheaf of blank paper toward him, apparently ready to start on the report this moment. Despite the dismissal she tried one more time.

"You are not a coward, William. You will have to face this sometime."

He did not pretend to misunderstand her. "I have faced it, madam. More than twenty years ago when my father sent me away, then last year when I met the Braedons in London, and even last summer when Morgan Braedon came here. I faced it and rejected them."

Since she would not leave the room, he did. She heard the carriage crunch down the drive and raced to the door, afraid he had left the Rise completely.

But he was standing on the drive talking with the boys. He had merely sent the carriage away.

Lavinia hurried to her bedchamber, propelled by both anger and frustration. Tears were not far but she would not give into them. She was in the right. She was certain of it.

She reached her room and closed the door with deliberate

quiet, resting her forehead against the wood as if it were possible to leave her heartache out in the hallway.

She wandered from bed to window and back until she stood staring at the quiet fire. If he would not listen to her, what could she do?

She did not know him well enough to understand how he handled this kind of anger, how long he would hold on to it. That was what came from too short a courtship. But there had been no governess to warn her of the consequences and Mrs. Newcomb had been too consumed with propriety when wisdom was what was needed.

She shuddered as she thought of the marriages that Mrs. Newcomb had told her about. The ones where the husband and wives rarely saw each other. Convenient, she said. And so could hers be. Why, the captain would spend months, even years at sea. Mrs. Newcomb said it as if it were to be greatly desired. She would be free to run her household and live a life of independence.

That might be a life that ladies of the ton favored, but it was not what she wanted. She longed for a family. Her own children as well as the three that were already part of her. She dreamed of a husband who would do more than provide a home but also be father, lover, and yes, friend. How foolish of her to pretend, if only to herself, that William wanted the same thing.

All he ever wanted was another person who would do his bidding, another person who would obey his orders.

For her part she would hold on to her anger for as long as she could. She would not cry. She was not powerless. She was not. And temper was so much less painful than tears.


William had no idea what to do with his anger. It gave him a blistering headache and made him restless and irritable and that was only the first hour. He could count on one hand the number of times he had been so infuriated. In the recounting he realized how he had handled it. With his fists.

But those incidents had been different. Never like this. Never had he allowed someone close enough to his heart to make it vulnerable. And here was the proof of why. Because they took advantage, pressed for more when you had already given all you could.

For all of five minutes he thought of returning to Portsmouth. He was ashore, but he could find some distraction there. Or go to London and ask the Admiralty for another assignment. Admiral Ingersoll went through more captains than powder in battle; surely he could find a ship under Ingersoll's command. William shook his head and decided that he wanted an escape, but not badly enough to end his days buried at sea.

He lay in the hammock at the boathouse, watching the almost full moon move across the sky, wondering how long it would be before they could be civil to each other again. It was not how he had hoped to spend his first night home.

During the days at sea when the sails were quiet and the *Splendid* rode the waves, becalmed and waiting for the wind, a dozen memories teased his brain. The way she would close her eyes and lose herself in the pleasure of some lovely smell or taste. The way she would listen to anyone—the children, himself, even Mrs. Newcomb—as though what they had to say mattered. The way she would stare at the water, sky, or flowers as though she had become part of their essence.

She had taken him to heart just as she had taken the children, Mrs. Wilcox, and everyone at Talford Rise. Why was he surprised that she had not had the sense to see through the cunning of Straemore? Her generosity was also a weakness. One that had allowed her to be used.

Angus and Harry rowed with also haphazard intent. It was only when they came a little too close to the spot where the ducks nested that they applied themselves to the oars and moved purposefully away from the reeds and back toward deeper water and the shore closer to the boathouse. They shipped their oars and climbed out of the boat and then settled themselves onto the grass under the trees closest to the waterline.

"It's damn hot out," Harry said.

"Let's eat."

"Right." Harry rose and went back to the boat and gently tossed Angus one of the two meat pies they had brought with them and then reached for the discarded cream cakes Mrs. Dolley had judged "not good enough for the tea tray."

"Do you wanna swim?"

"It's hot enough," Angus said, considering the water.

Harry began to unbutton his shirt.

"But we had better wait and see if Aunt Lavinia comes down. You know she said that we were not to swim alone."

"We aren't alone," Harry pointed out reasonably. "And she has yet to come down here even though it has been hot as blazes for a week."

Harry was pulling his shirt off when Angus reached out to stay him. "No, Harry."

"No? When did you become such a girl?"

"Take it back," Angus flushed. "I am not a girl."

"Oh, yes you are." Harry laughed. "You would not sneak over to the Vale with me to play a prank on the caretaker. You would not tie Mr. Arbuscam's coattail to his chair while he was snoring. Maybe you should learn needlework with Sara."

Anger crowned days of anxiety and guilt. Angus dropped his pie, stood up, and punched Harry in the stomach, satisfied when his best friend fell to the ground, gasping for air. Angus stood over him, fists raised. He stepped back when Harry reached out to grab his foot and drag him down for a muddy battle.

"Do not call me a girl again, Harry. Next time I will give you a black eye."

Before Harry had breath enough to answer, Angus took off.

He slowed when he was sure he was out of range of Harry's fists and slowed even more when he was completely out of sight. Detouring into the home woods, he walked along a seldom-used path he'd found last fall right after the captain left.

He knew something was wrong. Aunt Lavinia was busy with a dozen housekeeping details that had never been important before. At first he had not noticed since the captain had been spending a lot of time with them, just the way he had hoped he would. But after the first two days he had the feeling that the captain was trying to avoid something. Like when he and Harry pretended they had to care for the horses when Mr. Arbuscam suggested extra study. Horses were something they both liked, but it was an excuse nonetheless.

As much as he might hope otherwise, he was sure that the captain and Aunt Lavinia had had an argument about the marquis. And it was his fault. He wondered if she knew it and was keeping silent to protect him.

Had the captain brought a new switch home with him? It hardly mattered what the punishment would be. He could not keep silent any longer.

He would have to confess.

# **Chapter 27**

William sat at his desk, staring sightlessly at the paper, pen in hand, the ink on the nib having dried completely. Like the great cabin aboard ship, this room was entirely his. Only here he traded the echo of sea and sail for the far less familiar sounds of his household.

At this very moment Lavinia was with Dolley helping him direct the cleaning of the great crystal chandelier in the ballroom upstairs. The day was sunny and warm, almost too warm, and Dolley was completely capable of directing the crew, but Lavinia was with him.

His wife might be here but his mermaid was gone. He had yet to see her barefoot this spring, much less at the boathouse or swimming. It could be that she went late at night when he was abed, but he was not sleeping well and would surely have heard if she left the room so close to his.

Their marriage had been a mistake. They had rushed into it, he blinded by lust and she as much by a desire for family as by her fear for herself and the children.

A mistake, and an incurable one. He knew it in his head, but his heart was still pained by it. In time he would have to find some way to make it bearable, for both of them, and count himself lucky when he was called to sea again.

There was a light tap at the door.

"Enter."

Angus came into the room.

They had spent the better part of the last week together, William thought. How was it that he was only now noticing how the boy had grown?

There was maturity that he had not seen before. Perhaps Angus was like his midshipman. All boy when with friends and partway to man when they were invited to be with the officers at wardroom dinner.

"Sir, I must tell you something."

"Come in." When the boy only took a few steps closer the captain sat straighter. "I take it this is more than some prank gone awry. *Casus conscientiae?*"

"Yes, sir. It is a case of conscience."

When Angus did not smile or reply in Latin, William felt his heart sink. "Then sit down, tell me, and have done with it."

Angus swallowed and came to stand in front of the desk. "You cannot blame Aunt Lavinia. It was all my fault."

At first William was embarrassed that his personal life should be so obvious to everyone around him. What could the boy possibly have done to feel at fault?

"You see, sir, she was trying so hard to be brave. Like the first time one climbs to the top—really scared but not wanting to admit it."

"Indeed."

"It had been seven months, sir. She and Dolley were trying to decide who they could write to at the Admiralty. Dolley said that he did not think anyone would answer. That there were hundreds of post captains and a whole war to direct."

"Indeed."

"And then I remembered Lord Morgan, Lord Morgan Braedon." Angus could not meet his eyes, but then, with what William recognized as real effort, he faced him directly again. "When Lord Morgan was here that one time, he told me that I should watch out for you and write to him if you ever needed help."

"He did, did he?" *The interfering old woman.*

"Yes, sir. He said that you were like someone else he knew and that you would not even know you needed help." Angus drew a deep breath. "So I wrote to him. I asked him if he could give us the name of someone at the Admiralty. Anyone who would know where you were or what had happened."

"And the marquis came instead."

"Yes, sir. And I never meant for that to happen. Never."

"But it did, Angus. How like the Braedons to take advantage of you. And how unlike you to not understand where your loyalties lay."

He shook his head. "No, sir. I do know. I thought forever about what you would think. I thought of suggesting that Aunt Lavinia write to him but was afraid that she would not and then be even more unhappy."

"And is she any happier today?"

"No." It was not all he wanted to answer but he stopped a moment and then continued. "But she was happier, Captain. When Marquis Straemore told us you were alive and delayed by weather, she changed on the instant from someone worried to someone smiling and laughing. The marquis stayed for dinner and it was as much fun as your wedding breakfast. Do you remember how she was that day, sir?"

Yes, he thought, nodding to the boy. He had sketched that scene endlessly, capturing the joy of everyone there and especially Lavinia, all lit up, as bright as the chandelier.

"Captain, do you remember my father telling me never to forget my mother's laughter?"

He remembered the love the two MacDonalds shared, remembered how it shown from Jeannie's eyes.

"How my mother's laughter was her love run over? It was like that when the marquis told us you were safe. Aunt Lavinia was laughing and crying at the same time. But you are right, sir, she is not happy and that is as much my fault as her happiness was." He stopped, not anywhere near tears, but William could see how desperate he was to make amends.

"You can use the switch on me, sir."

"You know, Angus, you are more like your father than I ever gave you credit for."

"Really, sir?" he asked with some pride.

"Yes, but in this case I do not mean it as a compliment. You cannot always bear the burden of someone else's guilt. Angus, the truth is that the problems of a man are not always solved by three lashes."

"It works aboard ship."

"I want you to think on why it works there and not here." William knew and so would Angus after two minutes' thought. "I will consider your punishment."

"Aye, sir." This time the two words carried a wealth of woeful anticipation. He left the room, all boy, his head down.

William leaned back in his chair and rubbed his forehead with three fingers. It was women who made life ashore so different. At sea a breach in discipline could be solved with twelve lashes while at home the consequences dragged on for days because a woman made a man see that there was more to life than "aye, aye, sir."

In these circumstances, Angus would have had to be Solomon to make a decision that would have kept everyone happy.

Damn the Braedons. They had interfered in his life once again and near ruined it. What was it about the word family that made it his personal albatross?

The journals Straemore had left behind were stacked at the edge of the blotter, their worn bindings showing either neglect or abuse. Lavinia had told him of them at dinner with the children present. And he knew that she had done that quite deliberately. She need not have worried. He had himself under control.

He pulled one of them over and opened it, reading a few words. A fairy tale. An original one, about a trapped fairy

princess. Obviously written for a girl. He put it aside and ignored the other two volumes for a full three minutes.

The blank paper waited but he threw the pen down and
picked up the most worn of the three and opened it where
someone had left a marker.

*How can he be so stubborn, so cruel? William is his
son, his completely legitimate son, but he will not allow
him to stay.*

William closed the book, a flood of memories erasing his
headache but filling his heart with a pain so physical that he
closed his eyes and waited for it to ease.

He did not need to read another word to recall the scene
completely.

"He is your son, your legitimate son, my lord. You cannot
send him away." Even now he could picture the woman he
knew to be his father's second wife and his stepmother. He
had never seen her before that day and had never forgotten
her. She was like the trapped fairy princess, beautiful and sad,
desperately trying to find happiness.

"I can do as I chose, Gwyneth, and I will! I never knew he
existed until three days ago, until that man arrived at my door
with the boy."

At ten years of age William was a boy, but his height and
presence bespoke of more than childhood. Despite his size he
was in his heart too young to be anything more than afraid.

"He is James's brother. You have only to look at him to
see the resemblance."

"I tell you, Gwyneth, that he is no more a child of mine
than his brother is. Both have my blood but born from that
witch of a woman who even God has declared is no longer
my wife."

"She is dead, sir, and I am your wife. I would have us do

what is right. I have always treated James as dearly as the children born to us, and William deserves the same."

"Annabelle is dead and I want her and every memory of her to stay that way. She was the one who chose to leave and ran off with that fool. With his birth"—he pointed at William—"God condemned her to death as surely as he freed me."

"But it is hardly right that her son—your son—should be made to bear the sins of his mother. He has had enough burden, raised by strangers in France these last ten years."

"You try my patience." He spoke with quiet menace.

The woman glanced at the boy with her heart in her eyes. Apology and regret told him that she accepted defeat though she made one or two more efforts. Finally, when the marquis was becoming truly agitated, she stood up and curtseyed. "As you wish, my lord, but I would have a word with him."

His father waved a hand and walked to a far corner of the room as the woman walked to William's side. William could see that her eyes were filled with tears and he wondered if she was crying because she knew that a beating awaited her.

"I am sorry, my lady."

"*You* are sorry? But why?"

"You have defended me and he will beat you."

"No, he only ever threatens. He never raises a hand to me." She raised her own hand and gently cradled his cheek. "No, William, I am the one who must be sorry. But always know that you are loved."

William Braedon glanced at his father. It was as close as he could come to calling her a liar.

"Not the marquis. He has a family and a loyal wife but even with all those blessings he cannot let the past go. But always know that I will care for you and think of you and indeed pray for your reunion with this family."

He shifted in discomfort at her obvious emotion. Afraid that if she persisted he would start to cry himself.

She walked out, leaving the father with his unwanted son. The marquis shut the door firmly.

"She is a woman full of sensibility and determined to care for the world. But you are not part of that world and never will be. She is right. I cannot let the past go. Ever."

William nodded, wondering if the marquis was going to pull out a gun and shoot him. A man of his station could do anything and not pay the consequences.

"I am sending you away today. You will go to sea. My man of business will take you to Portsmouth to Captain Bessborough on the *Chartwell*. He will take you on as a servant and you can make your own way or die trying."

The boy who was then William Braedon understood this was rejection and felt nothing but relief.

William closed the book and cradled it with real tenderness. He had not thought of the marchioness in years. He had written to her twice but the letters were never answered and he made himself stop thinking of her and her kindness. It was so much less painful to hate the marquis.

*He cannot let the past go.*

The words stayed with him as he penned an advertisement for a valet, wrote a brief letter to his prize agent, and began a letter to the mother of a midshipman who had been lost overboard in the gale.

All the while one thought weighed on him: *even with the blessing of family and a loyal wife he cannot let the past go.*

By the stars, he was his father's son.

He finished the letter to Mrs. Dowd, recounting all his best memories of her boy, her son, her heart. Would this one piece of paper serve to convince her that the memory of her boy lived on? Small comfort, but it was the best he could offer.

The old marquis had once been someone's boy. Hard even to imagine what had come and gone in his life to make his father as he was. Far easier to see what had shaped his own life. Shaped it in a far different way and yet, William decided, there were similarities between his life and his father's.

This son also had a family and a loyal, if misguided, wife.

And then it hit him with all the force of a rogue wave. He was no more able to let the past go than his father had been. Like the old marquis, he was hanging on to the wrongs of the past and making the present a misery for all.

He was the guilty one. Far more guilty than Angus or Lavinia. For he was the one making them all unhappy. All it would take was forgiveness and they would have a chance at making a life together. All he had to do was let the past go. It was totally in his control, not anyone else's, and certainly not the father who had poisoned a generation with his bitterness.

"I will not share this hell with you!" he spoke aloud and then scanned the room as though his father's ghost would come at his command. "Do you hear me?" he all but shouted and then shook his head at his theatrics.

With the journal in hand, William went in search of his wife. The first step would be to make some kind of peace with her, to see if they could find a different path to the future. He wanted her laughing as she had at their wedding breakfast—laughing because her heart could not hold all the love it felt. Love for the children. Love for him.

He went up to the first floor and hesitated. There was a veritable crowd in the ballroom, laughing and talking as they unhooked each crystal, washed it in water and vinegar, and carefully dried it.

This was not the moment to call his wife to him. There was no privacy here. Hardly more than there was onboard ship, despite the greater space and the smaller crew. He would wait until later when she was changing or in the blue salon.

He would go for a walk along the downs. In his bedroom, struggling out of his jacket, he decided he would carry his letters to the village and post them immediately. He had enough energy to walk all the way to Portsmouth, but thought that to the village and back would serve.

He was searching through the armoire for his oldest, most comfortable jacket when he heard someone at the door. As he approached the door flew open, just missing his head.

Lavinia burst into the room, smelling like vinegar and dust, looking every bit as angry as an avenging goddess.

"You cannot beat him! You will not."

"What?"

She grabbed him by the arms, her fingers digging into him through the linen of his shirt. "I said that you will not raise a hand to Angus. I forbid it."

"Lavinia," he began, but she would not hear him and sank to her knees in front of him. My God, what was she doing?

Her head was bent but he could see her shoulders shake. A comb fell from her hair. Was she crying? Was she going to faint? He reached for her but stopped when she began to speak again. He picked up her comb instead and slipped it into his pocket. He could hear the tears through her words.

"Please, William, I beg you. If you are so angry that you must do violence, do it to me. I am the one who is at the root of this. Angus is only a boy who did what he thought was right."

"Lavinia, get up. Stand up right now." He hated to see her like this. More than humble. Because she was afraid for one of her boys. Afraid of him.

"No," she insisted on a sob, "not until you promise that you will not harm him."

"Of course I will not."

She looked at him then, her eyes swollen with dust and tears.

"Lavinia, I have no intention of taking the switch to him. Yes, I was angry, but what he did was out of the goodness of his heart and that certainly mitigates his behavior."

"All right," she said as though she were not kneeling at his feet, as though she was the one dictating the terms of surrender.

"Stand up." He reached out a hand to her and, to his surprise, she took it. "Your tears have more power than you know. When they come from a loving heart they are a weapon of unequalled might."

He handed her his handkerchief and she accepted that too, turning her back to him, blowing her nose, wiping her eyes, and finally straightening her shoulders.

Better, he thought. Not afraid any longer, but still unhappy.

"He was doing what he thought was right." She was calmer. "There seems to be an epidemic of that, William, for you see, I will apologize too, if that is the only way to win you back. I welcomed your brother because I thought it was right. It was not what you would have done. It may have been wrong but at that moment it did not seem so."

She put the handkerchief on the table nearest her and turned back to him, facing him. They were as close as they had been since he had kissed her hand three days ago. He memorized the fleck of color in her eyes that sometimes made them more green than brown and tortured himself with the feel of her skirt brushing against his knee.

"Until this very moment, Lavinia, I would have said that showing weakness is the sign of failure, but you come and abase yourself and make it the ultimate strength."

She closed her eyes and when she opened them there was a tenderness in them that relieved him as much as the end of her tears. "Until the marquis came I was so worried. You were gone so long, with no word from anyone. I was not afraid for myself, you do understand that?"

He nodded, not because he fully understood, but because he wanted to.

"I knew you had provided for us. That if something were to happen we would not want for food or home or any manner of worldly goods. But, you see, none of that is as important to me as you are."

He took a step closer, so that she had to raise her hands to push him away. She did raise her hands but did not push him. Her palms rested on his chest.

"Nothing—no one is as important to me as you are," she said again in almost a whisper.

*Not even the children?* he wanted to ask.

"Someday the children will grow out of their need for me, for us. But my dearest wish, my fondest hope is that our need for each other will only grow with our understanding."

Hope replaced unhappiness and his own heart swelled.

She played with the button on his shirt and would not look directly at him. "Our future is about the two of us and who we are when we are together." She raised her eyes to his. "And what we mean to each other even when we are apart."

"Oh, Lavinia." He pressed her close. "You give so fully, so freely." He held her tight and whispered into her hair. "Is this what women do? Is this why life ashore is so different from life at sea? You turn our world upside down so that we see our humanity and discover our ability to love?"

"Love?" He could feel her body tense at the word.

"But of course, mermaid. I had not thought of the last months as having any value whatever, but I see that it gave me the time I needed to reexamine life without you.

"You see, the epidemic extends to me as well. I am sorry that I compelled you to marry me for any other reason than the deep and abiding love I feel for you."

"William!" She dropped her hands and would have taken a step from him, but the door was pressing into her back.

This was awful, he thought. Like standing in front of a loaded nine pounder and waiting for death. Was she not supposed to return the sentiment?

"I love you, Lavinia Chartwell. There was not one day that

I did not think of you here waiting for me, keeping my house for me, my bed warm, my heart full."

"Oh, William." She threw her arms around him and buried her face in his neck. "How could we be so foolish? How could we not know from the start?"

It was not quite I love you, he thought, but he could wait. Not for long. But he could wait.

"Because it was not true from the start. Not until you wove your mermaid spell around me."

"And you captured me with kisses that were too bold to be forgotten." She kissed his chin and then his cheek. "I missed you so. I even slept in your bed." She kissed his mouth but before he could deepen the kiss she leaned back in his arms. "I love you."

Perfect, he thought, as his world ashore was made complete.

# Chapter 28

He drew back from the warmth of her body, resting on his side, and watched her stretch languorously and smiled at her catlike contentment. He did not know whether he drew more satisfaction from her obvious delight in the act or the pleasure she gave him.

If the first days of his homecoming had been a hell of misunderstanding and estrangement, these last few had been the opposite: complete sympathy and acceptance.

He was drifting into sleep when he felt her move. He opened his eyes to find her facing him, the sheet pulled decorously over her breasts that were as much a joy to look at as to taste.

A line of tension marred her attitude of relaxation. William brought himself fully awake as he had a hundred times in his life, though never before because his wife was troubled.

She stared up at the bed curtains. "Do you think I am wanton?"

"What?" He had heard her but had no idea where the preposterous thought had come from.

"Do you think I am a wanton woman, William? You know what I mean." She spoke with the first sign of irritation he had heard in three days.

"I am not entirely sure I do know what you mean. Explain yourself." He bit his lip trying not to laugh at her even more pained expression and rephrased his question. "Explain a bit more fully, if you please, my dear."

She was silent a moment longer then did as he asked, "Do you think I am the kind of woman who would find pleasure in the act—in sex—whether married or not?"

It felt like a trap.

"William, I enjoy it so much. Too much."

By the stars, he loved her, he thought. He wanted to gather her close, comfort and caress every inch of her, but instead he tried to consider this as a fear rather than the best news he had heard in a year.

"And that makes you think you are a trollop?"

"*Could* be a trollop." She emphasized the could even though there was no doubt she had been a virgin their first time together. "Trollop . . . hussy," she continued. "Yes, any one of those."

He pressed a kiss to her shoulder and she smiled a little, but did not move closer.

"William, half the reason I married you was because I wanted you."

She made it sound a confession, when she must know that it was more than half of his reason. Now *there* was a fire ship he had best avoid.

"Of course I was already insanely in love with you, only too naive to know it."

"Is that what it was? Naiveté? On my part it was fear."

She kissed his chin, a maternal gesture that lasted a moment. "While you were gone I ached so. Every time I let myself think about our one night together . . ." She blushed a little and he nodded.

"Oh, I understand completely, Lavinia, only I never realized that my wife would be as lonely as I was."

"Which is why I wonder if I am a hussy after all."

"Let me ask you this, Lavinia."

She turned toward him again with that honest intensity that had poured from her since the beginning.

He loved that look. Yes, he loved it. Had his rudeness that day grown from fear? Had he known even then that his life would never be the same again?

"Tell me, wife, would you sleep with Dolley if he came to your room?"

"No!" Her eyes widened with something like revulsion and shock.

"Would you have relations with a man if he offered you wealth and jewels?"

Her revulsion gave way to a sad guilt. "Not for money, but I married you for the wealth of safety."

"Indeed, but you *married* me for that. Even if sex was half the reason you married me, it was not the heart of it."

"No." She smiled. "But you see then, we are back to the same question. I had sex with you because I wanted it more than I wanted to see the next sunrise. Where is my self-control?"

Gone for good, he hoped. "Let me ask you this: if you saw a man in the field without a shirt on, would you think of sex?"

She blushed and stared at him for so long that his own smile dimmed a little.

She kept on looking at him directly as she said, "There was a seaman friend of Chasen's visiting and he was stripped to the waist, sitting under a tree mending the shirt he had been wearing."

She paused and he nodded encouragement. "And the very first thing I thought of was how you would look sitting in the sun with that fine sheen of sweat coating your body." Raising her hands she covered her eyes. "Oh, am I hopelessly depraved?"

"No, my darling, you are every husband's dream." She lowered her fingers and he framed her face with his hands.

"You make up for dozens of years in a damned hammock with a hundred other frustrated men snoring around me."

"Then Mrs. Newcomb was wrong about marriage," she said with some satisfaction and this time he did laugh out loud as he pulled her to him.

"She most certainly was." He was sure of it even though she had never spoken to him on the subject.

The kiss he gave her was for reassurance but soon became something more.

"We do have months and months of separation to make up for." He raised his head and found the answer in her eyes. Pulling her close once again he whispered, "Let's see precisely how wanton we can be."

William thought about his wife's confession a dozen times. It made him laugh. It made him happy. It made him long for bed. But threading its way through the joy of their reunion was a troublesome guilt. There was still a part of him that he held back, even as she gave him every bit of herself.

The journals. Stacked on the table near the fire. He had brought them up from his office to his bedroom and read them in the long night hours while she slept. The three were now as well read by him as by any Braedon. She must have seen the books there. Sometimes he thought she knew he was reading them, but she had not asked about them. Not once, even in their most intimate moments.

And she had had ample opportunity. They spent their first days together constantly, talking of every small detail of their new life. She would not let him demur but insisted he tell her his wants and his interests whether it was the plan to paint the entry hall or whether it was all right for the boys to swim without one of them there. It was as if she was making him practice for the more difficult discussion ahead.

She never once mentioned the journals and eventually he realized that she was waiting for him to speak first about them and about the part of his life that he would not let go. Until he did, he knew that the Braedons still came between them.

He moved the volumes to the bedside table even though the light was poor and reading difficult. And then left them there for two more days and nights.

Finally, one night when the moon was something less than full and its waning light filled the room, he moved them to the pillow where she would lie.

For she came to him each night. He knew it was not the norm that most husbands shared their wives' bed, but allowing her to choose to come was one more way to give her power, to make her feeling of helplessness a thing of the past.

Whatever the reason, he loved the moment when she would tap at the door and open it, usually not even waiting for his call. Sometimes she would tiptoe in as though this were some assignation, other times she would burst into the room as though love was as powerful a fuel as gun powder. Always she was his Lavinia—his love, his life.

Tonight she came in and walked right up where to he stood between the mirror and the clothes press. Their first kiss was long, sweet, and left them both breathless, but she was unwilling to stop. She pressed her mouth to the pulse at his neck, then trailed more kisses down the column of his throat, finally raising her mouth to his for a deep, hungry kiss that was torture and delight. He wanted her this moment—this instant—and he scooped her up and carried her to the bed.

He knew the moment she noticed the journals. He could feel the change as passion gave way to tenderness.

"You read them, William?" Her arms were around his neck but her eyes were on the worn volumes.

"I have." It took real effort to even speak the words and she must have known because she gave him that smile he could only call maternal and could not quite bring himself to hate.

He turned and sat on the bed with her in his arms, but she

had her own plan and wriggled from his arms and onto the covers.

She pulled off her slippers and tucked her bare feet under her. She would leave her hair loose until they were ready for sleep and she used both her hands to push it down her back. The movement showed off the elegant line of her neck and breasts and William felt his mouth go dry.

She smiled at him then, with such naive pleasure that he pulled his own stocking-clad feet up onto the bed and settled across from her.

"You read the journals," she repeated.

He reached over to take her hand. "I read them all."

She raised his hand and kissed it. He kept hold of hers and kissed the palm, then raised it and held it against his heart. "Lavinia, I never knew a woman's loving touch until you."

Tears filled her eyes and he hurried on.

"I came close once. When I met the marchioness. Close enough to know what I'd missed. Until I met her, I had no idea that women could be so kind." *Like you*, he thought but did not say. "I want you to read them, Lavinia." He handed one to her.

"Now?"

"One passage at least. I know it is selfish of me to insist when I made you wait days for me to speak of it."

She touched his hand lightly. "It's all right."

"Only you are generous enough to give me permission to be selfish."

"But you so rarely are. And this is so very," she paused, "so very like opening your heart to another. No one does that easily."

She opened to the spot he had marked. While she read, he thought of her sweet question, "Am I a wanton?" and realized that while he had been amused by it, it had taken courage on her part to even broach the question, to "open her heart" to him. Had that fueled his own nerve?

She read in silence but her attitude was as good as a commentary. When she was finished with the passage he had marked, the one and only time he had met his father, she moved to his side. He put his arm around her and let her cry.

When the tears had drowned her heartache she sat up, her eyes filled with a need for revenge.

"That miserable man. If he were not already dead I would beat him with a stick."

"As long as it is him you want to beat and not me."

"You will not distract me with your teasing. What he did was disgraceful."

"Lavinia, what my mother did was disgraceful. They were evenly matched in that."

She shook her head briskly as though she did not agree with him but would not be so crass as to argue.

"Can you see that I was afraid to love you, Lavinia? What did I know of it? Did my mother know love? If she did, it cost her everything to claim it. Was what my father knew with the marchioness love? If it was, the cost to the marchioness was too great. I did see love in the marriage of Angus's parents but Jeannie was taken from Carroll and that became its own cautionary tale. Care too much and you lose yourself or the one you love. I did not think it was worth the risk—until I met you."

"Only a man would see the navy as a safer place." She touched the scar on his face, the one at his collarbone that angled to his shoulder. "Never mind that you could die in battle or a storm or accident. Your heart was safe."

"Until you. Lavinia, you are the first woman to want something more than money or some other meaningless token."

Her hand stilled in its seductive progress. He did not think it was jealousy he saw in her eyes; how could it be? She knew that she was the one he loved.

"That night you asked if we could be friends all but broke my heart. What woman had ever wanted that from me before?

For us it was not love at first sight, but what we have is no less powerful for that. Even when we declared our love and shared it here in this bed I held back this last confession. I was afraid to trust your goodness and my own heart."

She blinked back tears. "I was afraid that you would never truly trust me again."

"How could you doubt it?" He was not sure he wanted that answer and hurried on. "Even unsure you were still willing to lie with me?"

"Well, I trusted you." She spoke as if she could trust enough for both of them.

"As I do you. Now and always." He hoped he would always remember that she needed words as much as action. "I will not say that I will never be angry again or speak rash words, but no matter, I will always love you."

She nestled closer to him and he put his arms around her. They sat for a long while like that, no passion between them, both lost in thought.

"I like this part second best," she said.

He laughed knowing what had first place.

"I love that in the last five days we have talked, truly talked with each other about everything from my roses to our children to the new housekeeper and whether she and Dolley will deal together. Sharing, William, I love sharing my life with you and you sharing in return."

He sighed and she nodded. Yes, she knew as well as he that there was one last thing that he must share. "You need to know that my idea of a perfect world does not quite match yours. I am willing to risk love with you. I trust you, but I am not ready for more than that."

"Not ready for the Braedons?" It was the first prompt she had given.

"I may never be ready for them." He shook his head. "You need to know that I am like my father in one thing and I pray to God it is the only way. I may never be able to let the past go. You need to know that, accept that."

"Of course I will. Your love and your happiness is more important to me than anything else. Even family."

He shook his head. "I hope that I do not demand too big a sacrifice, but I am too selfish to give you up. I love you, Lavinia, and my dearest wish is to make a life with you and a family."

"And we will. Wherever it takes us we will be together in all the ways that matter." He reached for her. As they fell back against the pillows Lavinia pulled him to her. "Welcome home, William."

# AUTHOR'S NOTE

Where is Rhys Braedon? He left England in 1811 for a European view of the Great Comet and has not been heard from since. He did send two letters to his brother detailing the particulars for the observatory James agreed to build and then nothing.

All the Braedons are worried. So am I. I do know what happened, but have no idea how he is going to find his way out of the fix. By the time you read *The Captain's Mermaid* I will be well on the way to discovering his secrets.

I must acknowledge the loan of a name. My friend Lavinia Klein once complained that no heroines were ever named Lavinia. I hope she no longer feels neglected.

The ten months it takes for me to write is plenty of time for changes in my world. This year it was Hurricane Isabel. By the time the storm and the power company were through, we lost eight large trees on or near our property. Our view of the bay is much improved and we have more sun in our yard, but the loss strikes me every time I go outside. I hope that the changes in your life have been more gentle.

You will note I still do not have a website, nor do I see one in the near future, but I can always be reached at PMaryBlayney@aol.com.

# More Regency Romance From Zebra

# Embrace the Romance of
# Shannon Drake